Praise for *Returnir*

"This book is certain to becom̲ ̲a ̲c̲l̲a̲s̲s̲i̲c̲ in Native American literature as well as a guide for anyone who seeks larger spiritual truths. Marshall, a Sicangu elder, is well on his way to becoming an elder for all of America."

—**Roger Welsch**, author of *Embracing Fry Bread: Confessions of a Wannabe*

"In this fine collection of stories, Marshall eloquently delivers some hard truths in a soft package. His message for today's world: we will surely sink beneath the floodwaters of tomorrow if we do not embrace the wisdom of yesterday."

—**Joseph Starita**, author of *"I Am a Man": Chief Standing Bear's Journey for Justice*

"Joseph Marshall is more than a great storyteller. He's also a very wise man. In these evocative vignettes from Lakota legend and rich personal experience, he reminds his readers that even in the overstimulated, overstressed 21st century, the greatest peace is to be found in simple, universal values and quiet contemplation."

—**Kirk Ellis**, writer/producer of TNT's *Into the West* and HBO's *John Adams*

"Through the beautiful teachings of his Lakota elders Joseph Marshall shares with the reader many of life's truths. He reminds us of the simplicity and the sanctity of life. There are no new magical answers or solutions to life's mysteries in this collection, but there are certainly powerful lessons that one can choose to embrace. When you read this book you will be motivated to rekindle the person you were when you began this journey."

—**Judi M. gaiashkibos**, an enrolled member of the Ponca Tribe of Nebraska and the executive director of the Nebraska Commission on Indian Affairs

RETURNING TO THE
LAKOTA WAY

ALSO BY JOSEPH M. MARSHALL III

The Lakota Way: Stories and Lessons for Living

*To You We Shall Return: Lessons About
Our Planet from the Lakota*

*The Day the World Ended at Little Bighorn:
A Lakota History*

The Power of Four: Leadership Lessons of Crazy Horse

Keep Going: The Art of Perseverance

Hundred in the Hand: A Novel

The Journey of Crazy Horse: A Lakota History

Walking with Grandfather: The Wisdom of Lakota Elders

The Long Knives Are Crying

Winter of the Holy Iron

On Behalf of the Wolf and the First Peoples

How Not to Catch a Fish: And Other Adventures of Iktomi

RETURNING TO THE
LAKOTA WAY

Old Values to Save a Modern World

Joseph M. Marshall III

HAY HOUSE

Carlsbad, California • New York City • London • Sydney
Johannesburg • Vancouver • Hong Kong • New Delhi

First published and distributed in the United Kingdom by:
Hay House UK Ltd, Astley House, 33 Notting Hill Gate, London W11 3JQ
Tel: +44 (0)20 3675 2450; Fax: +44 (0)20 3675 2451
www.hayhouse.co.uk

Published and distributed in the United States of America by:
Hay House Inc., PO Box 5100, Carlsbad, CA 92018-5100
Tel: (1) 760 431 7695 or (800) 654 5126
Fax: (1) 760 431 6948 or (800) 650 5115
www.hayhouse.com

Published and distributed in Australia by:
Hay House Australia Ltd, 18/36 Ralph St, Alexandria NSW 2015
Tel: (61) 2 9669 4299; Fax: (61) 2 9669 4144
www.hayhouse.com.au

Published and distributed in the Republic of South Africa by:
Hay House SA (Pty) Ltd, PO Box 990, Witkoppen 2068
Tel/Fax: (27) 11 467 8904
www.hayhouse.co.za

Published and distributed in India by:
Hay House Publishers India, Muskaan Complex, Plot No.3, B-2,
Vasant Kunj, New Delhi 110 070
Tel: (91) 11 4176 1620; Fax: (91) 11 4176 1630
www.hayhouse.co.in

Distributed in Canada by:
Raincoast, 9050 Shaughnessy St, Vancouver BC V6P 6E5
Tel: (1) 604 323 7100; Fax: (1) 604 323 2600

Interior design: Nick C. Welch

ISBN: 978-1-84850-436-3

Printed and bound in Great Britain by TJ International Ltd, Padstow, Cornwall

To my wife
Connie West Marshall
May 2, 1949 – February 14, 2013
You enriched my life and gave it meaning
because you loved me unconditionally.
You inspired me to reach deep into my writer's soul.
But most of all
you taught me how to be a good man.
For all of that, and more,
I will always love you.

CONTENTS

chapter one

The Gift of Silence

At the end of his life, when anyone asked Walks Alone how he had been a wise and caring head man for so many years, he always said it was because of his grandmother. Of course, none of those who asked him that question knew his grandmother, since she had died when he was still a young man. So he would tell them the story of the small, quiet woman who was such a powerful influence on him. It began when he was just a boy, and his name was Slow. His grandmother's name was Gray Grass.

Every kind of being that lived on the great northern prairie lands had to be strong in order to survive. Summers were extremely hot and winters were harsh and unforgiving. That meant that every kind of plant, tree, and shrub and every kind of creature that flew, swam, crawled, or walked on four legs or two had to know the ways and whims of Grandmother Earth. Two-leggeds—the people—were no different.

The people who lived on the prairie lands made their living by hunting and gathering. They hunted the animals whose flesh provided sustenance, strength, shelter, and comfort, and whose bones gave them weapons and utensils. They also gathered the various fruits and vegetables that grew on the flat-lands or along the rivers and streams, such as tubers, berries, wild oats, and peppermint. Life was good for the two-leggeds. But as for all the inhabitants of the land, it was also hard.

When Slow was ten years old, his mother and father were swept away together in a flash flood. They had been on their way to visit her parents in a distant village and had left Slow with his grandparents, so he was taken in by them. But the following winter, trag-edy visited the family once again. Slow's grandfather, a good and wise man, broke his leg while hunting. He was alone and far from help, and so he froze to death. Therefore, for many years, until Slow took a wife at the age of 20, it was only he and his grandmother in their lodge.

At the age of 12 he proved himself to be a per-sistent and skilled hunter during a very hard winter when game was scarce. He found a small herd of buf-falo after walking for many days in the bone-chilling cold and often hip-deep snow. It was a feat that even the adult hunters in the village would not attempt. The animals he found were enough to feed everyone in his village through the winter. Furthermore, it was his grandmother's advice and planning that had enabled him to travel so far and succeed at his mission.

Gray Grass knew that her grandson was always quiet, hardly talking even in the presence of other chil-dren and young people. And she knew why. Life had been hard on him and he had much to contemplate. Some of the other adults worried that he was too quiet. They wondered if the tragedies the boy had suffered might be too much to bear. The old woman, though, was glad for the boy's silence. She knew he sought solitude for the peace that it brought. After all, they had suffered heartbreak together. Though they had relatives in this village and another, each was really all the other had for support to face each day's trials and tribulations. So when anyone spoke about the boy's tendency to be alone and quiet, whether as worry or as criticism, she took such comments with a polite smile. As one who had lived a long life and endured much herself, she knew the healing value of silence. As for Slow, he trusted his grandmother without question.

The difficult circumstances that life had handed the boy and his grandmother made them closer than they would have been otherwise. Three people from the same family lost in such a short span of time left a big hole. Many people would have given up hope or spent the rest of their lives mourning. Yet in addition to the tragic losses, life had also given the old woman a new purpose; more than one, as a matter of fact. She had to become a parent again and take responsibility for being teacher to the boy the way his father and grandfather were to have been.

Like all the women in the village, Gray Grass knew the way of the hunter and the warrior—two roles fulfilled by every man and necessary to the survival of her people. Her husband and her son had honored that path. Therefore, though she had not taken to the hunting trail or the warpath herself, they had been a part of her life. Furthermore, in her grandson's face she saw her son and her husband, and that helped her to accept the difficult circumstances life had given them and to face whatever lay ahead.

Material wealth was not important among the people of the prairie. They moved often with the seasons, taking everything they owned with them each time. So it was not wise to own anything that was not absolutely necessary. Anything beyond that was a burden on people and dogs. After all, it was the dogs that carried most of the belongings on drag poles whenever the villages relocated. It was understandable, then, that the worth of a person was not measured in the things he or she owned, but in the deeds done on behalf of others.

All these things and more the old woman taught her grandson. But when it came to honing the skills he would need as a hunter and warrior, she asked men she knew and trusted to be good and patient teachers. As the years passed, the people in the village saw the boy grow into a quiet and respectful youth, and they knew it was entirely due to his grandmother. In time Slow came to be known as "his grandmother's son." It was a label that caused many to scratch their heads, trying to discern what it meant. But for those who understood, it meant that the old woman and the boy had turned tragedy into a strong bond, the kind of bond that many envied.

However it might have appeared to other people, there was a fear that haunted Slow every day of his life—that his grandmother would die just as his parents and grandfather had. Gray Grass suspected as much and realized that she must help her grandson face the day she knew would come. She decided to teach him to face two great fears that all people seemed to have—darkness and death. In order to do so, she would use another of life's realities that most people tended to overlook—silence—mostly because her grandson already spent much of his time in that realm.

She also decided to weave those lessons into the small events of everyday life. Of course, everyday life was full of the unexpected as well as the ordinary. There was always danger in one form or another. The weather was one. Though it behaved in certain predictable ways during each season of the year, it could change at any given moment. Animals were another, and the most dangerous among them were the bears and the big tawny cats. Though bears were not known to stalk or hunt people, the big cats did now and then. There were other creatures of lesser stature that could not be overlooked either, such as the rattling-tail snake with its poisonous bite.

All things great and small, dangerous or not, were part of the reality of living on the great prairie lands that stretched as far as the eye could see. Some realities were easy to perceive and understand, and others were not. Gray Grass was determined to teach her grandson about all the realities they lived with, seen or unseen. One of the ways she especially favored was to simply walk on the land, because it had much to teach all who knew how to heed its lessons.

So it was that one fine summer's day when Slow was 14, Gray Grass suggested they go for a walk. "Grandson," she said, "let us go for a walk tomorrow. It should be a day without wind or rain. We can leave at dawn."

Slow liked going for walks with his grandmother, even though he was a stalwart teenage boy on the verge of being a man. Because the people relocated their villages often, especially in the summer and autumn, their walks were not always over the same landscape or along trails they had walked before. Many times they found new trails. Those walks were precious to him, and he sensed that he needed to keep those memories inside of him.

For this particular outing the old woman had a plan. She packed plenty of food, filled the water skins, and quietly suggested that Slow take his lance and bow and arrows. At the next dawn, as the village was only starting to awaken, Gray Grass, her grandson, and their best dog crossed the nearby creek and headed north. Her plan was to walk a wide circle around the village. That route would take them through a variety of land-scapes and would not tax her old bones too much.

Straight north of the village they climbed a gradual slope that led to the top of a hill, the highest hill above the little valley. They met the young sentinels who had spent the night there on watch. Gray Grass visited briefly with the two young men and shared some of her food with them. The view from the hill made it easy to understand why the warrior leaders had placed senti-nels there. Not only was the whole village visible, but anyone approaching from any direction could be seen.

Yet it was not the breathtaking view that Gray Grass wanted her grandson to see. She told him to listen, so together they did. Somewhere to the east someone was pounding small drums, or so it seemed to Slow. After a moment he realized it was the male grouse doing their dances of courtship. Along the creek, birds were singing and calling out to the new day. Two voices were easiest to hear: that of the mead-owlark, with its lilting warble, and the redwing black-bird with its bright, ringing call. From beyond the many hills to the west came the bellow of a buffalo bull, diminished by the distance but still strong. And from the sky above them the red-tail hawk, one of the great hunters of the sky, sent its shrill cry. The calls and the voices were not loud, they were just there, carried on the breeze that gave itself voice from moving the grasses and leaves it caressed in its passing.

Gray Grass took them down off the hill and to the east, picking her way carefully with her chokecherry walking stick and waving to the young sentinels watching them go. As the morning wore on they stopped to rest in the shade of a buffalo-berry tree, one among many in a thicket. The berries were plentiful, but Gray Grass knew they were not yet sweet, because even the birds left them alone. "Two new moons from now those berries will be ready," she said. "Then the birds will take their pick before anyone else."

By the middle of the day they were straightaway east of the village, though it was too far away to see, hidden by intervening rises. Again they stopped, this time in the shade of a tall, thick cottonwood tree. It was not the only cottonwood along the creek, but it was the largest, with the widest trunk and many branches thick with leaves. Yet it was not only the size of the tree that mattered to Gray Grass. She wanted her grandson to hear its voice.

The voice of the cottonwood tree was a soft, shimmering rattle. Very soothing to most people, as it certainly was to the old woman. It was a quiet voice; perhaps that was why the song it sang was so soothing, especially to the old ones.

"A tree like this comforted me," she told the boy. "It was the summer after your grandfather died. I went to visit his burial scaffold, and I wept until I could weep no more. Walking back to the village I stopped beneath a tree like this. The breeze was blowing softly, just enough to make the leaves sing, like they are now. It seemed as though the tree was crying with me, in sharing my grief. So when I hear its song, like now, I think of your grandfather."

They sat, saying no more for many long moments, letting the tree sing to them. Slow had heard the song of the cottonwood many times, but now it had a meaning for him. He would always like cottonwood trees for what they meant to his grandmother.

After a small meal they gathered their things and turned their steps to the southwest. The dog, a strong and sturdy male, part coyote and part wolf, stayed close, as he always did. Gray Grass had in mind to reach another grove of trees that stood on either side of the same creek that flowed by their village, curving and meandering from far to the southwest. By the time they reached the grove, the sun was in the middle of the western sky, heading down to its meeting with the horizon.

More than a few times Gray Grass had picked berries in this grove. Chokecherry thickets and buffaloberry trees were numerous here, growing profusely on the bottomland watered by the creek. But there was more to this place than the berry trees and thickets.

Gray Grass pointed to the many small rings of stones arranged all along the creek bottom—old fire pits nearly hidden by the tall grass. Near just about every one of the fire pits lay large bones. The boy's curiosity rose immediately, while the dog was busy sniffing at the bones.

"What kind of bones are those?" Slow wanted to know.

"Buffalo," his grandmother replied, and pointed to a high cut bank behind them. "See that bank? It is as high as six men. Beyond it, to the south, is a long meadow between two long ridges. Buffalo were chased by hunters along that meadow to that cut bank and over the edge. Other hunters waited here, on the bottom. When the buffalo fell, the waiting hunters ran forward with their knives. They butchered and washed the meat in the creek, and they probably stayed for several days to feast and clean the hides."

"We do not hunt that way now," the boy pointed out.

"Some people did. People who lived on this land long before we came. Your grandfather brought me to this place. He liked to come here because he said it was a way to go back to the past."

"How old are those bones?" Slow asked.

"No one knows how many years they have been there, but I think it is far back beyond the memories we have of our people," she told him.

"That is a long time."

"Your grandfather said that if someone stayed here long enough, perhaps over a few nights, that it was possible to hear their voices. The voices of those people who hunted buffalo here."

Slow gazed around at the fire pits and the bones scattered about. He could tell rib bones from the leg bones, and the ridge bones that made the buffalo's hump stand high. "Someday I will come back here," he said. "Maybe I will hear those voices."

After they had rested for a while, Gray Grass soaked her tired feet in the cool waters of the creek.

With the sun dropping ever lower, they continued their walk, but not before the old woman left an offering of food for the spirits of those hunters from the days so long past.

Just before sundown, as she had hoped, they came to a small meadow guarded on three sides by low hills. The place resembled a bowl broken on one side, the opening to the east.

The ridge tops to the south, west, and north of it were covered with short grass and bristly soap weeds. There were no trees or shrubs. They paused to rest in the shade extending from the west slope.

Suddenly, it seemed as though they were the only three beings on the earth. They could not see the village, though it was not far. If dogs were barking or children laughing and shouting as they played, they could not hear. Everything was still and silent. Not a blade of grass moved, because there was not the slightest breeze. Such moments were rare, for on the prairie lands something was always on the move.

Slow found he liked this spot inside the shadowy bowl. Even the dog sat quietly.

"There are moments and places when everything becomes silent," his grandmother said, almost whispering. "Silence is a place," she went on. "A good place. We should not be afraid of it, or afraid to be silent."

"What is in that place?" Slow asked.

"Whatever you want, whoever you want," she told him. "It is a place where you can make things happen. You can bring people in. Many times I wake in the middle of the night and everything is quiet. Everyone is asleep, even the dogs. Everything is silent. At those times some people feel alone and do not like the feeling.

Not me—I like it, because it is when your grandfather comes to me, and we talk. Your father, too."

"I have done that," the boy admitted. "I have been in the silence."

"I know you have," she said. "That is good. This place," she said, gesturing at the meadow and the hills around them, "it is one kind of quiet. The silence here is of the outside, of the world. Sometimes, if we are in the right place, the whole earth falls quiet. All the animals, the birds, even the insects still their voices. The breeze stops. Grandmother Earth pauses, and there is peace."

The old woman paused and put a finger to her lips, and it seemed to be a sign for everything to be silent. Even a cricket that had been softly chirping nearby stopped.

Many times in his adult life, Slow would know such moments—a profound silence and the sense of peace it created. But this moment, sitting in that meadow with his grandmother, would be the one he would always remember first and most.

"Grandmother Earth has a heartbeat, you know," Gray Grass went on in a soft, gentle voice. "A moment like this happens in between her heartbeats. If you know where to be when that happens, you will find the silence."

Somewhere, many hills and meadows from where they sat, the muffled whistle of an elk floated on the breeze that rose gently. The moment was gone, but not forgotten.

"There is another kind of silence you can create anytime," the old woman told her grandson. "I think you already know how."

The boy nodded. "I think I do," he said.

"It is the place of inner silence, a place that is within each of us, or can be," she said. "We can go there anytime, and stay as long as we like."

Slow let out a small sigh of relief. He had thought he was the only one who ever went to that place. As if knowing his thoughts, Gray Grass waved her hand.

"That place is not where we live," she cautioned. "Look around, this is where we live, where our life's journey happens. But that inner silence can help us on that journey. Do you know how?"

Slow was not certain. "I do not think so."

"I have found that many people are afraid of three things most of all—death, darkness, and silence. I think we are born that way. But we can understand them if we truly search for their truth. Silence is the way to understand the other two; it is connected to death and darkness. There is something unknown about silence, like there is about death. There is something hidden about silence, the way darkness seems to hide things."

She reached out her small, gnarled hand and gently touched her grandson's chest. "In here," she said, "is that silent place. It is part of each of us, but not all of us go there. Many times it is a refuge, a place to hide from bad things or hard times. I want you to learn that it is more than that, something more than a sanctuary. It can be a place of strength, because there you can face grief and heartache, anger or loneliness the way you want to—because it is your place. A place that belongs only to you. You can hide there, yes, but it can also be like that high hill where the sentinels guard the village. You can stand guard on that hill and fight off anything that comes at you, like fear, self-doubt, or ridicule—anything.

"For me it has been a place to open my mind and find understanding. First, I had to find that utter silence, and in order to do that you must push all things out of your mind. That opens your mind up to thoughts, and to the spirits that are also part of our life's journey. Most of all to the Creator, the power that made everything. But nothing can come to you if you are afraid or do not open the way for it. That silence within each of us is one way these things can come to us. In that way you will begin to understand as much as you can what your life's journey is all about. You might come to understand that death is the ultimate reality because there is no turning aside from it. You might come to understand that darkness is a place for bad things to hide, but knowing that strengthens you.

"That silence is also where I go to send my thoughts and my wishes out, and to pray. Thoughts and wishes and prayers are strengthened by that silence, like you shooting an arrow on a calm day. The wind is not there to turn it aside. Anything that goes from your place of silence goes with unalterable purpose.

"There are two things you must always remember: your inner silence is not a place to hide from the reality of life, and it is a place where you must face yourself honestly. If you remember these things, then you will be given knowledge and your spirit will get stronger and stronger."

The old woman sighed. "I know this is much to think of for someone who has lived only fourteen years. Remember what I said, and remember these words—to those who calm the storms of life by using the silence to make peace, life will give good things now and then."

By the time dusk gave in to darkness, Slow and his grandmother and their dog were back in the village. The boy heeded his grandmother's advice and thought often of that day and the words she had spoken.

In the autumn and winter of that year, Slow began to take his turn as a sentinel to guard the village from enemies and danger. By the next year, he was accompanying warriors as they went out on patrol. All this happened because it was time for him to honor the path of the warrior, to take his place as a protector of the people. He was already a skilled hunter. He made certain his grandmother and the other elders were never hungry. Gray Grass, of course, saw all of this and was proud of her grandson.

In the summer of his 16th year, Slow faced an enemy in battle for the first time. Gray Grass had been waiting for just such a time, and she was especially pleased that he did not boast. In that way he was like his father and grandfather. After talking to other elders, Gray Grass put on a feast for the entire village, and she asked the oldest man to announce that her grandson would have his grandfather's name: Walks Alone.

The years passed and Walks Alone fulfilled his responsibility as one of the providers and protectors of his village. But the rigors of a long life began to show more and more on his grandmother. For the first time in his life the young man saw her struggle with simple things. Rising out of bed or from her chair was no longer easy. Her steps were slower and the amount of firewood she could carry was less and less. She held objects closer in order to see them clearly. Her hair turned white, strand by strand, it seemed, until her braids were like two snowy trails. But just as notice-able were the lines in her face—deep lines that sym-bolized the many trails she had walked.

As his grandmother grew older, Walks Alone's character emerged. He would gather and haul fire-wood after she had gone to bed, so she would not have to work as hard. From time to time he would cook for her, especially after he brought home fresh meat. He made certain her walking stick was always at hand, and he would walk beside her, patiently slowing his own pace to match hers. He asked other women to help take down his grandmother's lodge and pack their things whenever the village moved. When he was away on a hunt he arranged for someone to keep an eye on her.

In his 19th summer he courted and won the daughter of a good family from another village. By the next spring he took her as his wife. Then, instead of following the common practice, he did not live in her village. Redwing Woman saw her new husband's devo-tion to his grandmother and did not object. So their new lodge was pitched next to that of Gray Grass. As for Gray Grass, her grandson's new wife became the daughter she never had.

Over the winter the weight of her many years became too much for Gray Grass to bear. She grew frail with each passing day, and in the spring she was not strong enough to make the trek to the new vil-lage site. Walks Alone and Redwing stayed behind with her, along with two of Walks Alone's friends who were reluctant to leave the family unprotected.

They relocated their lodges to a valley guarded by thick groves of trees. There Walks Alone and his wife devoted themselves to their grandmother's comfort.

They passed the time listening to her stories, which she told with a voice that grew weaker and softer each day. Struggling to keep their grief from bursting, they watched the light in her eyes growing dim. On a bright afternoon as the breezes helped the cottonwood trees sing a soft song, the old woman took her last breath.

Walks Alone chose a secluded gully halfway up a slope, ringed by a grove of ash trees. There they laid her to rest on a four-post scaffold, her thin body wrapped in a fine elk robe.

True to the custom of his people, Walks Alone cut his hair short to signify that he was mourning his grandmother's passing. The following year, just into the Moon of Black Calves, he and his wife put on a feast and invited the entire village to eat with them, in honor of his grandmother. It was known as the Releasing of the Spirit, and thereafter the name Gray Grass was not spoken out loud, so as not to impede her journey to the spirit world.

Soon after the passing of Gray Grass, news came from people who spoke a different language and lived far to the south. They brought news of a strange animal, a large one with single round hooves unlike the split hooves of the buffalo, elk, and deer. It was said to be nearly as tall as a buffalo at the shoulder, with a large head without horns or antlers. Neither did it have fangs or claws, and its eyes were not those of a hunter. Such an animal was not known to the people and it was difficult to believe that such a thing could exist.

For a few years there were more rumors. A few travelers who said they had actually seen it scratched pictures in the dirt. The strange new animal was like a dog in that it learned to live with people and it could carry loads. Some of the people called it the Greater Dog.

Walks Alone's people continued to live their generations-old lifestyle, wandering over the prairies, moving their villages at least once each season. In the summer several villages joined and became one large town. In the autumn they pitched their conical hide lodges near the trails used by the buffalo. The autumn hunts were important and success meant sufficient stores of meat to last through the long, cold prairie winter.

Walks Alone was a stalwart and quiet man, one who always deliberated. He was a more than proficient hunter, and his knowledge of animal habits and game trails was second to none. Accordingly, the elders asked him to be the village's hunt leader. It was said that in the prime of his life his village did not once go hungry in the winter. It was Walks Alone who taught the young men to hunt buffalo in the winter. Walking on snowshoes made of hardwood was the way. It enabled hunters to find buffalo in deep snow, or drive them into snow-filled creeks or gullies. In deep snow the buffalo were vulnerable because they could not use their great speed to outrun the hunters, and their great strength was useless. Hunters, on the other hand, could maneuver atop the snow on their snowshoes.

A friend asked him how Walks Alone had been able to come up with the idea of hunting on snowshoes in deep snow. The reply was somewhat puzzling.

"It was there, in the silence," he said.

Two daughters were born to Walks Alone and Redwing Woman. A few of his friends were secretly disappointed for Walks Alone, because every man wanted sons to carry on his line. But he told no one he had prayed for daughters. He believed that the world needed more women like his wife and his mother and grandmother. So much so that his first daughter became Gray Grass Woman and his second daughter was Blue Stem Woman, which was his mother's name.

Walks Alone was known for his quiet ways almost as much as for his hunting prowess. It was not unusual for him to scout for game alone. It was a way for him to find solace in the silence of his inner being, just as his grandmother had. With his favorite dog as his only companion, he would find a secluded place and spend a day or more in quiet solitude to slip into that inner silence where he could contemplate life. There, as his grandmother had taught him, was the place to find strength, common sense, and enlightenment. It was on one of those solitary journeys that he found himself on the fringes of his people's territory. He came to a river that more or less marked the southern border and there along its banks his dog caught the scent of a stranger.

Standing among river willows was a large animal. One that Walks Alone had never seen in the flesh, though he had seen crude drawings of it. The animal that some people called the greater dog.

The hackles on his big black-and-gray dog stood up straight and a low growl rumbled from its throat. As far as he knew, in all the far-flung villages of Walks Alone's people there was not a single greater dog. Ever the cautious hunter-warrior, he blended into a thicket with his dog. For the better part of an afternoon they barely moved as they kept watch on the animal, which did nothing more than stand with its head down. Only occasionally it moved to switch its long tail to drive away flies. Finally, deciding to risk a closer look, Walks Alone took his dog and silently moved through the underbrush.

He knew nothing about the thing called the greater dog, except that it was rumored to be strong and was not a hunter. As they came closer, he did see that it was thick-bodied and tall—as tall as an elk. It nibbled at the grass around its feet now and then, and so Walks Alone surmised it was a grass eater like the elk, buffalo, deer, and antelope. When they were within a stone's throw it saw them, and hobbled away clumsily, as if injured. It was then that Walks Alone saw the cord tied around one of its front ankles.

The cord had been made by someone, of that there was no doubt. Walks Alone prepared his bow. When his dog growled, he was certain that an enemy was nearby. There was an enemy, but a lifeless one. Around his arm was tied the other end of the cord, thus revealing why the animal was not moving. It did not take long for Walks Alone to determine that the man lying under a tree had been bitten by a rattling-tail snake. Other signs indicated that the man had put a poultice on his leg. He had tried to draw out the poison.

From the man's clothing Walks Alone knew he was from a people who lived far to the south. A people with whom they had clashed, but not often. He buried the man, placing the weapons he found nearby with him in the shallow grave. The man was certainly someone's son, perhaps someone's husband and father. He was courageous enough to travel alone into an enemy's territory. For all those reasons Walks Alone gave him the courtesy and respect of a burial.

The greater dog was another thing, however. Not knowing what else to do, he cautiously untied the cord from around its ankle, though he was uncertain what the animal might do. Surprisingly, neither the dog nor the greater dog showed any animosity toward the other, only curiosity.

Walks Alone intended simply to set the animal free, so he was surprised when it followed them. At first he thought it would eventually go its own way, but it did not. She—from all indications it was a female—followed closely on their heels. And it some-how seemed appropriate that she and the black-and-gray dog showed no fear of each other. Furthermore, there was a gentleness in the greater dog's large brown eyes, and she responded to his voice.

As far as Walks Alone could determine, the greater dog had been well treated by her owner. That was the reason for her lack of fear, he surmised. Since he had kept the long cord, he tied it around her ankle when they camped for the night. As he had guessed, it was something she was familiar with and she grazed peacefully within the limits of the cord.

There was another cord tied loosely around her neck, just behind her jaws, at her throat. He could not imagine its purpose, but when he approached care-fully and pulled at the neck cord, she responded to its pull. Clearly, she had been taught things he did not know about. But he did decide that the neck cord might be a way to lead her, the way a dog could be led by a rope around its neck. He decided to try the next morning. Tying the long cord to the one around her neck, he cautiously pulled it and was pleasantly surprised when she responded and followed him.

At first Walks Alone did not consider what it would mean to have a greater dog become part of his life, or of his village. Information on them and how the southern peoples used them was limited at best. But it was natural to assume that whatever a dog could do, the greater dog could do many times over. He surmised that this animal could carry several rolled-up lodge covers, while a dog carried or dragged only one.

Encouraged by the gentle nature of the animal, Walks Alone boldly decided to lay his hands on her. So he carefully rubbed her neck and touched her ears. She tolerated it and even seemed to respond to it. Next he rubbed her shoulders, her back, and lastly her front legs. All of this the greater dog accepted without any apparent apprehension. More importantly, Walks Alone's own apprehensions about such a large and powerful animal dissipated. Trust, it was obvious to Walks Alone, had to be the basis of their interaction, as it was with dogs.

She was dark brown in color, with a black mane and tail, both long. Her hooves were black as well and very hard. Her demeanor was quiet—a kindred spirit, Walks Alone realized.

Thus in a curious procession they made their way back to the village, the black-and-gray dog in the lead, just ahead of Walks Alone, and the greater dog walking calmly behind him. As they came near the camp, he tried to anticipate what might happen. He considered leaving the greater dog hidden somewhere, but worried she might run away if left alone. Wherever she had come from and whatever people she had lived with, Walks Alone assumed she was familiar with dogs. He fervently hoped this was so, because he knew the village's dogs would be apprehensive of her. They had never encountered such an animal.

So the strange little procession entered the village and a new age entered the lives of the people of the prairies. Word spread faster than a wind-driven grass fire. Children and dogs were the first to gather. Most of the village's dogs barked at the appearance of a strange new creature. Walks Alone's dog, interestingly, took a defensive posture and prevented any of his fellows from approaching too closely. Among the people, curiosity outweighed apprehension. Throughout it all, though nervous, the greater dog stood calmly. Walks Alone stroked her neck and spoke to her soothingly.

Eventually most of the dogs realized that the large animal was not a threat and turned their attention elsewhere. But Walks Alone and his new companion and his dog were surrounded by a circle of curious people of all ages and sizes. Most of the adults in the crowd knew what he had brought home. The rumors and stories had been true.

An elder quieted the crowd and asked Walks Alone to tell his story. When he had finished, the elders gathered to talk about this auspicious and unexpected event. Walks Alone selected six young men he knew would do what he asked them without question. This was to form a large circle and sit around the greater dog, mainly to keep the onlookers from getting too close. Meanwhile, he and the elders sat nearby and talked.

The elders decided that the greater dog belonged to Walks Alone, since he had found it. He told them what he had been able to do with the animal and everyone agreed that to proceed with patience and caution was the sensible approach.

A large stake was pounded into the ground at Walks Alone's lodge. That night, and each night thereafter, the greater dog was tied to it by her ankle rope. During the day she was taken to nearby meadows to graze and to the creek for water. The animal formed an immediate attachment to Walks Alone's daughters. She seemed happy to see them every morning.

Even as the initial excitement diminished, most of the people knew that something important had happened. The elders discussed the possibility of sending young men to the south country, beyond the river where Walks Alone had found the greater dog. It was assumed that people who lived there might have greater dogs and know how to use them. Such a journey would be dangerous, but it was also necessary. Especially since more greater dogs might be obtained somehow.

Meanwhile the newcomer adapted well to her new home. Everyone doted on her. She was not uncomfortable when Walks Alone placed bundles on her back. Finally one day he jumped up and draped himself across her back. Though the people watching expected something to happen, the greater dog stood quietly, not the least bit alarmed.

As the days passed, the new arrival became part of the life of the village. The flames of excitement were fanned anew, though, when the village relocated to a new site. Walks Alone constructed longer and bigger drag poles for the greater dog to pull and fashioned the same kind of harness used for dogs. Much to everyone's surprise, she accepted the drag pole frame and harness and pulled the load. On the frame Walks Alone loaded not only his family's lodge and belongings, but those of two more families as well. The greater dog dutifully pulled the load. Now the elders began making plans in earnest to send young men to the south country, to find or trade for more like her.

In time, all of that happened, and by the time Walks Alone and Redwing Woman's daughters had children of their own, the village had 60 of the wonderful greater dogs. Not only did they pull great loads, they also carried people.

Over the years people talked about the summer when the greater dog came to the people. What they remembered most often was the quiet demeanor of Walks Alone. He had brought change to his people, yet he did not once boast of what he had done. Whenever he talked about finding the greater dog he would say that it was his unexpected good fortune, not anything that he set out to do.

Redwing Woman was proud of her husband. He was a good provider and he took to the war trail when it was necessary to defend the people. Both of which he did better than most men. The time came when both their daughters married and pitched new lodges next to their parents. And it was with love and pride that Walks Alone and Redwing welcomed grandchildren. One moment, on a cool autumn evening, as they sat at their outside fire sipping peppermint tea, Redwing Woman asked her husband what he thought of their life together. After a long, quiet moment of thought he replied gently.

"I have never forgotten what my grandmother told me when I was a boy," he said to his wife. "To those who calm the storms of life by using the silence to make peace, life will give good things now and then."

Woinila

(woh-ee-nee-lah)

Silence

CALMING THE STORMS

Anyone who knows the history of the native tribes and nations of the northern Great Plains is aware that the horse was a significant part of the story. Almost all the pre-European people of the northern plains were known for their horses and horsemanship. By the time Europeans reached the northern plains, the great "horse cultures" were in full bloom. However, exactly when and how the horse came to the northern plains is not known. Perhaps most of us assume that its arrival was a grand and notable event of some kind. We all want to believe that such a life-changing thing could not have happened without some noise.

Most enormous consequences, though, have innocuous beginnings. I recall my grandfather pointing out a gully running down the slope from the top of a grassy ridge to the river bottom. He said that some coyote, bear, badger, or wolf might have dug a hole just below the crest of the ridge, probably while digging for food, hundreds if not thousands of years before. Eventually the rains came, and water running down the slope slowly eroded and enlarged the cut until after eons of steady erosion it was long, wide, and deep.

I prefer to believe that the horse arrived like this, quietly, on the northern plains. It emphasizes the reality that there was a quiet side to life then. Many circumstances and moments epitomize quiet and silence to me, such as a cold winter night in the early 1950s on the prairie. The snow was a soft, hazy blanket on the land and the only sound was the very faint howl of a coyote. But people can be images of quiet and silence as well. First and foremost in that category was my maternal grandfather.

He was a soft-spoken man not given to large gestures. He never raised his voice to me and I never heard him do so to my grandmother. Just about everything he did was low-key and quiet. Once I saw him sear the palm of his hand with a thin, red-hot wire he was using to burn a hole through a piece of ash wood for a pipe stem. His reaction was a low grunt of surprise, even though the pain was excruciating. And I was constantly amazed as I watched him walk up to our horses and handle them practically at will. It was his quiet nature that reassured them. And these ways of his validated the stories he told about another man who was an image of quiet—Crazy Horse.

Indeed, every one of the old Lakota men in my childhood who spoke of Crazy Horse admired his ability to remain utterly calm in the midst of violence and chaos. To them that made him the very ideal of a fighting man. In today's vernacular Crazy Horse would be described as good at "keeping his cool." But my grandfather respected and admired Crazy Horse for his quiet ways off the battlefield at least as much as for his exploits as a fighting man. The way my grandfather described it, Crazy Horse almost unobtrusively saw to his duties and responsibilities as a man and as a leader looking after the welfare of others. During the winter he made certain that everyone, especially the elders and the widows, had enough food and firewood. He did not direct or order others to do these things; he hunted and gathered wood himself. He did those things quietly, without needing or expecting even a word of thanks.

There is a quiet side to life in the modern era as well. In 20th-century history, one person who is an example of quiet strength for me is Rosa Parks. Her contribution to the civil rights movement of the 1960s has been lauded, analyzed, discussed, debated, and written of from many perspectives, because everyone and every group espouses the point of view that most affects them. My perspective is that the prevailing racial attitudes of the time encountered a formidable force that lives in each person who is part of a beleaguered or oppressed group: quiet determination. A force that can be an immovable object under the right circumstances. Perhaps there was rage inside Rosa Parks at the injustice heaped on her people; nevertheless, her reaction at a critical moment in her life was almost understated. But the consequence was, in my estimation, more inspiring than the moon landing. That was a fear-driven technological accomplishment of one nation, afraid that their avowed enemy would do it first. Rosa Parks's quiet resistance to injustice was an example of the power of the human spirit shared by each and every one of us.

By and large, though, silence is not a virtue or a valued commodity in our fast-paced world. For us modern humans, especially those of us needful of, or immersed in technology, silence is virtually not an option. We have swapped the natural sounds that have been part of human existence over eons of time— breezes, wind, thunder, crackling fires, the rumble of landslides and avalanches, waves washing ashore, birdsongs, the laughter of children, animal growls, barks, bellows, whistles, yelps—for artificially generated noises. Our days now are filled with beeps, buzzes, clicks, radio, television, sirens, vehicular noises, and an unlimited variety of cellular telephone ringtones, all of which we accept as normal. Most Western households have at least 14 different kinds of appliances or electronic or mechanical devices that make noise. The list includes refrigerators, stoves, CD players, radios, televisions, electronic games, computers, telephones, doorbells, blenders, mixers, coffeepots, power tools, scanners, and printers. Several items we often have more than one of, such as telephones, computers, and televisions. This does not include the four or five devices we take with us when we leave our homes.

More alarming than constant noise is that apparent sense of normalcy and perhaps the possibility that we *need* constant noise. The fact of the matter is that we have adapted so well to the steady influx of noise, generation after generation since the advent of the industrial age, that it has evolved into a need. If that is true, then the *absence* of noise is no longer normal for us; it's something that causes nervousness, apprehension, and even fear.

Sound is part of our world and the particular environment that each of us lives in. Memories of my childhood are filled with my grandparents' voices, crackling fires, the ringing of axes, neighing of horses, the clunk of wagon wheels rolling, and so on. Like everything else in our environment, our existence, and our lives, sound and noise serve a purpose. Loud noise can signal confusion or impending chaos, just as other sounds can convey information, satisfaction, clarification, and pleasure. But there is a point when necessity gives way to excess. At that point, I believe the persistent presence of noise interferes with what we are as human beings.

In the story of Walks Alone and his grandmother Gray Grass, introspection is a part of their lives. It is, as far as I am concerned, another one of our senses as human beings, just like our five physical senses of touch, taste, sight, smell, and hearing. Of all our human abilities, introspection can be the foundation for the greatest emotional, mental, and spiritual strength—but it cannot make itself heard in a din. To be able to utilize this sense, we need to learn what silence is.

When I was a child, I lived with my maternal grandparents on a plateau above the Little White River in what was then the northern part of the Rosebud Sioux Indian Reservation, in South Dakota. Our home was a one-room log house my grandfather built. Our food came from the garden we planted and harvested, a few groceries we purchased or traded for in town, sometimes a hindquarter of beef (in lieu of cash payment for lease of my grandmother's land), and wild game. Our mode of transportation was primarily a wagon pulled by draft horses, or our feet if our destination was not that far—within three miles or so. Sometimes it was my parents' car, when they stopped by or stayed for a while. To say that the pace of our life was unhurried would be the understatement of my life.

My grandfather hunted deer in the fall after the garden was harvested. On the days he went out to hunt, my grandmother reminded me that we needed to be quiet. Everything we did in and around the house was done with as little noise as possible, even though my grandfather was miles away. Before I was able to hunt with him or on my own, that was my contribution to the hunt: to be quiet. This behavior was not something my grandparents concocted to trick me into staying quiet. It was rooted in an age-old belief that quiet begets quiet. (Probably in the same way that one yawn instigates another.)

In the past, quiet and silence were necessary for survival. Not only did hunters have to learn the skill to move over and through many kinds of obstacles and landscapes silently so as not to alarm the prey, silence was also critically necessary for detecting and avoiding enemies. Hence, for example, anyone who snored at night was gently but quickly prodded so that the noise stopped. The entire village was expected to refrain from making noise; babies and young children were kept close and their every need was attended to before they cried out too loudly.

Likewise, warriors who were sent out to scout for enemies used an ancient strategy. Old warriors believed that eyes had the power to "draw the eyes." In other words, if you stared at an enemy too intently for too long, sooner or later your stare would be felt, and you yourself would be seen. Therefore, young warriors were taught to interrupt their gaze once an enemy was spotted and put themselves into a state of absolute silence; a silence that emanated from deep within the spirit.

A favorite practice among northern plains tribes was to raid and steal horses from enemy tribes. There are stories of Lakota men who were able to infiltrate an enemy village in the dead of night. The objective was the horses tied at the very lodge doors, because those were the highly trained buffalo runners and war horses—the most prized of all—and in order to reach the objective, warriors had to be utterly silent both without and within. It was one thing to be able to move silently, but to remain virtually undetectable required the art of inner silence. That is, a man had to push all thoughts of anything but the mission at hand, including fear of failure, out of his mind. The physical skill and spiritual strength of silence was the only way to achieve success in this situation. Those men who did were able to calm the storms of doubt and fear that swirl when life itself is on the line and death hovers near.

Neither of my grandparents was given to doing or saying anything in a brash or loud manner. There was a look my grandmother sent in my direction when I was being a little too noisy. She was able to dissipate noise silently in that way. My grandfather, on the other hand, would simply pause whatever he was doing and wait for me to realize that I was being overly loud. And even as a child preoccupied with my own immediate needs and whims, I did notice that both of my grandparents were frequently deep in thought. At least that was my assumption when they were silent for extended periods of time; a correct one, as it turned out. As a teenager I asked each of them why they liked to be quiet. "To think," they told me.

During those moments of silence I, again even as a child, noticed something else. Their outward demeanor was different. There was a stillness about them, though not a trance. Sometimes they would be doing something, but it was easy to see that their focus was not entirely on the task. At other times they would be absolutely motionless and simply gazing in some direction. During those moments the stillness around them was like the proverbial thick fog one could cut with a knife. Though it certainly was not visible to the eye it was perceptible in every other way. So palpable that I did not want to disturb it.

Introspection wears two faces. One is light and one is dark, and the dark side scares people. But I also know for a fact that some of us can face that dark side, be it bad memories, grief, guilt, or anything else that we would turn and run from in the physical world. I know this to be true because my grandparents did just that.

I remember the day in the summer of 1959 when I found my grandmother at the kitchen table in the midst of some task, with a grief-stricken expression on her face that even a teenage boy could not mistake. She tearfully admitted that she had been thinking of her younger sister, who had died in 1919 during a reservation-wide Spanish influenza outbreak when she was 17 and my grandmother was 19. My grandmother said she could never think of her without remembering watching her waste away so rapidly before she finally died. Forty years later the memory was still vivid, and obviously still painful. Several years after that, I listened to my grandmother tell stories of her sister and punctuate them with soft sobs and a few tears.

She told me that certain memories had a way of presenting themselves, as it were. If we are lucky most of our memories are positive and pleasant. But the reality is there are the difficult memories that invoke grief, anger, regret, guilt, or denial. My grandmother was not afraid of facing bad, even ugly, memories, or her own mistakes. She would have understood an interesting but brief encounter my wife Connie and I had with a fellow restaurant patron in Santa Fe several years ago.

The restaurant, El Faro, was full one summer evening, situated as it was along a street saturated with art galleries. A band was playing loudly in the front room, which had a low ceiling, so normal conversation was impossible. A young woman asked to join us at our table, since we had the last empty chair in the room. After a few minutes she leaned across the table and shouted above the din: "Wherever you go, there you are."

That was the extent of the conversation with our table guest, whose name we do not know. But what she said is a reality. No matter who and what we are, or who and what we think we are or are not, there is no way to outrun ourselves. My grandmother's advice was to accept yourself as you are, and sometimes that meant confronting yourself. To do that we need to be introspective, to go to that place inside of ourselves where there is no room for anything but honesty.

When I think of this sort of introspection I am reminded of a morality tale, one of our Lakota Iktomi stories, that my grandmother often told me. Iktomi is the Trickster in many of our cultural stories—a ne'er-do-well who tries to slide by doing as little as possible and live by his wits, and consequently does not have much of a life except to serve as an example of how *not* to live it.

In this story he sees his reflection in a calm pond and admires himself. It is windy the next time he visits the pond and his reflection is misshapen, so he is certain he is not seeing himself. The next time it is raining and his reflection is dark and obscured, and again he is certain it is not him in the pond. A friend explains to him that each reflection, no matter how pretty or ugly, is him. The choice we have, my grandmother would say, is whether or not to accept the reality of who and what we are. And if we cannot face the reality of who and what we are in the deep silence of introspection, not to mention what we have done or not done, then we are like Iktomi. As my grandmother would also point out, if we cannot honestly accept ourselves as we are in the privacy of our own thoughts, than we will not be honest on the outside.

Both of my grandparents regarded that place of silence in our innermost being as a place of power. One reason to go there was to face and examine ourselves honestly. The other reason was to connect with everything around us. In traditional Lakota culture the simplest prayer we can say is *Mitakuye Oyasin* (mee-tah-koo-yeh oh-yah-sin), which means "All my relatives." With that short but profound prayer we invoke a connection with everything that is of the earth, including the earth. And what better way than to do that from a place of power? In meditating this way we are not only acknowledging the power of silence, but we are also using it as a way—as my grandparents would say—"to put our thoughts on the wind."

People approach meditation with a variety of rituals. My approach is simple and my time to meditate is in the very early morning when no one else in the household is awake (except for two cats). I usually burn sage or sweetgrass or bear root, then sit motionless. My first objective is to take myself to that place of profound silence. It is not a matter of descending or ascending; as a matter of fact, it has nothing to do with movement or space. It is simply an attainment, to achieve that dimension of silence where nothing of the physical world can intrude. Once there I say a prayer to ask for balance for the whole world. Then I open myself to allow whatever force, influence, or power chooses to come in. After that I may have something specific to ponder, or I may simply sit in that profound silence, in respect for all that was, and is, and will be in the world. Lastly, I pray for my family and relatives, especially those facing a significant life situation or difficulty of any kind. As I visualize my thoughts and my prayers lifted by the winds, my final thought is *Mitakuye Oyasin*.

As the old woman Gray Grass told her grandson, we humans are born with inherent fears. Fear of falling and of loud noises are obvious, but there is also the fear of darkness and death. Then there are the myriad fears depending on our individual circumstances: loneliness, poverty, powerlessness, bias, racism, hunger, pain, illness, obscurity, flying, and so on and so on. Strangely, compared to all of these there is less to fear in silence, yet we fear it as well. Like Gray

Grass, I believe, however, that in silence is the way or the key to understanding everything else we may fear.

Most of us grow accustomed to loud noises and understand that they can be useful as alerts to conditions around us. Likewise we probably realize that fear of falling is an inherent and significant survival instinct that serves us throughout life, especially as we grow older and more fragile. Fear of darkness is as old as our race, originating in our atavistic past when we realized every day and night that we were not the fastest or strongest physical being in our environment. Even as the predators we were then, we were nonetheless prey for bigger and faster predators, and many of those predators came for us out of the darkness.

Silence is a different matter. Even if we do not actively fear it, most of us, I believe, do not see it as useful in any way. Yet it can be a powerful ally against the trials and tribulations of our daily lives. If nothing else it can be a port in a storm, the calm eye of the hurricane, and otherwise a temporary respite from stress and care. For me starting a morning in quiet contemplation reminds me there is peace in the world.

Furthermore, silence enables me to delve into issues and questions that too often are sidelined or obfuscated by the noise of daily routine—such as death. It is in silence that I can contemplate, examine, and analyze any issue or question without fear of unreasonable response or ridicule, and where I can listen again to the voices of wisdom from the elders who live in my memories. It is in silence that I can reach my own conclusions.

It is in that silence that I have thought of death, and I have realized that all of my grandparents (and their generation of Lakota people) were right. Death is the ultimate truth. It says it will come one day and it does not waver from that truth. Once we accept that truth, it is then possible to truly live life without an unreasonable fear of it.

All of my grandparents died as they had lived. When their time came, they slipped into the next world with quiet dignity. Part of their ability to make that final transition from life to death was due, I firmly believe, to the fact that none of them were ever strangers to silence. In that silence they contemplated, examined, and relived the situations, issues, and events in their lives, not to mention people—especially family. They also took the opportunity to affirm or alter the basic values, realities, and beliefs they were taught and learned along the way. When used in this way, silence is a strength and an enabler.

It is entirely possible that silence is unexplored territory for some of us; perhaps many of us. Perhaps it is the undiscovered country for the generations who were born and grew up in the age of ever-changing technology. There is the very real possibility that silence—or the luxury of knowing it—will be their greatest loss, and perhaps their downfall.

I am not declaring that I grew up in a world devoid of noise, not at all. On the prairies of the northern part of the Rosebud Sioux Indian Reservation, there was an endless variety of sounds—wind, breezes, birds, animals, insects, thunder. And the noise level ranged from the soft buzz of a hummingbird to the thunder's earth-shaking boom. But there was also the absence of sound, the prolonged and profound periods of silence. In that world it is logical to me that we all have a voice, at least to announce that we are here, that we exist and are part of it all. In the technological and artificial realm, that logic does not work for me. Everything in the technological realm makes some kind of noise, from coffee pressers and pots to jumbo jets. In the constant cacophony, silence, it seems, does not have a snowball's chance in hell of making its presence known.

Yet silence is here. It is measurable in those milliseconds between the beeps, blasts, whistles, and blares our technology generates. And the amazing fact is that we humans have the power to push the off switch. Or we can separate ourselves from the noise by going within. Whether or not we choose to do either is the issue.

Growing up, it was not that I found all sounds offensive or intrusive; I understood that they were part of my environment. It was, rather, that I found silence to be comforting and peaceful. These days, it is that sense of comfort and that feeling of peace that I seek often. To find it, it is necessary to hit the off switch and remind myself that as wonderful and helpful as technology is, I can still control it within the confines of my home and office.

In other words, I have the power to enable silence.

chapter two

The Wolf
and the Raven

Long, long ago, it was said that all the people spoke the same language. This was in the days when things on the earth were as the Creator had intended. Each kind of people had its own language, of course, but it was also possible for the Bear People to understand the Hawk People, the Badger People to understand the Elk People, and so on. Even the Two-Legged People, those that call themselves humans these days, could understand and be understood. This did not mean that life for all things and beings was easy. It did not mean that some people were not enemies with others. Speaking the same language meant that they could get along now and then if they chose.

As any elder knows, life has a way of teaching lessons. Sometimes those lessons come in the most unexpected ways, and to those who expect them the least. So it happened for two beings whose peoples did not like each other at all.

There were two kinds of people who had spread over much of the earth: the Raven People and the Wolf

People. It was not that they were the most numerous; rather, they had abilities that others did not. They could and did adapt themselves to live in many places, such as the prairies, the desert, and the forests, and even the frozen north lands, which were under snow and ice much of the year. But there the similarities ended. The Wolf People were among the greatest of the hunting peoples, which included the Hawk, Eagle, and Short-Tail and Long-Tail Cat Peoples. Hunting people were feared and respected by other people. Then there were those, such as the Raven People, who made their living by scavenging and were not feared. It could be said that they were looked down upon, at times even ridiculed because they depended on the efforts and skills of others, mainly the hunters. So it is easy to understand why the hunting peoples looked down their noses at scavengers, and the scavengers stayed out of the hunters' way.

Furthermore, where the wolves were swift, strong, and silent, the ravens were not the swiftest among the flying peoples and had—as far as many were concerned—the most annoying and unpleasant voices of anyone. Their raucous squawk could be heard over great distances and wake even the diggers who lived in dens in the ground.

So it was that on a fine autumn day one of the Raven People, known as Screech, landed on the bare branches of a mountain aspen tree, his black feathers glistening in the sun. He saw a wolf feeding on the succulent meat from his successful hunt. The wolf's name was Long Runner, for he was known for his endurance among a people who prided themselves on their ability to run tirelessly.

Long Runner had seen the raven and even heard the *whoosh-whoosh* of the air passing beneath the bird's wings as he flopped his clumsy way through the forest. He knew one scavenger or another, such as the brown buzzard, would be along. They had their ways of knowing when hunters had had a good hunt and food was at hand. So he was not surprised to see a raven perched in a nearby tree.

Screech had not eaten for several days, and he was hungry. Flying high above the forested slopes of the mountains he had seen a large herd of grazers—deer—being stalked by a large wolf. Wolves, he knew, were persistent as well as skilled hunters. So it was only a matter of time before the hunt was over and food available. He knew wolves could not climb trees, but he stayed on a high branch, just to be certain he was safely out of reach.

Screech saw other wolves appear out of the forest and guessed they were the hunter's family. His stomach growled as he watched them feast, hoping they would leave a little something for him. Hunters always did, not because they were generous but because they would eat so much they could eat no more. So the hungry raven waited, hoping that no other scavengers could catch the tantalizing scent of fresh food.

The raven watched the hunter, the wolf who had brought down the deer. He was bigger than the others and looked very strong. His coat was gray but flecked with black and his eyes were yellow. After he ate, he sat back and let the smaller and younger wolves eat as well. Finally, when Screech's stomach was beginning to sound like thunder, the wolves had their fill and left. The raven left his perch and flew above the trees to make sure the wolves were indeed leaving. Then, gliding back down into the forest, he tore hungrily at the carcass. It had been stripped nearly to the bones, but it was food nevertheless, and such was the life of a scavenger.

Screech was able to eat his fill until other opportunists arrived. First it was the big brown buzzards, the black and white magpies, and then the little wingeds, like the flies. But no matter, Screech was satisfied and food would not be a worry at least for a day or two. He found a hidden perch in the branches of a big cedar. There, beneath layers of wide, flat needles, he took a nap.

Two days later he was hungry again and had the brilliant idea of looking for that one wolf, the big gray hunter with the yellow eyes. Screech suspected that the forested mountain slopes over which he flew were that hunter's territory. If so, it would be good to find a place to live here as well. There was no better benefactor a scavenger could have than a skilled hunter.

As luck would have it, he spotted a wolf trotting through the trees. Screech followed above, staying high.

On this day, things were very still in the forest, no breeze to carry sounds and scents. Far ahead of the wolf, a large grazer was resting in the deep shadows provided by the thick trees. Grazers, such as deer and elk, usually rested in the day when the sun was out and did their feeding at night. This grazer was an elk, and he was counting on a calm day to stay hidden from hunters with keen noses and sharp ears. Screech saw that the wolf was likely to pass by the hidden elk, given the direction he was taking. If the hunter could not find the elk, that meant both he and the raven would go hungry.

An idea came to the bird—from where, it did not matter. It was there and very intriguing, especially to a being who was very hungry. Screech could never be a hunter. He would be hard-pressed to catch anything. Even chasing and catching mice was next to impossible for him. It was exceedingly frustrating for him to be above everyone and everything, to have that vantage point and not be able to use it. Perhaps these were the reasons the idea came. Whatever the reasons, there it was, so he decided to use it.

Gliding down through the trees as silently as he could manage, Screech alighted on a branch directly above the elk. When he guessed the hunting wolf was close, he let out the most annoying squawk he could muster.

"SQUAAAWWK!"

Screech startled even himself, and he certainly startled the elk. The grazer leaped up and ran, not wanting to know what sort of creature was capable of making such a frightening sound. He crashed through the trees and underbrush, making more than a little noise himself. Screech flew up through the trees, squawking at the top of his lungs, making as much noise as he could to keep the grazer moving. The first part of his idea was working.

Rising above the treetops, the raven looked for the hunting wolf. No one was happier than he when he saw the wolf sprinting through the trees after the elk. Nevertheless, it was only the beginning. After a long pursuit the tireless wolf finally wore down his prey in a clearing, and took him down. Then he paused and called his family, his resonant howl floating across the mountain valleys.

Screech knew he had to wait his turn, but he knew how to be patient. Such was the life of a scavenger. He watched enviously as the wolf ate, along with the other members of his family as they arrived. When the hunter had his fill and moved off to wait, Screech saw his chance.

Long Runner watched with mild interest as a raven descended clumsily from tree to tree, branch to branch, until it was near enough for him to see its reddish-brown eyes. Those scavengers seemed always to be the first to appear after a successful hunt. A few were even bold enough to come close, to push their luck in order to get food. The wolf sighed and turned disdainfully away, until the bird spoke.

"I did that," it said.

All the wolves paused for a moment, surprised that a raven would dare speak to Long Runner. Since there was no danger from the scruffy-looking bird, they returned to their feast.

"Did what?" Long Runner scoffed.

"I frightened that elk, there. Made him run," asserted Screech. "Otherwise you would have gone past him, past where he was hiding."

Long Runner chuckled. "What does that mean to me?"

"I thought perhaps a succulent piece of meat," ventured the bird.

"You know how it is," the wolf reminded the raven. "Scavengers wait their turn. You can have what is left, if we leave anything at all."

"I thank you for that," Screech said, trying a diplomatic approach. "I know how it is. But I think there is a way I can help you. In return for a bigger share, of course."

Long Runner chuckled again. "You think you can help me. That is almost something to laugh about. How can a scavenger help a hunter?"

"Since you ask," the raven replied, keeping a courteous tone in his voice, "I can do something that you cannot. Something that no four-legged hunter can do."

The wolf was beginning to be annoyed. He did not like scavengers of any sort, be they furred or feathered. "I know one thing," he said haughtily. "You cannot hunt."

"True," allowed Screech. "But I can fly, and up there I see things. I see trees, rocks, creeks. I see hunters, I see grazers. I saw that elk hiding and I saw you passing it by."

"So you came to ridicule me? Is that it?"

"No. I came to say I can help you."

"I do not see how that is possible," retorted the wolf. "I have never seen a raven take down an elk."

"True. But I have never seen a wolf spot a grazer from above, in the sky," Screech pointed out.

Long Runner saw that the raven was up in the tree well out of reach, even if he were to jump as high as he could. On a whim, he decided to follow along with what the bird seemed to be suggesting.

"So," the wolf said, "are you telling me you will find grazers for me?"

"Yes," the raven replied confidently.

"What happens after you find them? You scare them and I give chase?"

Screech decided to take a risk and flopped down to a lower branch, so he and the wolf could be eye to eye. "No," he said. "When I see anything, one or many grazers, I will fly in a circle above them. That will tell you where they are. If they are moving I will swoop down at them and point them out. Then you can move in and bring them down."

Long Runner realized that the raven was serious. "Really? You would do all of that in return for a meal?"

"You will not be giving me anything I do not earn," replied Screech.

The last thing Long Runner expected from a scavenger was common sense. But he was not about to be taken in by something unexpected, even if it did seem sensible. "I will talk with my wife and family," he said. "What you are offering seems to be a good thing. But these kinds of things must be discussed."

"Yes, speak with your family," the raven agreed. "I will take this up with my family as well. Perhaps we can meet two sunrises from now. My name is Screech."

"My name is Long Runner. There is a rock-covered ridge not far from here. If I am not there two sunrises from now, you will know my answer."

The wolves finished their meal and left. Screech moved in and ate as much as he could, then carried a large piece of meat back to his mate. When he told her how he had helped the wolves with their hunt, and his idea to help them in return for food, she laughed.

"All of the hunters, the wolves, the foxes, the big cats, the hawks, the falcons, all of them laugh at us because we are scavengers," she reminded him. "We wait to see what they leave behind. If they leave nothing or not enough, we dig for grub worms. What makes you think you can change the way things are?"

The Wolf and the Raven

"I am not trying to change the way things are," he replied, wilting slightly in the face of her logic. "I am simply trying to strike a bargain between us and one family of wolves so we can have food. I do not think that will change how things are."

"I do not see the wolves agreeing to this thing," she said. "They do not need us to help them. Wolves, of all people, are likely the best hunters anywhere. Besides, they think they are better than we are."

"I do not care what they think," Screech told her. "I care about the bargain I want to make with them. If we strike that bargain, I will do my part, they will do theirs. I will keep my opinion to myself and I will not care what they think."

The conversation that took place in the home of Long Runner and his wife, Gray Legs, was not unlike the one between Screech and his wife.

"Do you think we are poor hunters because of what one raven said?" she wondered. "Everyone knows we are great hunters. Even the Bear People think so."

"Tell me," Long Runner said patiently. "Do we bring down a grazer every time we hunt?"

"No," she said. "Many times we do not."

"Yes," he reasoned. "Even great hunters do not succeed each time. We fail more than we succeed. So what if the raven can do what he says he can do? With his help, perhaps we can be better hunters."

"What will others think?" Gray Legs fretted. "What will our relatives think, the foxes and the coyotes?"

"Perhaps I will ask them," decided Long Runner.

And ask them he did. He met with his cousins, Lives in the Hill, the coyote, and Black Whiskers, the fox. Long Runner told them of the raven's offer.

"I have never known ravens to be anything but bothersome," Black Whiskers said. "And loud, very loud."

"I have never spoken to one," snickered Lives in the Hill. "They are nothing but scavengers. They benefit from our hunting. Why do they not hunt, like many of us do? Perhaps it is because hunting is not easy, and it is much easier just to wait. If it was not for us, they would starve."

"I would have nothing to do with them," advised Black Whiskers. "A scavenger can never be a friend to anyone, except another scavenger. Scavengers are what they are, we are what we are, and that is the way things are. It is not our place to change anything."

Long Runner was neither pleased nor disappointed by what his cousins had to say. After all, he truly wanted to know their thoughts. But, unfortunately, coyotes were not known for keeping things to themselves. So on his way home Long Runner was accosted by Stone Roller, the biggest bear in the forest. The distinct hump on his back, common to big brown bears, was the mark of enormous strength. Stone Roller's people were powerful hunters and afraid of no one, and he had earned his name because he was so strong he could roll large boulders with ease.

"My friend," called out Stone Roller. "Is it true what I heard? Are you teaching ravens how to hunt?"

Long Runner laughed. "No, that is not true. It is true that I have spoken to a raven, and he made an offer to help me hunt."

It was the bear's turn to laugh. "You? A raven will help you hunt? That is the funniest thing I have ever heard!"

Long Runner waited for the bear to have his laugh.

"I have not heard that you are losing your skills," the bear continued. "Unless there is something I do not know. The only one who is a better hunter than you is me. What can a scavenger teach you, or me? This is a funny thing indeed!"

Without waiting for a reply, Stone Roller ambled away, chuckling to himself.

Long Runner trotted home to his den and told his wife what his cousins and the bear had to say about the raven.

"All hunters think that way," she told him. "What have you decided?"

"My cousins do not hunt for us, neither does the bear. We take care of ourselves; that is our way. What others think does not feed us or keep us warm or safe. We do those things for ourselves as well. So I think I will go and talk to the raven."

In spite of her own doubts, Screech's wife flew with him to the rocky hilltop, and there they found Long Runner and his wife. And the bargain was struck.

"I cannot help you when you hunt at night," Screech pointed out. "But I am awake and flying when the sun rises. If you tell me when you are hunting, and where, I will find the grazers and point them out to you."

Long Runner raised his nose to the sky and emitted a series of yips and a howl. "That is my signal to my family that we are on the hunt," he said. "Other wolf families do the same, but you will know my voice."

"On the way here we saw a herd of grazers resting in a gully, that way," Screech said, pointing. "I think they spend the nights there and will likely be there tomorrow when the sun comes up. Gather your family and bring them. If the grazers are there, we will be circling above them."

So in spite of the opinions of other hunters still burning in his ears, or perhaps because of them, Long Runner kept his bargain. The next morning he and Gray Legs led their children and a cousin, seven hunters in all, on a hunt. True to his word, Screech and his wife and several members of their family were circling high above the gully. The hunt was successful and Long Runner left enough meat to feed Screech and his entire family.

It was a good beginning to an arrangement that served the two families well. Not every hunt ended successfully, because grazers were just as adept at eluding hunters as the hunters were at pursuit. But Screech and his family never failed to find something for Long Runner and his family to chase. The arrangement proved especially necessary when winter came with deep snow and powerful winds. When that happened, the grazers were even more difficult to find and pursue. In spite of harsh conditions Screech and his family proved to be strong and resourceful.

In the beginning, many of the other peoples warned that it was not wise to change the way things were. "Who knows what might happen?" some said. Other hunters, and some other scavengers as well, ridiculed Long Runner and his family for befriending the ravens. But neither Screech nor Long Runner paid any heed to the laughter often ringing through the forest—derisive laughter taunting the strange relationship.

One autumn day, after many years of keeping their bargain, Long Runner and Screech sat together on a rocky pinnacle overlooking a broad valley. The raven was no longer afraid of the wolf, and the mighty wolf no longer looked down on the bird. As a matter of fact, they were good friends.

"I have found, lately," admitted Long Runner, "that my strength and endurance are not what they once were. I cannot run as far as I once did and it is easier for some grazers to elude my bite. I am getting old."

The raven chuckled sympathetically. "Yes, I know what you mean. My arms become tired more quickly now," he agreed. "I cannot keep my wings outstretched as long as I once did. Now I find I must rest more often and it is harder for me to get high into the sky. I fear I am getting old as well."

"Our bargain has served us well," said the wolf. "But I am afraid there are some things we truly cannot change. Like getting old. There is no bargain we can make with life to keep us young and strong."

"True enough," agreed the raven. "Several days ago I spoke with Stink Head, the buzzard. He is still angry with me for helping you. According to him, scavengers and hunters are as different as night and day and should keep their places. I do not think he is complaining because he is wise and knows something I do not. He is complaining because he is afraid."

"Yes," Long Runner replied. "He is afraid of something he does not know. As I was in the beginning. But I am still a wolf and you are still a raven. Our bargain has not changed that. Since you and I are getting old, what will happen to that bargain?"

"I have considered that," Screech assured him. "I think we should pass it on to our children. They will reap the rewards of what we have done. Perhaps they will pass it on to their children, too."

So it was that a simple bargain became one for the ages, one that is honored to this day.

For those who have not separated themselves from the realities of Grandmother Earth, the relationship between the Wolf People and the Raven People is still there to see. Sadly, the Wolf People are not as many as they once were. That is because the Two-Legged People took it upon themselves to change the way of things. They stepped out of the realities that all the other kinds of people still honor and became the most feared hunters of all. As such they hunted because they could, not because they must. The two-leggeds turned on the Wolf People because of ancient misunderstandings, and they still cling to that misunderstanding.

The Raven People seem to be flourishing still, though surely they are saddened to see what has happened to their old friends, the wolves. Yet wherever they find one another, the wolves and ravens still honor their ancient bargain. The wolves still watch the sky whenever they hunt, to see what the ravens see that they cannot.

One day, back in the mists of time, Screech climbed into the sky and soared on tired wings until he found his old friend. Long Runner was basking in the warm sun of a fine summer day, to chase away the ache in his old bones.

"I came to ask you a question," Screech said to his friend. "I have wondered these many years."

"Ask," replied the old wolf.

"Long ago, you accepted my suggestion that we help one another. My question is: why?"

"Oh," said Long Runner, after a deep sigh. "Because I was curious. There was only one way to learn if we could help one another, and that was to try, to walk a road that others were afraid of. In doing so, I learned something. I think you learned it as well."

"Of course," Screech said without hesitation. "Tolerance. I learned that you are not bad, as hunters go."

"And you are not the needful creature everyone says you are. You are good and wise, as scavengers go."

Laughter filled the forests. The laughter of old friends laughing with each other.

Woicu

(woh-ee-choo)

to tolerate, to accept

The Road of Tolerance

Experience has taught me that there are two kinds of tolerance: that which comes out of genuine fairness and that which comes out of a need to survive. I have known both.

An Indian reservation in the period from the late 1940s to the mid-1960s was a cross section of social and racial attitudes and emotions. By the time I was a freshman in high school I began to understand that we Lakota were not in control of our lives. Even though I had experienced my share of racial epithets and attitudes in elementary school, I did not fully grasp their underlying cause. Not until late in high school did I realize that it all came from a sense of impunity on the part of whites because they were in control. The fact that we lived on Indian land, a place called the Rosebud Sioux Indian Reservation, was not relevant. It was still a white world, an uncomfortable reality that we Lakota had to tolerate in order to survive in it. Thus it was in high school that I learned about *survival tolerance*.

Survival tolerance kicks in anytime one realizes one is outnumbered, or when the prevailing attitudes or rules or expectations are too powerful to challenge, much less overcome. As an eight-year-old in a Bureau of Indian Affairs (BIA) school I learned almost immediately that punishment was the consequence of any misbehavior, real or perceived. I also learned there was nothing I could do to change it. In the interest of survival, I learned to go along with the program, no matter how ridiculous, distasteful, or embarrassing I thought it was. Practically from my first day of school I learned to be afraid of those who were in control of the school—white adults.

For me as a young student, teachers were symbols of white authority. They were in control of me, my time, and my activities from the moment I set foot on the school grounds until I left (escaped) it. Riding the bus *to* school on the Pine Ridge Indian Reservation was nearly an hour of dread because there was very little in the approaching school day that I could directly control. I could raise my hand and ask to go to the bathroom, and I could choose who to play with during recess. Beyond that I was powerless. During lunch I went through a line carrying a metal tray, and food was placed on it.

Some of which I did not like, such as stewed tomatoes. The rule was that every student was to eat every morsel on his or her tray and could not leave the lunchroom until that happened. On the days stewed tomatoes were served, I was one of the last students, and often *the* last, to finish eating. Every bite of stewed tomato was an adventure in the exercise of willpower. I had to force myself to eat it while a teacher stood nearby, watching with a stern expression.

I learned to tolerate stewed tomatoes, though it was frequently a stomach-turning tolerance. Sometime during the school year I realized that a day without stewed tomatoes was a good day, and I could tolerate whatever else happened that day. Survival tolerance at its best.

It would be misleading for me to say that there were no positive experiences in those years in school from kindergarten to 12th grade. There were, but few and far between. Overall, those years for me were more moments of being suspicious, guarded, defensive, and uncomfortable. And in order to get through it, I was the one who had to be tolerant. But while I exhibited *survival tolerance* there was another kind on the other side of the issue. I describe it as *tolerance of privilege.*

The tolerance of privilege is exercised by those people who are of the ruling or controlling group or class. They are aware—sometimes painfully, sometimes grudgingly—that there are people who are different for various reasons or circumstances, such as race, religion, physical handicap, poverty, or sexual orientation. The ruling group may not like anyone who is different, or they may dislike only some who are different. In any case, if they cannot remove anyone who is different, they tolerate (often under protest) being part of the same community, or riding on the same plane or train, or being in the same building, or working for the same company as those they perceive to be different. This may be tolerance, but it is not acceptance. People guided by this kind of tolerance avoid or limit contact with the different ones, all the while thinking they are better somehow.

Several of the white teachers in my BIA school set a powerful example of the tolerance of privilege. There was another kind of authority figure who exhibited it, too: a priest. Several white Episcopalian priests, to be specific, whom I had personal experience with—though I daresay in the 1940s, '50s, and '60s (and perhaps to this day) there were probably men of the cloth from several denominations with intentions of "saving" native souls who took the same attitude toward us.

Priests had two ways of treating us. One was a sort of gentle condescension. These priests treated and spoke to everyone—including elders—as if we were children. The others were like stern fathers, quick to scold us for the sins (according to them) we had committed and would surely commit in the future. Of course the scolding sermons were delivered in English that was better suited to a formally educated non-native congregation, not one whose grasp of the language was intermediate at best. During the years of my childhood, English was a second language for everyone in my generation and before.

I compared this behavior to that of Lakota men who were lay ministers or ordained clergy. My paternal grandfather was among the first Lakota men to be ordained—he was a deacon—and in 1957 my mother's younger brother was ordained a priest. None of the Lakota clergy—lay or ordained—were ever condescending or scolding, and all treated elders with the utmost respect. The inherent values of their ethnic heritage and culture were apparently much too strong in them for an adopted set of beliefs to alter. Furthermore, they conducted services in the Lakota language.

In retrospect I am still appalled at how a few younger priests spoke to and treated my grandparents and their age group. These were not isolated incidents of ill-mannered individuals; it was a pattern of behavior for many of them, probably because they felt that sense of impunity I mentioned. Yet I am not surprised that those elders—though taken aback at such discourtesy—handled the situation with graciousness. They *always* demonstrated the utmost civility and courtesy toward the priests. I heard many elders, including my grandparents, rationalize disrespectful or discourteous behavior with the comment, "He does not know our ways." They were being tolerant, in a genuine way, in a spirit of fairness. And they were able to hear the message in spite of the messenger.

To be sure, not all Episcopalian priests were condescending or stern. There were those who considered their calling to work among the Lakota (and Dakota) a privilege. A few took the trouble to learn the Lakota language. And it must be noted that a Dakota priest, Creighton Robertson, was elected Bishop of South Dakota Diocese of the Episcopal Church in 1994 and served in that post until he retired in 2009. But many of the priests I observed as a child were authoritative and paternalistic in their relationship with Lakota congregations on the Rosebud Reservation. That was the same as white teachers with native students, all enduring examples of the tolerance of privilege.

I learned, however, that even that was preferable to intolerance.

Intolerance is the common thread that weaves its way through ethnocentrism, homophobia, arrogance, anthropomorphism, and racism. It is a tendency to feel uncomfortable with anyone or anything that looks, acts, or thinks differently than we do. Under the right conditions it is the fuse that ignites the powder keg. And just as dangerous and damaging as intolerance on the part of individuals is institutional intolerance. At the age of nine I recall hearing a voice over a loudspeaker in a small South Dakota town just before a Fourth of July parade. The voice said, "No Indians allowed on Main Street." I remember asking my father what that meant, and I recall that he and one of his brothers-in-law (my uncle by marriage) both chuckled, shaking their heads. Survival tolerance to diffuse institutional intolerance. Though my father was three-quarters Lakota and one-quarter French blood, in appearance he was a throwback to his French paternal grandfather (Joseph Marshall I), with blue eyes, lighter skin, and sandy hair. In defiance of the announcement (and much to my mother's angst) he mingled with the white crowds on Main Street, purchased treats for my cousins and me and a six-pack of beer for himself and my uncle. No one was the wiser. If my uncle, with his dark skin and classic

Lakota features, had dared to do the same, he would have been spotted at once.

Later I asked my mother why the white people did not allow Indians to watch the parade and walk on Main Street. She shrugged and said, "It is the way they are." Not until years later, as a young adult, did I begin to give serious thought to that incident. I have pondered it many, many times since and still do. The same question was and is always there: why?

The answer was and is always the same: because they can.

If by happenstance someone who knew my father had recognized him for who and what he was and reported him to the authorities, he would have been escorted off of Main Street at the very least, and perhaps even arrested and thrown in jail. Most of the white people in that small town would probably have thought it was acceptable to punish an Indian person in some way for violating a rule established for that day. On July 3rd and on July 5th and on every other day, Indians could walk down Main Street without any repercussions. On July 4th, we were not welcome because that was what law enforcement officers, or the city council, or the mayor decided. They could do that because they were in control.

It was immaterial to them that my father and my uncle were combat veterans of World War II, both having served in the Pacific against the Japanese. They probably would not have cared that my father's younger brother had died at age 19 as a result of wounds suffered in combat in June of 1945, on the island of Luzon in the Philippines. The town fathers of that small community would not have cared that my paternal grandmother was a Gold Star Mother (a mother whose child had been killed in a combat action). It was more important to them that Main Street be free of Indians. Intolerance sanctioned and empowered by the community.

As human beings we are shaped by our experiences, especially those out of the ordinary. Survival tolerance is still part of my nature and always will be. For me, and likely other native people, it's a learned mechanism that is hard to shed.

But tolerance is positive as well. My grandparents were extremely tolerant of me, especially in my early childhood. They were tolerant of my moods, behavior, and habits because they cared about me. They had raised my mother and my uncle, after all, and understood how children were. My moods and my behavior were nothing new to them, just part of the reality of childhood. They were part of what I was in those years, and they were not (as I recall) overwhelming or constant problems. The point is that my grandparents sometimes (probably often) had to be tolerant of unacceptable behavior, but never did they have to be tolerant of me as a person. It did not enter their minds, or later mine, that they had to "tolerate" the part of me that was white, my one-eighth French blood. That seemingly innocuous reality opened a window to a broader understanding for me; it taught me that tolerance for any reason is a good thing because it can be the first step toward the absence of prejudice.

To take this first step, it is not necessary to like one another, as long as we know that we all have the same right to exist. After all, the story that opens this chapter begins with the words "Long, long ago it was said that all the people spoke the same language." If they had not, the wolf and the raven would not have been able to communicate. And perhaps that language has nothing to do with words after all, but with the simple act of tolerance.

The wolf and the raven disliked one another for reasons that were right and logical for each of them. Their initial tolerance was very limited, based on what each could gain from the other. As their relationship progressed they both learned that they stood to gain much more from each other than that practical exchange. In the end they became friends. They did not tolerate each other in spite of what the other was. As far as I am concerned, they tolerated each other because their friendship far exceeded the perceptions and limitations of "not as good as" or "less than." Those factors no longer mattered. What mattered was the value each saw in the other as a fellow being who was part of the world.

Recently my oldest son texted a photograph of his son, my grandson, who is five and in kindergarten. The caption was "Tokahe and his kola." *Kola* is "friend" in Lakota. In the photograph my black-haired and brown-skinned grandson (Lakota and Navajo) is standing with his arm around his best friend, who has blond hair and light skin. I doubt that either of these good friends realizes that they are exhibiting unconditional tolerance. At their age, being friends is not a matter of race, creed, or color. It is two kindred spirits forming a bond and having the adventure of kindergarten. For them there is absolutely nothing about each other they need to tolerate. For them it is total acceptance of what the other is. No more and no less.

Innocence is the power that children have, one that we all have but lose when the world shows us what life is really all about—or so we are told. But the memory of the sanctity of innocence should motivate us to strive for it: a full circle back to a state of mind when we could and did look at the world around us without the burden of prejudices. Sadly, many of us cannot divest ourselves of the prejudices we have acquired and learned. We are not strong enough, or courageous enough, to consider that something, or someone, or some situation or circumstance could be different than we believe. We would rather be comfortable with our perceptions, even if they are wrong.

Most of us who have been kicked around by life (and who has not been?) probably think that innocence has no place in the world as we know it to be. Consequently we limit ourselves by looking at life and the world through the small window of our reality. We find a certain amount of security in that. Innocence, though, was the realm wherein we had the ability to see without limits and perceive without prejudice. If we had that ability as adults, we could look at the world as it really is with all its foibles and endless variety. That is tolerance. To be tolerant we do not have to be innocent, we simply have to remember what it was like to be innocent.

chapter three

Iktomi Flies

Anyone and everyone who lives on the great northern prairies knows that winter is the harshest season of the year. Deep snow and intense cold combine with wind to punish the land and its beings with blizzard after blizzard. In a flat place with few rolling hills and few trees to block the wind, it is a dangerous and sometimes deadly time. There are four ways to survive: Some, like many of the birds, simply fly to warmer places and return in the spring. There are a few, like bears, frogs, lizards, and snakes, who find a snug place and sleep through the entire winter. Everyone else makes preparations through the summer and autumn either by laying away stores of food and improving their dwellings or eating and eating and to fatten up their bodies for when food is scarce. In one way or another, everyone does their best to survive until spring.

However, there was one being who never prepared for winter, and there were many reasons he did not. For one, he was afraid of hard work. For another, he thought he was smarter than he really was and could use his wits to survive. As a result, he had a hard life, always on the edge of starvation, with no place to call his own.

This being was Iktomi (eek-toh-me). Many of the prairie dwellers felt he really did not belong on the prairie lands. As a matter of fact, it was hard to know where he belonged. No one was sure where he had come from. There were rumors that he and his twin brother had fallen from the sky. Their mother, Moon, had grown tired of their misbehaving, so she cast them down to the earth. There was no way to know what kind of beings they had been in the sky, but on the earth Iktomi was a small, weak, and always disheveled little creature, while his twin brother, Iya, was a giant and the complete opposite of Iktomi. They were alike in one way, however: both were unpredictable.

So it was that one day late in the autumn, skinny, hungry little Iktomi sat in an old hillside den, shivering in the cold wind. The fire he had built the night before had long since gone out, because he had not gathered enough firewood. He had eaten the last morsel of food he had stolen from a raven. Prospects were not good, to say the least, not only for this day but because winter was nearly here.

He crawled as far back into the deep as he could, to get out of the wind. Days ago he had traded away the only robe he had for a bit of food. Now he wished he had not as the wind pushed its way into the shallow cave. Suddenly he heard a slight noise outside. Iktomi held his breath, but the noise did not sound like it was made by a large being, like a bear or a long-tailed cat or a wolf. Taking a chance, he poked his head out.

"I was wondering if you were still here," said a friendly voice. It was Digs, the prairie dog. He and his people had great villages of underground dens. He carried a large bundle of seeds to add to his supply of winter food. Iktomi eyed the bundle. Though seeds were not among his favorite foods, any food was good when one did not have any.

Digs saw where Iktomi's beady little eyes were gazing. "How are things with you?" he asked. "Are you ready for winter?" The last question he asked with a bit of a smirk on his face, because he knew the answer.

"I am still in the planning stage," replied Iktomi.

"Yes, well," chuckled the prairie dog, "I am afraid that circumstances are far past that. I can feel winter's presence in this autumn wind. My family and I are still busy. We want to take advantage of these last days before the snow comes."

"Might you have some room in your village?" ventured Iktomi, hopefully.

"I am afraid even our largest dens are much too small for you," Digs said, secretly thankful for that reality. Iktomi was a bottomless hole when it came to food. Though he felt pity for him, the prairie dog knew that Iktomi's situation was of his own making. Everyone knew that winter always came, and everyone prepared one way or another. Everyone, that is, except for this forlorn creature who sat shivering in the wind.

"There is nothing good about winter," Iktomi spat, as he shivered and looked up at the gray skies.

"Not true," countered the prairie dog. "Our people make the best of it, like many others do. We spend our days listening to our grandparents tell stories, and we eat the food we have stored. The winds may howl above us and the snow may fall heavily, but deep inside our dens we are snug and warm."

"That is easy for you to say," growled Iktomi.

"Because we have prepared," Digs reminded him, patiently.

Iktomi watched the prairie dog ambling away with the bundle of seeds on his back toward his warm and snug dwelling. He kicked at the ground. Why had he not prepared? Of course, he had asked himself the same question last autumn. With a deep sigh, he decided to go to one of the villages of the Two-Legged People. Perhaps they would take him in. There was nothing to lose by asking.

Along the way he came to a deep pond and found Slaps, the beaver, patching his lodge with slabs of mud.

"Greetings to you, Iktomi," sang out the beaver. "How goes it with you?"

"I am on my way to see the two-leggeds," Iktomi replied.

"Then you have a long walk," warned Slaps. "They have moved to a valley a long way from here, to their winter camp."

It was not news Iktomi wanted to hear. This was not the kind of a day to make a long journey, especially when he was not certain the two-leggeds would take him in. "No matter," he lied, "I was also planning on looking at a den above the river."

"Good journey to you," said Slaps, too busy working to watch Iktomi leaving.

Dejectedly, Iktomi trudged across the meadows and hills until he was too tired to walk any more. Along the way he had picked the last bits of fruit from several berry thickets. But they were small and bitter and far from enough. Not knowing what else to do, he found shelter out of the wind on the lee side of a bank.

A cold sun hung behind a thin covering of clouds, making everything seem colder. Iktomi sighed deeply. There was nothing for him to do but make the long trek to the village of the Two-Legged People. There were times when they were kind to him, but mostly they ridiculed him. He knew they referred to him as the Tricky One. But he would endure just about anything for food and a warm place to sleep over the winter. Who was he trying to fool? He would do anything not to starve and freeze.

Suddenly the sound of the wind was different. Iktomi instinctively curled himself into a ball, not knowing what to expect. He certainly was not prepared for a gray form that flashed past him and came to earth in the grass nearby. A large goose with a black head and neck and a white throat. It looked around and immediately saw Iktomi.

"Who are you?" Iktomi asked, relieved that it was not one of the sky hunters, like the great eagle.

"I am called Traveler," replied the goose, his voice resonant and clear. "I am a scout for some of my people. We are the last to go south."

Iktomi knew about geese. He had seen many of them in long lines flying overhead, practically filling the skies. They flew south in the autumn and north in the spring.

"What are you doing here?" the Tricky One wondered.

"Looking for a place to rest for the night and find some food. We have a long journey to make," Traveler replied.

"Tell me," said Iktomi. "Where do your people go for the winter?"

"Far, far to the south," the goose told him. "We spend the winter along the great water. There it is warm, even hot, and there is plenty of food."

"My, my," was all Iktomi could say. "Would that I could fly, so I could go there, too."

The big gray goose looked at the skinny, unkempt being huddled against the bank. He had never seen anyone or anything so forlorn. "Do you live here?" he asked.

"Yes," admitted Iktomi. "I do."

"As far as I know, prairie dwellers prepare for winter," said the goose. "I assume you have done so, since you live here."

"Whether I am prepared or not," countered Iktomi, sidestepping the truth, "I would much prefer spending the winter where it is warm and where there is plenty of food."

"Then you are welcome to accompany us," offered Traveler.

"Very kind of you, but, alas, I cannot fly," Iktomi whined. "You are born to it, I am not."

"Have you tried?" the goose wanted to know.

"No," Iktomi said. "Flying has never entered my mind."

"Then perhaps it is time you give it some thought," the big bird suggested.

"You are mocking me," protested the Tricky One. "I am not made to fly. The Creator gave you wings."

"True," agreed the goose. "But when we are still small, our mothers teach us to fly. More than feathers is necessary. One must also have the will."

"That is all very well for you," Iktomi insisted. "A bird mustering up the will to fly is one thing, but for me it is impossible."

"Then what have you got to lose by trying?" Traveler reasoned. "Unless you have a snug dwelling and an endless supply of food waiting for you."

The goose had no way of knowing Iktomi's real situation, of course, but the Tricky One winced. *Perhaps this bird is magic somehow,* he thought. *Or he is teasing me so he can laugh.*

"I know not why you are telling me I should learn how to fly," he said, suspiciously. "But I can think of nothing more useless. It would be a waste of effort."

The goose turned and gazed at the landscape, appearing to lose interest in the conversation. He sighed. "Just as well," he said. "Flying is not for fools or the weak of heart. Besides, I need to find food for my friends and relatives who will be here soon." He walked down the slope. "I cannot waste my time trying to teach you to do anything you do not want to do. Be well."

"I would not know how to begin!" shouted Iktomi.

The goose did not stop but glanced back. "I will be here at dawn tomorrow," he called out. "If you want to learn to fly, be here."

That evening Iktomi surprised himself with his own industriousness. He managed to dig a shelter, with his bare hands, into a cut bank, just wide enough to fit him and deep enough to block most of the wind. Then he gathered grass, brush, and twigs enough for a small fire. Though he was starving he did manage to ward off the night's cold. A last little flicker of flame sputtered out just as dawn broke over the eastern horizon.

True to his word the goose descended from the gray sky and landed near the bank. Iktomi stiffly left his shelter and approached the waiting bird.

"This is a good beginning," said the goose. "You have exceeded my expectations simply by being here."

After two days without food Iktomi wondered if his ability to reason was weakened, because he heard himself say, "I want to learn how to fly and go south where it is warm."

"Then I trust you have had a good night's rest," cried the goose. "If you are not flying by the time the sun goes down again, you will spend the winter here."

Traveler led the trembling Iktomi to the top of a hill with a long downward slope. Near a knot of bushes was a strange-looking object. Two, as a matter of fact. Two thin poles with long goose-wing feathers attached in a line, side by side.

"My friends and relatives and I donated two feathers each, one from each wing," Traveler said, pointing to the feathered poles. "We will tie one to each arm."

Iktomi felt just a little foolish as he stood at the top of the hill, a feathered pole attached to each arm. "What do I do now?" he asked with some trepidation.

"Two things, at once," advised the goose. "You will run down this hill as fast as you can. As you are running you must move your arms up and down. The faster you run and the faster you move your arms, the better chance you have of lifting yourself into the sky."

"Lifting?"

"Yes, it is precisely how we do it. How any bird does it."

A wave of doubt coursed through Iktomi's thin frame and appeared in his close-set eyes, not unnoticed by the big goose. He stepped up and faced the Tricky One, eye to eye.

"Do you know what faith is?" he asked.

"Faith?"

"Yes, faith."

"What does faith have to do with feathers and flying?" Iktomi demanded.

"Everything," replied the goose, resolutely. "Faith is just as necessary as feathers. We gave you the feathers, but we cannot give you the faith. That is for you to find."

"Where do I find it?"

Fortunately, Traveler was a wise old goose, and patient. "What do you believe in?" he asked. "Do you believe in right, or goodness, perhaps kindness? Or do you believe in taking care of only yourself?"

"All I want to do is fly and go south with you, where it is warm," stammered Iktomi.

"Indeed. That is why you need faith. Faith enables you to believe. You must believe that you can fly, that you will fly."

Iktomi looked at the feathered poles tied to his arms, and then down the long slope. "But something tells me there is also some effort to be made," he said, fearfully.

"As I said, run down the hill, flap your wings, believe that you will fly, and lift yourself into the sky."

Iktomi laughed though nothing was funny. "Last winter I nearly froze in my den," he recalled.

"And nearly starved." After a deep sigh, he lifted his feathered arms high and began to run.

"Move them up and down, like wings!" Traveler called out.

Iktomi had never run faster than a trot in his entire life, at least not since he had been cast down to the earth. His spindly legs were not accustomed to such sudden and strenuous activity. Moving his arms like wings was not easy either. Neither was performing those two simple movements together. He was managing to coordinate them when he stumbled over a bristly soapweed. In the next heartbeat he plowed a furrow in the dirt with his face.

A sudden errant thought flashed through his mind, before his anger exploded. Flying was above the Earth, not in it.

Iktomi rose on his trembling legs spitting dirt and shaking his head. A stream of indistinguishable sounds erupted from his mouth. What he assumed was a show of righteous rage was not perceived as such by the goose.

Traveler had never seen anything so comical in his life, but he stifled his laughter and endeavored to look wise and caring.

"These things happen," he counseled. "I recall falling before I was able to fly for the first time."

"That . . . that is comforting," spat the Tricky One. "What do I do now?"

"Come back to the top and try again," said the goose.

Iktomi was about to protest when he saw the first snowflake float past his face. In an instant he envisioned the entire prairie covered in snow as far as the eye could see. Somewhere, far, far to the south was a land where there was no snow. A warm land.

With renewed energy he hurried back to the top of the hill.

"Now," advised the goose. "It is not necessary to do anything different. Run, move your arms, and believe."

"Run, move my arms, and believe," Iktomi repeated, though not with much conviction.

"Remember," Traveler encouraged, "believing is doing, not the other way around."

Iktomi nearly reached the bottom of the slope before he tripped once again. This time he did not fall as hard, and he thought he felt a bit of lift, but he could not be certain. After he picked himself up and loosed an exasperated sigh, he trudged back to the top.

He did not fall the next time, or the next, or the next. Each time he climbed back to the top, however, it was harder and harder to do.

"You are doing everything right," Traveler pointed out. "However, I do not think you believe that you can actually fly."

"I think you are right," admitted Iktomi. "All I can think about is not falling."

"This time," the goose persisted, "imagine yourself flying. Imagine it. Think of nothing else. Imagine yourself above the ground, above the trees."

Iktomi sighed. "I will, I will."

And so he did, and so he flew.

In that first instant it was like a dream. He was flying, he was above the ground. The bottom of the hill seemed to be falling away, then he realized that he was getting higher—and higher! Realization nearly gave way to disbelief. He reacted by moving his arms faster, and recovered. He was flying.

Astonishment and disbelief nibbled at the edges of his awareness, but he allowed himself to accept the reality of the moment. Then he heard a rush of wind and saw a big gray goose next to him. Traveler was smiling proudly.

"What do we do now?" Iktomi shouted.

"Practice!" replied the goose. "Keep moving your arms so you can climb higher. Then we will simply glide. Look ahead, not down, and just do what I do."

Iktomi pushed back the fear nipping at him and mimicked every movement of his fellow flier. Before he knew it the land below him became larger, and he realized he was higher than the tallest tree or the highest hill.

I am flying. I am flying, he told himself over and over. For some reason he was afraid to close his eyes, but found he had to squint against the wind on his face.

Following Traveler's every lead, Iktomi learned how to bank and make a turn and bend his lower legs up to climb higher. Moment after moment he gained more confidence. Then he began to worry about getting back to the ground, knowing that he could not fly all day without getting tired. He shouted his concern to Traveler.

"Landing is simply gliding down," the goose said. "The big test will be to get back into the air again. Let us try."

Iktomi's first landing was a little sudden, mainly because he glided in at too sharp an angle. But he did manage. After a moment's rest, Traveler led him to the top of a hill for another takeoff.

The goose had been right all along. One simply had to believe that one could fly. So it was that Iktomi managed to get off the ground again. Soon enough he was high above the land. As a matter of fact he was beginning to feel very pleased with himself. He was enjoying the view immensely.

Suddenly they were surrounded by numerous geese—Traveler's friends and relatives. "We must now turn and head south," the big goose said. "Just get in line behind me."

Iktomi took his place behind Traveler. Looking around he realized that he was now part of a great arrowhead-shaped formation, the kind he had seen only from the ground before. His joy knew no bounds. The air rushing past his thin little body was cold, but he knew that he was headed for warmer climes. He could not wait.

The landscape passed beneath. Hills, meadows, creeks, prairie, trees, and grass. In the sky around them were snowflakes. Winter was indeed coming soon. As he settled in and began to feel more at ease, Iktomi realized that there was a line between not believing he was actually flying and believing it—accepting the reality of what was happening. The secret to staying in the air was to *believe,* to have faith.

All too soon, his faith was tested. Above a river they were approaching a large village of two-leggeds.

As two-leggeds do, they paused in whatever they were doing to watch the long lines of geese pass overhead. It was not too long before one of the two-leggeds saw something unusual in the sight. Among the geese was a strange creature. A strange creature that was, of all things, Iktomi!

RETURNING TO THE LAKOTA WAY

Word spread quickly in the village, and soon crowds were watching, pointing at the non-goose flying with the geese.

Iktomi and the geese were passing directly over the village. The Tricky One was continuing to marvel at the view of everything from the sky. It was a perspective he never imagined. But how could he? Flying was for the birds and a few insects.

Iktomi looked down and saw the village and recognized the dwellings. They looked round from his perspective. He also saw the two-leggeds looking up and pointing. He had been in a village before and knew the dwellings to be snug. But he had to leave, in the interest of his own safety, because he had been less than honest. It was a memory Iktomi did not want to revisit.

Then he heard laughter, and voices.

"Look! It's that skinny little trickster, Iktomi! He is flying with the geese! Who does he think he is?"

For some reason Iktomi heard the laughter and the voices clearly. He looked to his left and then the right. The geese were paying no mind to the sounds rising from the village. But the voices rang in his head. Voices laughing, at him.

He looked ahead at the land that stretched away as far as he could see. Yet, he could not make the voices go away.

"Look! Iktomi is flying! That is hard to believe!"

It was almost as if a hand he could not see reached up from the ground, and grabbed him by the ankles. Traveler looked back and saw Iktomi wavering in the air. The wise old goose quickly knew what was happening.

"Do not pay attention to them," he warned. "They cannot believe what they are seeing."

But it was too late. The thought, *This is too good to be true* had been lurking in the back of his mind, a tiny grain of doubt that Iktomi had been able to ignore. In an instant it became a boulder. He felt himself falling.

Iktomi screamed and flapped his arms desperately but all he managed to do was slow his descent. For one awful, sad moment, he saw the V-shaped lines of geese above him. *Thud!* He bounced on a grassy hillside. Every part of his skinny little body was in pain and he had to struggle to catch his breath.

The geese circled back and descended to help him, but the two-leggeds from the village were already on the scene of Iktomi's crash. Traveler and his companions had no choice but to fly away. There were too many among the two-leggeds who thought of geese as a delicacy. And some of them who had Iktomi surrounded carried their hunting weapons. The geese had to leave Iktomi behind.

The two-leggeds looked at the little trickster. After several moments they decided that Iktomi would probably survive his fall, and that—miraculously—his body was still in one piece.

"He has the luck of fools," someone declared.

"What shall we do with him?" another asked.

"Leave him," came the suggestion. "He is nothing but trouble."

"Wait," said an older man. "Several years ago he told us where to find a herd of buffalo, in a hidden valley. So we gave him food. When we went to the valley, all we found was old and dried buffalo droppings. No buffalo had been there for years. He fooled us, and sneaked away before we came back."

"Yes, I remember," said a second man. "I think he needs to pay us for the food we gave him."

So it was decided. Iktomi would spend the winter in the village working off his debt. He was taken to the lodge of an old woman, a widow. She was a good woman and lived alone, so there was no one to help her. Until Iktomi was given to her.

The good thing was that Iktomi had a place to spend the winter, where he was warm and had food. The difficult part of it was he had to gather firewood and keep the old woman's fire going. When a hunter gave the old woman meat, it was Iktomi's task to cut it up and cook it. Then he had to haul water from the river. After the river froze and the ice was thick, it was harder and harder to cut a hole and keep it open.

Escape was impossible. Boys on the verge of manhood were assigned to watch Iktomi, one at a time. But as hard as he had to work, Iktomi had no intention of leaving. There was nothing for him out there; no food, no shelter—nothing.

The old woman was kind to him. She thanked him for his hard work and told him stories. Every night when his chores were finally done and he could curl up beneath his warm robe, Iktomi thought of flying. It seemed impossible to him that he had actually flown. He had kept some of the wing feathers the geese had given him, and he certainly remembered what the land looked like from the sky. It was a hard thing to believe.

Spring came, as it always did. New grass came up out of the earth and new leaves to the trees. One day

Iktomi heard the high, clarion call of geese. Looking up he saw many, many lines of them flying in their arrowhead formations. He wondered what lands they were returning from, and if his friend Traveler was among them.

Elders of the village declared that Iktomi had paid his debt, and said he could go. The old woman gave him a bundle of food and sent him on his way.

Iktomi forgot the old woman as soon as he was over the hill behind the village. He was only worried what would happen when his food ran out. It was a worry not new to him. He knew that some women from the village were planting corn along the river bottoms. In the autumn there would be ears of corn ready for picking. This would be something to remember when the hungry times came, as they surely would.

He did not know where he was going, but he was not in a hurry to get there. There was one thing he was absolutely certain of. He would never fly again.

Needless to say, he never did.

Wowicala
(woh-wee-jah-lah)
Faith

FLYING AND OTHER POSSIBILITIES

In most dictionaries, the first two definitions of the word *faith* are: *confidence or trust in a person or thing* and *belief that is not based on proof.*

The first definition implies that proof is necessary to some extent. We have faith that the sun will rise, for example, because we have seen it do so all of our lives. Or investors have faith that the stock market will behave in a certain way when a given set of factors come into play, determining whether it will be a "bear" or "bull" market. During World War II the Allied nations had faith they could win the war in Europe against Hitler and in the Pacific against Japan, likely based on the fact that they had defeated Germany in World War I. They had done it before and could probably do it again.

Faith in some contexts has become synonymous with *religion,* but of the two definitions only the second hints at this. Most people who are part of an organized religion (or an unorganized one, for that matter) believe in the existence of an all-knowing, all-powerful deity, though they have no proof that such a deity exists. They take it on faith that one does.

As a child I had faith in my grandparents. I knew that they would take care of me, although neither of them ever said that taking care of me was their responsibility. I knew I belonged with them. At that age I had no idea, of course, what religion was, although they took me to church on Sundays. Church was for me simply an activity my grandparents participated in with other people. They told me it was necessary for me to go with them and behave respectfully and be polite to the white man who came to pray. While in church I did what my grandparents asked, for a number of reasons. They had never put me in a situation where I felt threatened, uncomfortable, or embarrassed. I was not so analytical about circumstances at the age of five and six, of course, but I did know or feel that everything was good. Therefore there was no reason to doubt my grandparents.

Faith in my grandparents involved more than their ability or obligation to care for me. It took on added dimensions over time. As my ability to think and discern grew, I began to see them as two individuals with different habits and views, but basically operating—living life—from the same set of values: honesty, compassion, humility, generosity, and tolerance. They did not once invoke religion as the only way to live or look at life. Nor did their actions and statements ever approach what could be described as pious.

They were both members of the Episcopal Church, but what I find compelling now, from the perspective of my 67 years, is that their values reflected cultural influence more than Christian doctrine. Their interaction with the community (the village, as it were) was a reflection of being Lakota rather than being Christian. Something that I could not ascertain when I was a boy was that those Lakota people who adopted Christianity did so for one primary reason: many teachings and beliefs espoused by Christianity happened to coincide with Lakota beliefs. Among them were respect for elders, as in "honor thy father and thy mother," and another was the idea of sacrificing for others, which was represented in the Sun Dance. Therefore, in my early teen years I was confused when white priests and other white Episcopalians implied or stated outright that following the teachings of Jesus Christ—thus being Episcopalian—was preferable to being Lakota. In other words, I had to let go of being Lakota and embrace Christianity. I never got that same message from my grandparents, either in so many words or through their actions. It was important to them that I learned respect for other people (especially elders) and practiced the values they themselves lived by. While those values are not exclusive to the Lakota culture, neither are they exclusive to Christianity. It follows, then, to my way of thinking that faith is not exclusive to religion.

However any dictionary might define faith, all of us who include it in our philosophies of life have our own insight into what it is. Faith is one of those factors in life that cannot be generalized, because it rises out of experience and what we believe, what life has taught us. Thus it takes different forms.

People frequently comment that "faith" has helped them through a difficult situation. Obviously it is easier to make such a statement when the situation turns out positively, because the outcome seems to support the power of faith. But not every situation turns out well for everyone. The same circumstance or event that one person is able to emerge from unharmed may be disastrous for someone else, causing loss, injury, or death. Some might believe that faith prevented the situation from being worse than it was. Logically, they call on faith, too, to help them through the aftermath of a disastrous event. Surviving a natural disaster is often only the prelude to difficult consequences, such as the loss of a house or the deaths of friends and relatives—a sudden and complete change in everything that had been comfortable and "normal" up to the moment the disaster struck. At that juncture, faith is sorely needed.

When people talk about faith in these situations, they're obviously making reference to religion and an all-powerful deity. It is natural and understandable for those of us who believe in a god, whether we call that god Jehovah or Allah or Wakan Tanka, to ask for help in moments of stress, uncertainty, and imminent danger. If we survive the storm, as we saw above, we ascribe the outcome to the merciful intervention of that deity. Sometimes, however, we question why that deity would allow such a thing to happen. Therefore, out of the same circumstance we have an assertion or confirmation of faith and a feeling of doubt, and perhaps the latter shakes our faith a bit.

There are many unrelenting realities throughout this journey we call life, realities that are reaffirmed the longer we live. One of them is the unpredictability of life and another is the fact that there is bad as well as good. Though it seems to be an inherent human desire for all things to go well, or as we think they should, that does not happen every time. When situations do not go well or as we think they should—or we are faced with a sudden and unexpected catastrophic event or possibility—we may doubt the fairness of life. Often, in those instances, doubt may seem more powerful than faith.

A popular movie titled *Signs* explores the loss of faith. A priest (presumably an Episcopalian or Lutheran) loses faith in God as a consequence of his wife's death, after she is struck by a car while jogging. The priest experiences more than mere doubt, however. He renounces his faith and is angry with his god for allowing his wife's death. A priest, of all people, should know and understand that life is not always fair—but even he falls to the power of doubt.

Having faith is the foundation of hope. When we realize that a situation is far beyond our ability to change or rectify it, many of us give in to it. Some of us, however, even in the worst of times, hope for some kind of relief or resolution that will bring light into the darkness or end the uncertainty or pain. That grain of hope, I believe, arises from our basic instinct for survival. Faith drives that instinct and enables us—at least most of us—to cling to it no matter what because there is a fundamental human belief in goodness, the eternal hope that good will overcome evil, that right will prevail over wrong.

My grandparents taught me to believe that there is good in life, that good things do happen. By and large this is what every society or set of beliefs teaches us. It is certainly not a lie, but there's another side to this reality: bad things happen as well, ranging from disappointment (such as not getting a raise or a date with the object of your dreams) to setbacks (such as losing a job) to tragedy (such as a serious illness). We are taught that good is preferable, that we should strive to do good, to do the right thing, and to enable good. Therefore, given who my grandparents were and considering that their basic values were rooted in the Lakota culture, I choose to have faith in the strength of that culture and the best ideals it stood for and still does.

My grandparents also taught me that faith is believing in something without question—for example, compassion, truth, morality, generosity. It is knowing that those values—those human characteristics, if you will—do exist in the world.

Furthermore, faith is believing that those values will be exercised more often than not.

Faith is also putting one's own sense of compassion, truth, morality, or generosity into the mix when it is necessary. When we do, we are adding it to the sum total of those characteristics in the world, something like a snowball rolling down a hill, getting larger and more powerful as it goes. We do this any time we are compassionate, or truthful, or selfless. And if we believe that God created us and gave us—or enabled us to arrive at through our life's path, lessons, and choices—the values that we have, then having faith in our own strengths is having faith in God.

My kind of faith was not given to me because I was born a Lakota or because I was baptized an Episcopalian. It was taught to me a little at a time as I learned about the realities of my world, realities that I could perceive and were affirmed by the adults in my immediate family, primarily my grandparents. The environment that I enjoyed as a child—the prairie, river valley, rolling hills, gullies, and trees—was populated by other beings, such as birds, coyotes, foxes, prairie dogs, deer, antelope, raccoons, and squirrels, and everything and everyone functioned and behaved according to what they were. Trees, for example, could grow anywhere but were found predominantly near water, meaning along creeks and rivers and near springs. Certain kinds of thick-bladed grasses, or rushes, always grew only along creeks, rivers, and around springs. Redwing blackbirds were always found near water, but meadowlarks and grouse built their nests on the open prairies. Rattlesnakes and burrowing (or screech) owls lived with prairie dogs in underground burrows. When horses grew thicker-than-usual hair in the autumn, it was a sure sign that a harsh winter was coming. They were never wrong. The same could be said of caterpillars.

Although there were variables, these realities always occurred basically in the same way and generally at the same time of the yearly cycle when conditions were right (regardless of man's calendar). They could be counted on. One had faith in those realities, faith that they would always be part of the overall reality of life on the plains. There was a greater lesson, as well. One learned that faith in something was an operative and necessary part of being alive and having a life.

But to enable faith to work for us, we must know what we believe in. It has to be a part of each of us individually. Over my 67 years I have learned that the values my parents and all my grandparents tried to teach me are, in many ways, the foundation of faith. They taught me that with those values I am capable of facing, understanding, and enduring the negative aspects of life.

At the core of it, I believe faith is our very human instinct for things to be good and right, to turn out well. Faith is the one force that pushes or guides us toward the positive, to enable us to believe that good will win more times than bad. And if that belief inspires us individually to do what is right and good and moral and ethical at the moment it needs to be done, then faith is definitely a factor. For me, though, faith is more than hoping and believing that good will always win out, or that circumstances will always turn out the way I want them to. Faith is knowing that within me is the strength and ability to deal with the tough times, because I have been taught to do that, and I have done that. And as Iktomi shows us beyond a doubt, faith is just as necessary as feathers if we want to fly.

chapter four

The People of the Great Ones

It is said that everything has a beginning. This is true for every kind of being and every nation on the face of Grandmother Earth. Now and then there is more than one beginning. This is certainly true of those who once called themselves the Buffalo Nation. But we should not overlook the story behind the name.

Long, long ago, before the people called themselves the Buffalo Nation, they lived in the earth. How and when they came to the place they would eventually call the Heart of All Things, no one can remember. It happened so long ago that it is beyond the reach of memory, so long ago that it is on the other side of memory. Also lost in the mists of the past is the reason the people had become dwellers beneath the earth in the first place. There are some who think one of their ancestors, a young man, married a young woman whose people lived beneath mountains that rose from the prairie floor. Those mountains were sacred to the people, a place exceedingly beautiful to behold. From a distance the pine trees covering their slopes appeared black, so the mountains were called the Black Hills.

However they had come to live in a cave in the Black Hills, those-who-lived-in-the-earth had a good life. Other beings also lived in the cave but the people shared the place with them. Everyone in that underworld lived on the myriad of plants that grew there, near the creeks and around the springs, which were plentiful. All the beings, including the people, wanted for nothing.

Change comes in the most unexpected ways, however, and sometimes when it is least expected. One day one of those-who-lived-in-the-earth happened to be curious about a path that led upward, and he followed it. There were many great caverns, and a wind came in from some mysterious place and went out just as mysteriously. It was the wind that led this young man to a narrow passageway. He followed it up and up, listening to the sound of the wind. To the young man it was as if the earth itself was breathing, in and out.

After a long, long climb, the passageway narrowed until it was not much more than a low crack in the rock, and the young man had to crawl to fit into it. Suddenly, he was nearly blinded by bright light. Resisting the urge to flee back down into the cave, he covered his face until he could see again. Looking around, he saw strange sights and colors, and he nearly did retreat into the cave. But he was an adventurous young man and his curiosity overcame his fear.

Stretching before him was a meadow covered with grass and dotted with small groves of trees. On a distant slope were tall, dark trees through which breezes sighed and whispered. Over it all floated thin, wispy clouds beneath a sky of bright blue. In that same sky was a brilliant, glistening orb that seemed to beckon to the young man. He wondered if perhaps it was the reason for a kind of warmth he had never felt in his life.

Time was not important in those days on the other side of memory, and certainly not for a person who had spent his entire life beneath the earth where there was no sun or moon, no sunrises or sunsets. The young man wandered across the meadow to one hill and then another, staring at trees and plants and things he had never seen before. Here was a place he had heard of only in stories—stories he thought were only bits and pieces of old people's imaginations.

He wandered around gazing, gawking, and touching, almost as if he were a child again, discovering new things. The light was fading when he remembered he was in a place not his home, so he hurried back to the opening in the ground. Deep in the caverns of the cave he excitedly told the elders what had happened. He told them of the things he had seen beyond the opening at the top of the cave.

Some of the elders were angry with the young man. They scolded him for his impetuousness. Nevertheless, the news spread quickly. There was a different place—a different world—if the young man was telling the truth.

One thing was certain: curiosity was something everyone was born with—it was the way to explore life. In spite of the elders' warnings and advice that the situation should be approached with care, some begged the young man to take them up to the new world. After preparing food and filling water containers, they followed him to the opening. But not all of them were ready to make a bold leap. At the crucial moment, most of them gave in to their fears and stayed behind. Only three went out.

Those who stayed waited below the opening, sitting inside the narrow space and looking toward the light. The young man and the others had disappeared into that light. Impatience turned to apprehension as the four did not immediately return. But after a while the hesitant ones fell asleep, and suddenly, it seemed, they were being shaken awake by the four explorers.

Like the young man who had gone out first into the outer world, the three with him were excited, all trying to tell their stories at once. Their enthusiasm spread. The elders listened and suggested a plan. Eight of the ablest men were to go out and explore as far as they dared, then return to report.

And so it was done. Outside the eight men went in pairs in different directions. After a few days they returned. They brought with them a variety of plants and a container of water from a flowing stream, and they described everything they had seen. Most wondrous of all was the sun coming up in one place, traversing the sky, and going down in another.

Again the elders devised a plan, perhaps the most important one in the lives of their people. It was a simple plan: to leave their underground world. If all went well they would never again call themselves those-who-lived-in-the-earth. So it was that the people packed all their belongings and their tools. After one final gathering and a meal in the great, high cavern that had been their meeting place, everyone trekked upward toward the light. Everyone, that is, except for one woman.

Nothing that anyone said could entice her to change her mind. She simply and steadfastly refused to leave. Two of the elders stayed with her awhile—the oldest man and the oldest woman. They could see that she was at peace with her decision to stay behind. The elders knew that everything happened for a reason; life had a purpose and there was a power that had made the world. So they honored the woman's wish to remain.

The first days on the surface were full of uncertainty. Everything they saw, touched, tasted, or smelled was new, and they were overwhelmed by the sheer size of the landscape and the endless sky. Some of their all-but-forgotten stories told how they had once lived in this world that was new to them now. But even the oldest among them could not remember.

Little by little they grew accustomed to the new surroundings, adjusting to circumstances and conditions day by day. Occurrences such as wind and rain were a shock, and thunder and lightning were outright terrifying. But under the steady influence of the elders, the people learned how to get along on the surface. There was one unfailing truth: the sun came up each day, sometimes hiding behind different manners of cloud, it traveled across the sky, and went down. Sometimes another kind of light filled the night sky. Its light was not as bright nor as reliable as the sun's, but it was another reality for the people to embrace. Over time the people would come to understand those great powers in the sky, but those days were yet to come.

The people were not unused to cold and hunger. As gray clouds filled the skies and the breezes blew colder, the elders directed shelters to be built and food stored. Their wise counsel served the people well as the snows and cold of their first winter above the ground came. It was a deep cold they had not felt, but they knew how to build fires, and somehow the days passed and warmth returned to the land.

Over the warmer days of spring and into that first summer they explored the great mountains. They learned what manner of plants grew where, and there was enough bounty to feed them well, though they had to share it with other beings. By the next spring they were looking to the unknown lands stretching away beyond the edges of the mountains, their curiosity rising once more.

The elders knew they could not keep the young men back, no matter the weight of the wisdom and depth of the reason with which the old ones spoke. Young men were always most intrigued by the unknown; they could not resist its allure. So as the seasons went on, several young men—and it could be said they were both foolish and brave—turned their footsteps toward the distant horizons. Some went north, some east, others south, and still others west. Not all of them returned, but those who did told of a world that was endless: of mountains, valleys, gorges, prairies, and of rivers great and small.

Not all the people were ready or willing to leave their great mountains, a place of beauty as well as plenty, a place that became for them like the heart of Grandmother Earth herself. There were those, however, who yearned to see what waited beyond the far horizons. After generations of living within the limits of a cavern beneath the ground, they did not want to stop moving. So they became wanderers, never staying an entire season in one place, moving their dwellings often. Some young men captured wild dog pups and tamed them to be friends and companions, and to carry loads as well.

Years passed. The elders who had led the people out of the cave passed into the spirit world, and others took their place. The new elders did not feel the connection to their old world as their predecessors had, and they forgot that one of their people had stayed behind. Now no one went back to that world beneath the ground to visit her. As the years passed, anyone who did remember her assumed that she had passed into the spirit world as well.

Life was good. The people learned to adapt to the seasons and whims of the natural world, learning from the animals who long preceded them there. They learned that it was necessary to do more than planting and gathering to have enough food to survive. So they learned to hunt, again following the examples of the animals who hunted. The power that had created the world and everything in it also gave them the ability to reason and adapt. So they did.

One night a man, a thinker and a philosopher, had been gazing at the thinnest sliver of waning moon. Suddenly he envisioned a weapon in that shape. Cutting down a slender ash tree, he whittled and carved it to look like the waning moon, and thus the bow was born. Next he adapted the lance, making it slender and shorter to fit the bow. Then he showed the moon's gift to his fellow hunters. With the new weapon the hunters became more effective at procuring food for their families.

Nevertheless, as often happens in the natural world with its whims and cycles, circumstances changed. Less snow fell one winter, followed by fewer rains in the spring, which meant that the summer and autumn were dry. When it happened again, plants that were the source of sustenance for many animals did not grow. After the third or fourth cycle of dry seasons, the lack of water spelled doom for everyone and every thing.

Since the people now relied mainly on hunting to procure food, they had no choice but to range far and wide after the animals they hunted. And the animals in turn had to travel great distances to find food and water. Yet no matter how far the animals and the people searched, the land was dry and food was scarce. People and animals starved and died of thirst.

In times of need and distress, it is a primal force in everyone to yearn for home, and those who were still strong enough struggled with their last vestiges of strength to make their way back to their mountains and their cave. Not all survived the trek. The very few who did were met by the Woman-Who-Stayed—who was still alive after all—and her heart was broken by the news she heard. Her people were suffering and dying.

The woman left the cave and went out over the land and saw for herself. Dried-up creeks, plants, and trees withered from too much heat and not enough water were testament to the change that held the land and its inhabitants in a merciless grip. The woman returned to the shelter of the cave, her heart torn, her spirit feeling the pain of her people. She wept.

True desperation and heartache have a force. They are honest and primeval expressions that cannot be ignored. So as the Woman-Who-Stayed wept for her people, not knowing what to do to help or comfort them, her anguish reached the Power that had created everything. Something entered her awareness then, something like a whisper but carrying the power of thunder. There were no words she heard, only a sense of what she had to do.

After preparing herself according to her vision, the woman left the cave. In the open between two mountain ridges, she performed a simple ritual. Singing a song, she walked in a circle, sunwise, that is, in the direction the sun traveled across the sky. Once, twice, three times, and on the fourth circle she became a different being, one never seen on the face of the earth. She stood on four legs, taller at the shoulder than a man, her back curving up into a hump. Her hump sloped down into a great head with two black horns that curved upward, one on each side. She stood on four legs with black split hooves, and she was dark brown in color. The once all-but-forgotten Woman-Who-Stayed had turned into the most powerful creature on the land.

Not only did she become a different being, she was turned into many. As she continued to circle—as she had been told to do by the Power that entered her spirit—her song became a bellow that echoed across the land, and as she completed each circle another being like her appeared. Each of those new beings danced in its own circle, creating itself over and over again. By the time the sun had gone down, there were so many of these new beings that they filled the mountain meadows.

As the sun rose again, the wondrous new creatures left the great mountains and scattered themselves across the land. There were so many that they came out of the mountains in seemingly endless streams.

Hunters among the people were the first to see them. They were afraid because they had never seen four-legged beings so large. Wisely they hid and watched. They realized that the new creatures were not hunters. Hunters among the animals had fangs and claws, and their eyes were on the front of their heads—like the great cat and the wolf—while these beings' eyes were set on the sides. Furthermore, the new creatures nibbled on what little grass there was.

After days of observing the new creatures, the hunters devised a plan. Working as a group they took one down. Many arrows were necessary, but their hopes were realized because the flesh of the creature provided so much meat. Soon word spread across the land and hope was rekindled. Hunters took meat home to their families and the people were saved from starvation. Not only that, they were reinvigorated.

Elders among the people sensed that the appearance of the large four-legged creatures was much more than a fortuitous turn. Whatever had brought it about, for them it was nothing less than the gift of life. Not only had the animals appeared at just the right moment to save the people, they had appeared in astonishing numbers. There was certainly a wondrous mystery to it, something profound that they could not yet fully understand. As if in affirmation, the rains returned and when winter came the snows fell again. Even the land itself was reborn. Grasses, shrubs, tree, and berry thickets flourished anew, and creeks and rivers filled again.

Since the obvious reason for the reprieve was the great animal that seemed to arrive out of nowhere, the people turned their efforts to knowing it as well as they could. Because there were so many of the great beasts and their main food was grass, they were not hard to find. Their domain was the great prairies. Scouts were sent to watch them, day and night, and it was not long before they became familiar with the habits of the largest four-leggeds on the prairie.

These animals that had saved them now became the main source of the people's livelihood. In addition to being so plentiful that they were difficult to count, their sheer size was astonishing. One could feed a family from one new moon to the next. But as the days and seasons went by the people saw that there was more to these creatures than a source of food. There was more than the power that comes from strength and sheer size. They also symbolized the very spirit of survival and the ability to thrive on a land that separated the weak from the strong.

Various names arose to refer to them. One was the High-Backed Ones, which aptly described the high hump on their backs. Another was the Great Grass Eaters, because among the grazing animals they were the largest of all. Those two names, and others, eventually evolved into the Great Ones, a simple name that aptly described what they meant to the people.

The Great Ones roamed across the land in herds, some larger than others. Some herds were so numerous that it would take a day for them to cross a river. The people saw that each herd established its own territory and wandered throughout it, going where the grass was good. Every spring their young were born, their coats a reddish brown, so the cycle of the moon when the calves were born came to be known as the Moon of the Red Calves. No beings were better at surviving the deep snow and cold of the harsh prairie winter than the Great Ones. With their large split hooves they could dig through crusted snow to the grass beneath. Their hair grew long and thick for the winter, protecting them from intense cold. And when enemies came, though they had only a few, the Great Ones formed circles with the young in the center, making a protective wall of heads and sharp horns that nothing could breach.

The Great Ones were strong of body and spirit, virtues that the people knew they could take for themselves along with the sustenance. In time there was very little in the everyday lives of the people that did not show the mark of the Great Ones. They had discarded the old lodges made of brush and wood in favor of a new kind made from a few of the Great Ones' hides scraped and sewn together. From the rawhide they made containers of every sort, for food, clothing, and household items. With the hair left on, the hides were warm sleeping robes. But there was much more. The people fashioned cups and spoons from the horns, toys from the backbones, and sled runners from the long rib bones.

Among the elders, some harbored a secret worry that the Great Ones might one day leave. They had come and saved the people. What would happen if they were to leave as suddenly and as mystically as they came? It was a question that could not be answered. But every elder knew that if the Great Ones did leave, circumstances for the people would change. Perhaps they would suffer again.

There arose another thought. Without the Great Ones the people might never have recovered from the extreme hardships that had befallen them. They might have all died of thirst and starvation. To some of the elders it was as if the Great Ones had been *sent* to save them, perhaps by the Power that had made the world. Especially since such an animal had never been seen before.

The truth came with an old woman who arrived at a summer gathering one day. She was one of those who had returned to the cave in the mountains during the darkest days of hardship. She told how the woman who had stayed in the cave was heartbroken by the pain of her people, so heartbroken that she could not be comforted, but offered herself to the Power that had created them all to stop the suffering. Though she was not certain that anyone would believe her, the old woman described how the Woman-Who-Stayed sang and danced and turned into the great animal that had saved the people.

Among the elders there was no doubt that the old woman's story was true. One of them pointed out that among the great herds it was the cows who led; it was the mothers among them who protected their offspring so ferociously. The elders were awed and humbled that the Woman-Who-Stayed had been so selfless. The wisest of them suggested that they might establish ways to show that they were grateful. Another suggested that they must honor the great animals for all that they meant to the people. At the same time, the elders knew that they had to acknowledge the realities of the world around them. Not to do so would be to invite imbalance.

One reality was that the Great Ones had to be killed in order for the people to realize the gifts of life and comfort. The Great Ones had become the primary source for the basic needs of food, shelter, and clothing, gifts that were given after the sacrifice of life itself. So after much contemplation the elders devised rituals to honor that sacrifice.

They were simple rituals, but the elders advised, indeed begged, the people to perform them with humility and respect. First was the Calling Ceremony. Young men were chosen to be scouts, and it was their task to know where the herds were at all times during every season of the year, but it was an older man, one humble and respected among the people, who was charged with calling the Great Ones when it was time to hunt. The caller humbled himself and prayed to the spirit of the great animals to make themselves available, to bless the people with the gift of life.

The other ritual was one of thanksgiving. Every hunter was instructed to carry red willow bark and water with him on the hunt. After one of the great animals was taken, the hunter was to beg forgiveness for taking its life, then leave the bark and water as an offering.

Furthermore, no part of the animal's body was to be wasted, and the people were to always think and speak of the Great Ones with respect. Over time many of them began to think of themselves as People of the Great Ones, since the great animals' strength of spirit and the sustenance derived from their flesh had made the people a strong nation. The Buffalo Nation.

Thus on the great prairie lands that stretched as far as the eye could see, the Great Ones flourished, and so did the people. From west to east, from north to south, numberless herds covered the land, so numerous that when they ran, the earth shook.

In time the people would know hardship again, but this time it was due to a weakness that caused imbalance. A weakness that occurred because the people forgot who they were and where they had come from. As before it was one of the Great Ones who came and guided them back onto the proper path. She appeared in the form of a white cow and taught the people how to strengthen themselves and to remember who they were. She taught them important and necessary rituals in order that they could remain strong.

One of the rituals was known as They-Look-at-the-Sun-and-Dance. Men who participated in the ritual would literally stare into the sun and dance while making a sacrifice of pain and selflessness on behalf of their people. If any ritual could define the spirit of the people, it would be this, because it symbolized the importance and necessity of selflessness and sacrifice, and to remind the people that it was those realities that had saved them and then made them who they were.

Wiiciglusna

(wee-ee-chee-gloo-shnah)

**Selflessness or to let oneself fall,
to give of oneself**

To Look at the Sun and Dance

No tradition or ceremony is more readily associated with the Lakota people than the Sun Dance. Non-native people tend to characterize it as archaic, primitive, pagan, and even barbaric, based on misinformation or a sense of superiority or something in between. But these reactions obscure both the overall purpose of the Sun Dance and the core reason for the aspect that the misinformed most object to: the piercing done to the actual Sun Dancers who are the crux of the ritual. In so many words, the Lakota Sun Dance is the very representation and demonstration of *selflessness*.

Sun Dancers, who are male, willingly and intentionally undergo the piercing in the upper chest area, through the skin and into the upper layer of the pectoral muscles. To be pierced means to experience pain on behalf of the people. To be sure, the entire experience of dancing for four days on rough ground in bare feet, from sunup to sundown, while staring at the sun, is not exactly pain-free. In many cases the participants do not take food or water during the day.

In pre-reservation days, Sun Dancers pledged many months ahead to do the Sun Dance. In the months leading up to the ritual, under the guidance and instruction of medicine men, they participated in ceremonies and rituals to prepare them. When the time came, therefore, they were ready mentally, physically, and spiritually to honor and demonstrate the tenets of selflessness.

Selflessness was obviously a necessary value in pre-reservation Lakota society, and it is important to understand why. What did *selflessness* mean in that day and age and what impact did it have on the everyday lives of people?

The story in this chapter, "The People of the Great Ones," is part of the answer. If it had not been for the total selflessness of one person, the people would have died during the hard times of drought and starvation. The Woman-Who-Stayed became *pte*—the bison (or buffalo)—after she offered herself to Wakan Tanka to end the suffering of her people. It is no secret to those of us Lakota who are aware of our history that the buffalo were the backbone of our lifestyle and culture on the northern plains. Practically speaking, they were the source of food, shelter, and clothing. There was also a long list of tools, utensils, weapons, and household goods made from their flesh and bones. That physical connection led to a symbiotic and spiritual relationship. In the eyes and hearts of our ancestors, the selfless generosity of the buffalo defined and enabled who we were as a people. So much so that we called ourselves *Pte Taoyate*, or the "People of the Buffalo"—the Buffalo Nation.

There are, of course, slight variations in the story of how the Lakota people and the bison formed such a symbiotic relationship. But the basic realities of the relationship are true. The bison were a source of sustenance and spiritual strength. And we Lakota do still think of ourselves as Pte Taoyate, and one of our oldest stories tells us we were created because of one individual's selflessness. Therefore, because we believe that we owe our very existence to *selflessness*, it is a value that is part of our cultural identity and essential to our spirit as a people.

In pre-reservation Lakota society, selflessness was such an essential value that it was an integral part of expectations for a small segment of the community. Though everyone was expected to be selfless, a certain group was expected to set the example for the rest. Those were young men selected to be Shirt Men.

The elders, on behalf of the community, decided which young men were eligible. They had to be of exemplary character and building reputations as leaders in the community. Though selections were sometimes influenced by politics or pressure from prominent individuals or families—since being a Shirt Man carried a certain amount of prestige—for the most part young men of good character were selected.

At a public ceremony after the young men accepted the honor (now and then a young man did decline), a wise old man told them of their duties as Shirt Men. Part of what he said to them was this:

> To wear the Shirts you must . . . help others before you think of yourselves.
>
> Help the widows and the orphans and those who have little to wear and to eat and have no one to speak for them.
>
> Do not look down on others or see those who look down on you . . .

In other words, anyone given to arrogance and a self-serving attitude need not apply, because to be a Shirt Man was to constantly give of oneself for others' good.

No privileges came with the status of Shirt Man and certainly no authority, only the responsibility to live a life of service. The old stories say that not all young men given the distinction lived up to the expectations the people had, but most did. Interestingly, the last time Shirt Men were selected by the Oglala Lakota was around 1865, and one of those in the last group was an up-and-coming warrior leader by the name *Tasunke Witko*, or "His Crazy Horse." He is known to history simply as Crazy Horse.

Though Crazy Horse is known mostly for his exploits on the battlefield in the turbulent history of the northern plains in the latter part of the 19th century, there was another side to the man. As reckless and courageous as he was in battle, he was quiet, shy, and humble in all other respects. There were many Lakota men of the day, young and not so young, who were brave in battle. Because combat was the best way to build a record of achievement, and hence a strong reputation, on the way to attaining leadership, many men wanted to be known as formidable men capable of being leaders. Crazy Horse, on the other hand, did not turn his back on the responsibility of being a Shirt Man. Given what we know about his character, he would have been selfless without that status.

Suffice to say that his herd of horses was always smaller than other men's, because he regularly gave horses to those who needed them. Likewise, he and his wife, Black Shawl, did not hesitate to give away their own food to families in need. Consequently their food containers were always nearly empty. But selflessness involved more than material generosity. By all accounts Crazy Horse treated everyone with courtesy and respect and did not expect preferential treatment because he was a leader. As a matter of fact, he consistently and actively demonstrated that a leader's first responsibility was service to his community.

Crazy Horse's selflessness was also demonstrated on the field of battle. He was consistently the first to charge the enemy—also part of the Shirt Man's creed—and he was the last to leave the field, always leading the rear guard. Any man who followed him on a military patrol knew that Crazy Horse did not leave anyone behind, alive or dead.

To be sure, Crazy Horse was not the only person who acted selflessly. In a culture where actions were much more important than things, giving of oneself ensured that no one was left behind, or went cold or hungry, or was forgotten because he or she could not pay a material price. Each and every time the sacred tradition of the Sun Dance is conducted, it serves as a powerful reminder that the buffalo gave of themselves to make us strong.

Selflessness is a virtue that cannot be legislated. Its value and impact must be learned firsthand. The best way to learn it is to benefit from someone else's selfless action. When we do, we learn that selflessness needs little more than sincere effort to have an effect.

In our time, however, it would seem that the world teaches us not selflessness but self-indulgence, primarily because technology makes things easier, perhaps too easy. As far as I am concerned, there is a point at which technology crosses the line between making life easier and teaching us to be lazy and feel entitled. The consequence of being lazy and feeling entitled is helplessness.

The telephone, for example, made voice communication easier, initially with the help of an operator who had to connect calls. Then rotary dialing enabled local calls without operators and we had to remember numbers (or write them down) and dial them on the phone. Dialing became punching when buttons replaced the rotary dial, but it still required us to perform the task. However, when "speed dial" was invented and telephone numbers could be stored in the phone's memory and all we had to do was touch four to call Aunt Mary, then we began to feel powerful and entitled. Now we program numbers into our cellular phones and hit "Okay." No need to even remember Aunt Mary's number now. But there's a consequence overlooked in the excitement over how innovative and convenient such a technology is. It seduces people into losing self-reliance. And self-reliance, in my humble opinion, teaches selflessness.

In the early 1950s I lived with my maternal grandparents in a log house on a grassy plateau above the Little White River on what was then the northern part of the Rosebud Sioux Indian Reservation. Our house had neither electricity nor running water and I had no definitive idea that such conveniences existed. Light came from kerosene and gas lamps, and my grandfather had dug a shallow well from a natural spring in a nearby gully. We took water from it in buckets and poured it into a large wooden barrel. We burned wood for heating and cooking. For transportation we used our own feet or a horse-drawn wagon.

My grandfather plowed in the spring, walking behind a single-bottom plow pulled by two large draft horses. After he pulled a harrow over the large windrows of turned earth, we planted potatoes, corn, squash, pumpkins, green beans, and watermelons. Once those crops were growing, we had to cultivate them. One of my least favorite chores was picking potato bugs off by hand. If we did not, they would have eaten everything. We hauled water in barrels on a sled from the spring to water the rows of crops. All this in addition to the water we needed for drinking, cooking, washing, bathing, and doing the laundry.

Chopping and splitting wood was a continuous chore, but first we had to gather it. In late summer and early autumn we walked the draws and wooded areas along the river to pile downed branches. Later we returned with the horses and wagon to haul the wood back to our place. Larger branches had to be cut with a saw and thinner branches chopped to the proper length with an axe or hatchet. Later the thick pieces were split lengthwise.

Late fall meant harvesting the garden, picking wild berries, and digging prairie turnips. Whatever was not designated for giveaway to friends and relatives or trade at the grocery store in town, we prepared for drying or stored it in the root cellar. A successful deer hunt meant transporting the carcass back home and butchering it, which my grandfather did. After that my grandmother sliced the meat—whatever we did not consume immediately—into thin strips for air-drying.

The last bit of warm weather in the fall was the time for re-chinking the log walls of the house with mud or plaster, sealing windows, doing whatever repairs were necessary to the wagon, and oiling the leather harnesses the horses wore to pull it. Late autumn was also the last opportunity to haul wood. Cold weather did not necessarily mean more work, but some chores were different and done sometimes under daunting conditions. Keeping the open, shallow well from freezing over meant breaking the ice every day.

Everything we had or enjoyed, even the simplest necessity, was produced or obtained with some amount of effort. There were no dials or switches we could turn. When I was six or seven, my chores and tasks were not as difficult as those either of my grandparents had to do, though they were just as critical. Trimming the cotton wicks on kerosene lamps was not heavy work, for example. But it meant that they gave out steady light without smoking. Also making sure that the hot-water reservoir on the cook stove was always full meant that my grandmother could heat water whenever she needed. This was a period in my life that laid the foundation for the values I would learn and live by, and if there is one that stands apart from the others, it is self-reliance.

And in my opinion, anyone who has learned self-reliance has already learned selflessness. Self-reliant people know firsthand how much effort is required to live life, to make a living, to accomplish anything day in and day out. They know how to make that effort. Therefore, doing for others, directly or indirectly, is not out of the norm for them. And doing for others is a necessity that many of us do understand, especially given the state of the world at the present time. Much of that state is mired in need.

The fact of the matter is there is always someone in need. No economic system in any society ensures that we will all have what we need materially. Furthermore, not all of us have everything we need emotionally or spiritually. Pre-reservation Lakota society knew and understood these realities—as did other societies and cultures throughout time the world over. And over time ways, means, and values were established to mitigate the realities of want, need, and insufficiency. Meeting need could be as simple as a bundle of food, a drink of water, a sympathetic ear to listen, or a shoulder for someone to cry on.

All of my grandparents, and my parents, not only explained what selflessness was, they showed me. And the list of ways I benefited from their selflessness goes on and on. They, of course, have not been the only people in my life to help me. Others have given of themselves with time, money, understanding, advice, sympathy, and many instances of propping up when I needed it. These are the gifts I will never forget, yet the greatest gift of all is the lesson of selflessness. When I am able to return the gift, I do it to honor the memory of my grandparents.

The world is far from perfect. Wars, famine, rape and genocide, natural disasters, poverty, disease . . . you name it, we got it. All of these, and more, shout the need for selflessness. No nation in the world, affluent, powerful, or otherwise, is immune from hardships within its borders, the kind of hardship that suppresses hope and tests human resolve. People of every race, creed, and age group face a daily crucible of hunger, homelessness, and despair. Politicians, sociologists, clerics, and others may debate solutions for the problems, but answers cannot come fast enough. While sincere and constructive debate in and of itself is necessary, acting swiftly and appropriately to mitigate problems is critical, too. And it is more often than not the people closest to the problem who are the first to act, usually those who have the least to give materially but do not hesitate to give of their time and effort. Those are the people who help in food kitchens and halfway houses, distribute meals and blankets, and man the phone lines for suicide prevention programs. They exhibit the kind of selflessness that should be an example for politicians and others who are more concerned with image and political compromise than with making decisions and taking action. Selflessness is alive where it is needed, but we need more of it.

The vociferousness of history sometimes drowns out simple lessons that would serve us well, if we could only remember. And selflessness on the part of leaders is just as necessary now as it was in pre-reservation Lakota society, if not more. The fact of the matter is, it worked then and it can work now. Anyone who wants to be a leader or wears the title of leadership, especially at any level of government, should perform his or her job and live up to its responsibilities selflessly. All leaders, especially those who are responsible for seeing to the welfare of others—such as senators, congressmen, cabinet secretaries, governors, mayors, city council members, presidents, and so on—should understand and have demonstrated selflessness in private life before winning the offices or being appointed to the jobs they hold. We cannot afford leaders who learn selflessness on the job, because when that happens it is always for political expediency and gain, and not for selflessness' own sake.

The Lakota Sun Dance has seen a resurgence in popularity in the past few decades. On one level it is an affirmation of identity, an assertion that enough of a culture rooted in antiquity still exists to give meaning to that sacred ceremony. But to understand its real purpose, as far as I am concerned, we need to realize that it is not, or should not be, done as a source of prestige or recognition for those who "look at the sun and dance." Indeed, participants should not seek recognition at all, because that is what selflessness is. I know that many of them do look at the sun and dance for their families, their communities, their people, their culture, and for the world at large.

To look at the sun and dance is one of the most physically, emotionally, and spiritually demanding commitments there is in the world. Any Sun Dancer can tell you that one of the reasons they dance is the hope that their sacrifice of pain will continue to be the inspirational lesson in selflessness it was meant to be.

As a people, we Lakota are not obviously the same as our ancestors were. Our lifestyle is much different as a consequence of the interaction with Europeans and Euro-Americans. Gone are the villages of buffalo-hide tipis (tee-pee; from *otipi* meaning "they live in" or "something to live in") that dotted the endless prairies, and gone are the vast herds of the Great Ones, the very beings that symbolized selflessness. They no longer blanket an endless line of hilltops or fill entire river valleys with their sheer numbers, and Grandmother Earth no longer feels the thunder, the rhythm, and the power of their motion.

But it is, I firmly believe, necessary to remember that the buffalo *are* still here. Their numbers are nowhere near the same as they once were—in the tens of millions. But the fact that they have survived into the 21st century should remind us that what they were and the essence of what they meant for us—the lesson and gift of the Woman-Who-Stayed—are still here as well. If we Lakota do not heed that lesson, shame on us.

chapter five

Lessons from the Grasshopper

In the days far beyond the reach of memory, there was purpose to everything the people thought, and believed, and did. There was also purpose in what the people were as a group and as individual men and women. Girls grew up and became the mothers and nurturers of children, perhaps the most important purpose of all. Boys grew up to be the providers and protectors, also called hunter-warriors. Whatever girls had to learn to become good women, and whatever boys had to learn to become good men, was all intended to make them useful to the family, to the community, and to themselves.

A boy was left to his mother, his grandmothers, and his aunts—and really to the influence of all the women in the village—until he was strong enough to pull back a bow, usually around the age of five. During those years he learned many necessary lessons under the tutelage of women. After that he was guided onto the path of the hunter-warrior and placed under the tutelage of men. There was a reason for this. It was said that a boy learned the way of the hunter-warrior from his father and grandfathers and uncles, but from his mothers and grandmothers he learned the courage and compassion he would need on that path.

Lessons on the path to becoming a hunter and warrior were in two different realms: those that could be seen and felt and those that could not. Weapons and how to make and use them were in the first realm. So when he was strong enough a boy was given his own bow and a set of arrows. By the time he was five he had already watched his father, grandfathers, and uncles carrying and using those very necessary weapons. Other weapons included the war lance, the buffalo lance, the knife, the sling for throwing stones, and the curved rabbit stick for hunting smaller animals. But of all of these it was the bow and the arrow that most defined the hunter-warrior.

No one knew exactly when the bow and the arrow had come to the people. For certain, it was told, the bow was a gift from the moon and the arrow a gift of the sun. Since the moon was a woman, the bow was female. Likewise, since the sun was a man, the arrow was male. It was so because all things worked best in balance. Up needed down, night needed day, cold needed hot, good needed bad, and so on. And so it was that impetuousness needed patience. If boys had anything in abundance it was impetuousness, and if there was anything they would need in abundance to be good hunters and warriors, it was patience. That was the challenge for those who taught them. But those teachers often reached beyond themselves to train impetuous boys.

A certain boy was his father's pride, mainly because he had two older sisters and his father had more or less given up hope of having a son. Not that he loved his daughters less, but because a man always wanted to pass on his line through a son. The boy was named Little Arm by his grandmother, for he was slight and probably would not grow to be as tall as his stalwart father. But as Hawk Wing's father counseled, the size of the man was a poor second to the size of the will in the man.

So it was that Little Arm began his journey on the path of the hunter-warrior. He was not as strong as other boys his age, nor could he run as fast. But when it came to the bow and arrow, he would develop a skill second to none. It began with his grandfather, Wolf Eyes.

Wolf Eyes was Little Arm's mother's father, and he was not a tall man. But his reputation and his accomplishments as a hunter and warrior were as notable as any, and likely more than most, and he was known above all for his patience. In Little Arm the old man saw himself, and he became the boy's first and most important teacher.

A familiar sight for a few years was the little boy leaving the village on the heels of his grandfather. Little Arm would follow his grandfather anywhere, it was said among the people. And the boy was willing to follow the old man to more than a place or a landmark—he also followed his grandfather to a way of being, to the realm of the lessons that could not be seen or felt. In this way he became a good man.

By the time Little Arm was seven his grandfather had taught him the basics of making his own bow and arrows. It began with finding the right kind of wood. They prowled creek and river bottoms to find slender ash trees. The boy looked for trees that were straight, as thick as his grandfather's forearm, and stood at least as tall as a grown man.

The old man chose chokecherry saplings for hunting arrows and a thicker softwood like river willow for war arrows. Every kind of feather would do for fletching so long as it was long enough—except for owl and eagle. Goose feathers were preferable for arrows used in winter or wet weather, since their natural oils repelled water. Along riverbanks they found the hard stones—chert and flint—for arrow points. At first Wolf Eyes shaped them for him, but eventually Little Arm would make his own. By the time he was ten, he was making his own bows and arrows with a quality that surpassed most boys older than he.

By then he had also mastered the basic techniques of shooting, but his marksmanship was not as good as his craftsmanship. Both Wolf Eyes and Hawk Wing saw that Little Arm was frustrated because his skill with the bow was not as good as other boys. His grandfather knew that the basic problem was a lack of patience.

One day, after he missed what he thought was an easy shot at a rabbit, the boy threw down his bow in frustration. "I will never be as good as everyone else!" he exclaimed.

Wolf Eyes waited until the boy had retrieved his bow. "Then I guess we'll have to take this matter up with the grasshoppers," he told his grandson.

The next day, in the middle of a warm summer afternoon, the old man took his grandson to a meadow not far from the village. Wolf Eyes had chosen that particular spot for two reasons: there were plenty of grasshoppers and no curious onlookers.

Grasshoppers are the kinds of small beings that can be so plentiful no one bothers to look at each one of them. Rather, there is a tendency to perceive them as a bothersome group. But the characteristics that made them invaluable to Wolf Eyes—and to generations of Lakota warriors and archers—was their wariness and erratic flying. They were always on the alert since they were the favorite food of just about any bird that flew, and for that very reason they never flew in a straight line. They were masters at the art of changing direction because their very survival depended on how well and how often they did. These were characteristics that seemed simple enough, until a boy tried to outwit and outmaneuver even one grasshopper.

As the old man and his grandson walked across the meadow, grasshoppers took wing all around them. It was dizzying just to watch them flutter about, making a strange little buzzing noise as they flew. Wolf Eyes stopped and put his hand on the boy's shoulder.

"Let us stand and be still," he told the boy. "Here is what I want you to do after the grasshoppers settle down. Stand quietly, as we are now, and do not move no matter what. Then, after a while has passed, take one step. One very, very slow step. If you make grasshoppers fly, then you are not moving slowly enough."

Though puzzled, the boy understood the instructions.

"I will wait for you in the shade over there," said the old man. "Wait for the grasshoppers to settle down, then take a step. Take as many steps as you can without scaring them. Remember, if even just one flies, you are moving too fast."

As Wolf Eyes found a comfortable place to sit under a nearby oak tree and watch, Little Arm looked around and waited for the grasshoppers to settle back down again. The nearest ones were a pebble's toss away. But as he knew well, the slightest sound or movement sent them flying. After several long moments of waiting and standing like a stone, he lifted a foot. The entire field of grasshoppers flew up, filling the air with an annoying buzz. The boy took a deep, exasperated breath and stopped. From his grandfather he heard not a word.

The boy waited longer the second time. An errant breeze tugged at loose wisps of his hair and gnats buzzed around his nose and eyes. He nearly lifted a hand to swat them away but stopped himself. Instead he calmed himself with a slow, deep breath, and then concentrated on the heel of his right foot. Then ever so slightly he brought up the heel, but no more than the width of his finger. Next he lifted all but his big toe. Balance would be critical, once he lifted his toe off the ground. If he lost his balance he would likely frighten the grasshoppers. Which is exactly what happened. The meadow came alive again with a flurry of flying grasshoppers with buzzing wings. Little Arm decided that the trick was not to step so far, but to keep his step short.

The next time he tried he managed a short step without frightening a single grasshopper. But when he tried again he was a bit too satisfied, became careless, and the air above the meadow was full of grasshoppers again.

That night, sitting at his grandfather's fire, Little Arm vowed that he could learn to move so slowly that no grasshopper would hear or see him.

"Summer is nearly over," his grandfather said, "and by the middle of autumn most of the grasshoppers will be gone."

So the next day and the next and for many days after that, Wolf Eyes took his grandson to wherever the grasshoppers gathered, in order to learn the valuable lessons that grasshoppers could teach. After many days Little Arm was able to move more than 20 paces across a field without frightening a single grasshopper. He had learned to control his movements to slow them down until it seemed he was not moving at all.

Before he could become too pleased with himself, the old man revealed the next part of the lesson. "Now," he said, "you must find one grasshopper, one that is away from his fellows, and you must do so with your bow strung and an arrow on the string, ready to shoot. After you are five to six paces away, frighten the grasshopper into taking wing, then shoot at it."

Little Arm was not overly concerned with this turn of events. He had, after all, learned the art of stealth. What could be more difficult than that?

"Your task is to pull, aim, and shoot as soon as the grasshopper flies. You must hit it before it alights again," the old man went on. "Your stealth must get you close, and then you will work on improving your skill with the bow."

By the next afternoon, Little Arm was more frustrated than he had ever been in his life. Sneaking up on a grasshopper was one thing. Hitting it as it flew was next to impossible. Every grasshopper had the same annoying habit. Each flew in one direction for less than a heartbeat, and then abruptly turned. There was no predicting which way it would turn. As a result any shot he attempted went awry. None of the arrows he shot at a dodging grasshopper came close.

Shoulders slumping, the boy returned and dropped down next to his grandfather, who was sitting in the shade of a tree. "I will never hit one of those things," he whined. "It is much too difficult."

Without a word, Wolf Eyes rose slowly to his feet. Taking his bow from its case, he strung it and slid an arrow out of his quiver.

"Follow me," he said to the boy, and walked into a grassy swale.

Little Arm did as he was told, keeping a close eye on his grandfather as he held the bow at the ready. After a long pause, the old man shuffled his feet and sent a grasshopper flying. With smooth, practiced motion born of years of shooting bows and arrows, he pulled and released. The boy had to concentrate on the flashing arrow and was astonished when it came no less than a finger width from hitting the insect.

"*Never* is a word that should not be used by anyone who wants to be a hunter and warrior," Wolf Eyes said gently. "Except to say 'I will never give up.' I have hit a grasshopper, perhaps twice. I will never stop trying, so I may hit one again. The important thing is this. Shoot to hit one. Do not shoot to come close."

Almost every day until the last days of summer gave way to autumn and the grasshoppers were fewer and fewer, Little Arm prowled the meadows and watercourses. No grasshoppers fell to his arrows, but his eyes were picking up and following the movement of each one he shot at. Furthermore, he was learning to withdraw an arrow from the quiver and place it on the string without looking, since his concentration was on the grasshoppers.

In the late autumn and winter the boy accompanied his father and grandfathers as they pursued elk and deer. Though he carried his bow and arrows along each time, he was expected to simply watch and learn from experienced hunters. Closer to home he was free to hunt rabbits anytime he chose. Owing to days of practice on grasshoppers, he was able to bring home rabbits more often than not. Rabbits were fast, he told himself, but nowhere near as fast and unpredictable as grasshoppers. He was anxious for summer and more practice on the wily little insects.

Every summer for the next three years Little Arm pursued grasshoppers. He became adept at an approach so slow and deliberate that it seemed to anyone watching that he was not moving at all. The boy could walk across a grassy meadow full of the insects without disturbing a single one. To Wolf Eyes it was plain to see that his grandson's skill at handling his bow and arrows was improving, nearly day by day. No other boy his age was as smooth and quick.

Little Arm was growing just as the other boys were. He was filling out and becoming stronger, but he would always be slight and shorter than boys his own age. Even as his grandfather Wolf Eyes continued to quietly advise the boy, an uncle—a man known for his endurance—taught Little Arm to develop his stamina. Grass Runner's ability as a long distance runner was known far and wide, and his physical stature was the same as the boy's.

"Everyone has an ability that sets him apart from others," Wolf Eyes told the boy. "Your uncle is not the biggest or the strongest man in the village. But the bigger or stronger men cannot run without stopping like he can. Endurance and stamina are a different kind of strength."

With those words ringing in his ears, Little Arm followed his uncle across meadows and up and down hills. Speed was not their goal, however. The boy learned that a steady pace could conserve his strength. The more he ran, the stronger his legs and his lungs became. All in all, in spite of his small size, Little Arm was developing into a young man with formidable physical skills.

But every summer and autumn, bow and arrows in hand, Little Arm pursued the elusive grasshoppers. At the end of every autumn Wolf Eyes could see improvement in the boy's abilities. Now there was no one, man or boy, who was as smooth or as quick with a bow. In the autumn of his 16th year, those abilities would save his older sister's life.

White Shell Woman was nearly two years older, with many suitors who came calling, young men eager to weave themselves into her awareness. So much so that White Shell could not wander any distance from her parents' lodge without someone accosting her. For that reason, when her mother sent her to pick chokecherries one day, she dispatched Little Arm to accompany her. She knew her son would guard his sister well.

But on this day it was not an anxious suitor who was interested in the comely young woman, it was a large mountain lion with intense yellow eyes. Little Arm and his sister were far enough away from the village for the big cat not to fear the presence of people, and for some reason they had not taken a dog with them. Although he kept watch for any kind of danger as his sister talked amiably and filled her bags with chokecherries, Little Arm did not see the tawny animal lying flat in the grass. This was because it was the same color as the grass, and it was not moving.

The long-tailed cats were numerous across the land and were known as ambush hunters. They could wait interminably for unsuspecting prey to get close to them. As Shell Woman finished at one chokecherry tree, she tied up her full bag, opened an empty one, and walked toward the next tree. Just beyond that tree lay the cat.

Little Arm followed his sister, his eyes probing shrubs and thickets nearby. Fortunately his bow was strung. He took a second arrow from his quiver as he listened to his sister's chatter, and placed it in his bow hand. At the moment he was mostly concerned that one of the young men interested in his sister might jump out from the brush, so he was not entirely surprised when he noticed a slight movement out of the corner of his eye. Instinctively he raised his bow and flicked an arrow toward the string.

Something long and large erupted from the grass, a blurred shadow hurling itself toward Shell Woman. Without a thought, Little Arm pulled his bow and released the arrow. In the next instant, even as the arrow struck its target, another arrow was on the string. In the instant after that, it was a flash barely seen in its short flight.

The mortally wounded cat collided with Shell Woman, who had her back to her attacker and could not see it. The collision sent her into the chokecherry tree as the cat fell, its life already draining. Little Arm drew another arrow, placed himself between the fallen lion and his sister, and released the third arrow into the struggling animal's throat. Though the enraged lion rose on trembling legs, it was too weak to move. Emitting a low growl, it toppled on its side, no more to rise.

Shell Woman's only injuries were scratches to her face when the lion had shoved her into the choke-cherry thicket. Back in the village she told her mother and other women how her younger brother had killed the lion and saved her life. Men hurried to the thicket and found the carcass. It was one of the largest lions ever seen, but more astonishing was that two of Little Arm's arrows were buried in its heart. An extraordinary feat of marksmanship.

For days the village was buzzing with talk about Little Arm's victory over the lion. His grandfather and two other old men skinned the animal and the hide was tanned. In the meantime Little Arm went hunting to get away from the sudden attention. His sister told the story of her younger brother's brave act to anyone who asked.

In the middle days of autumn Little Arm's family invited everyone in the village to a feast to honor their youngest child and only son. Though thoroughly embarrassed by the attention, the boy endured the festivities to please his parents. He did not expect the two gifts he was given. First, the tanned hide of the lion had been made into a bow case and arrow quiver, the product of the exquisite skills of his grandfathers and grandmothers. It was the finest anyone had ever seen, decorated with porcupine quills dyed red, yellow, and blue.

The second gift was nothing the boy could carry in his hand, and it was more important than any object he could own. He was given a new name to signify he had left his boyhood behind. He would be known as Yellow Eyes, a name that would link his accomplishment with the strength and spirit of the lion.

After the feasting and dancing was over, the women in his family asked Yellow Eyes to help with a few tasks. It was not that they were unable to do the tasks on their own; they wanted him to spend quiet moments with them to learn that humility was the path to being a good man. A lesson he took to heart.

When winter came, his father invited him along as several warriors went on patrol to the edges of their territories, and thus he was no longer regarded as a boy. He was now a young man, though he was reminded that he had far to go to attain the kind of accomplishments and gain the experience of the mature warriors in the village.

His grandfather Wolf Eyes's advice was simple: "Do not forget what you learned from the grasshoppers."

Two years after he killed the mountain lion and saved his sister, he got the chance to prove his mettle as a warrior and show how well he remembered that lesson.

He and his closest friend Elk Knife were on their way home from an autumn hunt, pulling deer carcasses on drag poles. In an area where there were no villages, the barest whiff of smoke came on the breeze. Assuming that enemies were about, the two young men hid the carcasses and set out to learn who had made a fire. Following the faint odor of smoke, they came to a creek along which stood several thin groves of trees. From one of the groves rose a thin wisp of smoke, barely seen among the bare branches. The two friends hid themselves in a swatch of tall grass and watched. It was late in the day, and it was apparent that the four men they saw in the trees were making camp for the night. Voices drifted on the breeze, speaking words they could not understand.

As sundown came and dusk settled over the land, the soft glow of a small fire could be seen, even though the flames burned inside a pit dug into the ground. Around the camp four strangers were visible as they moved about, and the smell of roasting meat was easily detected. Darkness came and the fire was extinguished, a sure sign that the strangers were being cautious.

"What shall we do?" whispered Elk Knife.

"You must go back to the village," decided Yellow Eyes. "Tell our war leader that enemies are in our territory. I will keep watch until you return with other warriors."

"I will not reach the village until morning," Elk Knife pointed out. "Do not forget that there are four of them, and only one of you."

Elk Knife departed and Yellow Eyes considered what he should do. When daylight came the strangers would certainly encroach toward the village. If so, there was little he could do to stop them, since he was outnumbered. A thought entered his mind, but he immediately dismissed it. It returned, though, and after several moments it began to make sense. If he could sneak in and take the strangers' weapons, they might leave.

What he was thinking of doing was extremely risky, to say the least. If the strangers were seasoned warriors, as they probably were, it would not be easy to get close, and it would be next to impossible to take their weapons. But after more long moments of pondering, trying to talk himself out of taking a foolish risk, Yellow Eyes could not ignore the challenge.

He was no more than a long arrow cast from the strangers' camp. So he worked quietly. Though the night was cool he stripped down to only his breechclout and moccasins. Then he rubbed himself thoroughly with dirt to mask his scent. Deciding that it would be best to carry as little as possible, he left his bow and arrows and lance behind. With only his knife in its sheath at his belt, and heart pounding heavily, Yellow Eyes started walking toward the strangers' camp.

His eyes were well accustomed to the dark, and fortunately it was a moonless night. From the hills and prairies all around came the usual night sounds of coyotes barking and wolves howling. Most of the insects were gone by this time. After several deliberate steps, he would pause and listen for sounds from the camp. In this manner he proceeded until he was close enough to toss a stone at the four forms he saw beneath robes. They appeared as not much more than shadows, but nonetheless discernible. Edging closer with one deliberate step after another, he stopped when he could hear them breathing. One of them was snoring lightly, and all of them seemed to be asleep.

Yellow Eyes stood motionless for a very long while, studying the camp. The strangers were lying head to toe in a sort of circle around the cold ashes in the fire pit. He risked several more slow, almost imperceptible steps, waited, and then took several more. From his new and closer vantage point, he could discern that each man's weapons were behind him, on the side away from the fire pit. Each seemed to have a bow and arrows, a war club, and a lance. A simple plan formed in his mind.

From the position of the Three Sisters star formation in the sky, morning was a long way off. But he wanted to be gone by the time dawn broke. He would move silently sunwise around the sleeping strangers, squat at each form to take the weapons, and move on. As long as he made absolutely no noise and moved as though he were not moving, he knew he had a good chance of seeing the sun set the next day.

He stopped above the first sleeping form and studied where the man's weapons were. Luckily, he was not lying on them. Squatting down to keep his balance centered over his hips, Yellow Eyes laid hands on the weapons, first the lance and then the bow in its case and the quiver full of arrows. He left the war club and knife, since they were bundled under the man's head.

His luck held and he was able to silently lift the second man's lance and bow and arrows. He paused to tie everything into a tight bundle, which he carefully slung across his back. It was not until after he had taken the weapons from the third man that trouble reared its head. The second man moved. He rolled over noisily and pulled his robe up over his shoulders. Then he propped himself on an elbow and stared off into the darkness.

Yellow Eyes stayed absolutely motionless, holding his breath, waiting for the man to realize that his weapons were gone. But after a moment, the man lay back down, and the camp was quiet once more. Though in an awkward kneeling position, Yellow Eyes stayed motionless until he heard the man's even sleeping breaths. After another long while, he moved into a more comfortable position and waited some more. He had three sets of weapons and debated if it was wise to push his luck. Dawn was still a long way off and there was time, but he had been incredibly lucky up to this point. Still, he did want that fourth set.

When the Three Sisters were close to the black outline of the southern horizon, Yellow Eyes had the last bow, quiver, and lance in hand. Now he was starting his withdrawal, reminding himself that any impatience or carelessness now would undo his deed. Once again moving so slowly that he did not seem to be moving at all, he made his way out of the strangers' camp.

By the time dawn broke Yellow Eyes was safely in a thicket, having hidden himself and his booty. From his hiding place he had a good view of the strangers. The first man who awoke was in the middle of making a fire when he seemed to notice that something was wrong. He quickly woke the others, and soon they were all on their feet and searching around the fire pit. Yellow Eyes knew they were looking for their weapons.

He knew the strangers had to be perplexed, and he assumed they were angry as well. They conducted another wider and more thorough search around the camp, but of course they found nothing. Their next action showed that the strangers were intelligent, if nothing else, other than heavy sleepers. They departed, heading north, away from the village.

Yellow Eyes followed them for part of the morning, but the strangers did not turn aside from the direction they were taking. When they disappeared over a distant hill, he turned his footsteps home. Near where the strangers had camped he met Elk Knife and a group of warriors. He showed them the deserted camp with the cold ashes in the fire pit.

"Where are they?" asked Fast Dog, the war leader.

"They went away," replied Yellow Eyes. "Just after dawn." The strangers' footprints were plain to see, validating what Yellow Eyes said.

"Why?" asked Elk Knife.

Yellow Eyes shrugged. "Perhaps because I took their weapons."

The men exchanged puzzled glances, not certain they could believe the young warrior. Without a backward glance Yellow Knife hurried to the thicket where he had hidden the cache of weapons and took them back to the warriors.

Fast Dog examined the weapons closely. "These are the weapons of a people from the north," he said. He pointed to markings on one of the lances. "I have seen this before. They live along the Big River in large earthen lodges." He turned to Yellow Eyes. "How did you do this?"

"I sneaked in and took them. They are heavy sleepers," he explained.

Good-natured laughter flowed through the knot of warriors, but there were also nods and glances acknowledging respect for an extremely brave deed.

The elders awarded the captured weapons to Yellow Eyes. He kept one set and gave away the others to his father and grandfathers. Before the next new moon he was invited to join the Wolf Men Society. It was a small warrior society, its members known for their scouting prowess. They were the eyes and ears of the other warriors, often venturing alone deep into enemy territory. Yellow Eyes accepted the honor. The Wolf Men made a feast and presented their newest member to the village and gave him the symbol of his new status—a wolf-hide cape to be worn over the head and shoulders. As everyone knew, wolves were known for their keen senses, persistence, and patience.

Three more winters passed and Yellow Eyes courted and won the love of a beautiful young woman, and in the ensuing years they raised a daughter and a son. Throughout the prime of his life Yellow Eyes was never the strongest or the fastest warrior, but no one was a better scout and few could match his skill with the bow and arrow.

In time he became a teacher and young men were influenced by his calm and deliberate approach to all things. Now and then a young man would ask Yellow Eyes how he had learned to be such a formidable warrior and scout. To such questions he always had the same answer.

"Let me tell you about grasshoppers."

Wacintanka
(wah-chin-tan-kah)
Patience

LOOKING AT MOCCASINS

A pair of moccasins sits on a table in our living room and sometimes in my office. They were to have been my father's, but after he died they were given to me. They are a colorful pair, with red, white, dark blue, and medium blue beads in classic Lakota geometric patterns.

Traditional moccasins like these are still made by Lakota artisans. The basic components are brain-tanned leather, glass beads, thread, and rawhide. Soft-tanned leather forms the top of the moccasin and rawhide the sole. Yet there is another component that cannot be seen, but it is every bit as critical to the construction of the moccasin—patience.

On the pair I have, there are three bands of small beads that circle the moccasin from the toe to the heel and back to the toe. The second band is not quite as long as the first and consequently the third not as long as the second. In each of these bands are vertical rows of 8 beads, with 13 rows to the inch, or 104 beads per inch. Given that the three bands of beads put together are about 68 inches in length, there are approximately 7,072 beads.

On the upper part of the moccasin, from the toe to the instep, are nine bands. Once again each band is eight beads across, and there are ten bands, tapering to a point near the toe to fit into the curve above the first three bands of beads. Combined, the nine bands are approximately 28 inches long. With 104 beads to an inch, there are about 2,912 beads. This means that on each moccasin there are nearly 10,000 beads, and nearly 20,000 on the pair.

The task of making moccasins is simple but time consuming. A pattern is lightly drawn on the hide, then cut. Before the upper and sole are sewn together, the beads are sewn on. After holes are punched in the soft-tanned hide with a sharp awl, the artisan places eight beads, one at a time on a needle, threading it through the hole in the center of each bead. Each line of eight beads is then sewn directly onto the tanned hide through the punched holes. This is known as appliqué beading.

Each artisan who does this kind of craft works at her own pace, so it is difficult to say how long each moccasin takes to bead as a rule. Suffice it to say it is anywhere from 24 to 48 hours of beading. Or each pair of fully beaded moccasins represents 48 to 96 hours of effort. Furthermore, not only is it stringing and sewing on beads row by row, it is also necessary to incorporate the different colored patterns, so a row of eight beads may contain several different colors. It is difficult to say which is more important in the process—skill or patience—but good work cannot be done without both. Without patience, even consummate skill will not realize its full potential.

Patience has applications far beyond making cultural artifacts. Patient people are much less apt to make snap judgments or act impulsively, and they rarely stick their feet in their mouths. They will likely move over and let an impatient driver pass, understanding that getting there is more important than getting there first. Furthermore, patience is a precursor to thoroughness, deliberation, and coolness under pressure. Yet it seems in these times to be ever more rare.

We have become cultures and societies that rely on instant gratification. Like speed-dialing on our phones, as we saw in the last chapter, effect follows cause in less than the blink of an eye. Our technology-dependent existence has taught us that having to wait for anything is an annoyance. Consequently, patience

RETURNING TO THE LAKOTA WAY

is no longer the necessary virtue it once was. A mere 60 years ago—at least in my world—it was critical.

I watched both of my grandmothers do beadwork. My paternal grandmother beaded traditional moccasins, and my maternal grandmother beaded prayer book covers and once a stole for my uncle, her son, the priest. It seemed to me, as an impatient boy, that they were maddeningly slow. Poke two holes with an awl in the soft-tanned leather, pull a single strand of thread through one hole, pick the beads with the point of a needle, slide them up the thread, push the needle through the second hole, tighten down the thread and set the beads in place, and then inspect that one row of beads. Then repeat the process several hundred, if not several thousand, times. But somehow hours, or sometimes days, later, the piece of hide was covered with beads in intricate multicolored designs and patterns.

My grandfathers showed patience as well. My maternal grandfather walked behind a single-bottom, horse-drawn plow for hours, turning the black prairie loam into furrows. The next day he hooked up the harrow to break down the windrows of dirt. After that he marked out rows so that seeds could be planted. That was only the beginning. After the seeds were planted, I lost track of the days before the first light-green shoots pushed up out of the earth.

My paternal grandfather was an avid fisherman. He was constantly arranging and rearranging his gear in the various compartments in his tackle boxes: lures, hooks, lead weights (sinkers), bobbers, string, and leaders. He would sit for hours, sometimes barely moving, on the shores of a dam, a lake, or the Missouri River, waiting for that tug on his line. Then there were the hours he sat writing his sermon for Sunday service, since he was an ordained Episcopalian deacon. There were times when his pencil remained poised for long, long minutes before he wrote his thoughts on the paper.

I know that my grandparents were not born patient. I know they showed impatience when they were children, as I did, because they told stories on themselves. They learned about patience from their own parents and grandparents. My grandparents and their generation were at most the second to be born on the reservation, and their lives were still tied to the cycles of nature; enough firewood had to be gathered and laid in to last through the winter, for example. In order to do that and everything else that ensured survival and enabled comfort, patience was a necessary virtue.

Their parents and grandparents taught them, and they in turn taught me, what kinds of twigs made the best kindling for starting fires and how to look for just the right kind in thickets in the gullies and in the trees along the creeks and the river. This was always a task requiring several days, resulting in piles of twigs that we then carried to the wagon or came back to pick up later. If I was in a hurry to finish and picked up a branch that was too large, it was relegated to a different pile. After kindling came larger sticks and branches that would be cut to lengths of about 12 to 18 inches to fit into the stoves. After that it was log-size dry wood, six inches thick and wider, that would be split.

In order to be warm and cook food and boil water, certain tasks had to be done, and in a certain order. In following that process I learned the meaning of patience. I knew that the food we cooked, the water we boiled, and the warmth of the heating stove through the long winter nights were just as much a consequence of patience as they were of good, dry wood. I am reminded of that each and every time I use the fireplace in our home.

Before the Industrial Age, people lived in closer association with the natural cycles and whims of nature. Events in nature occurred (and still do) when conditions are favorable or reach a certain point, regardless of any calendar; our ancestors could not affect that process, so in order to go along with nature's program, patience was a necessary virtue. Impatience, however, has always been a human trait, and at some point it evolved into a defining factor in human societies. My grandfather theorized that mankind learned the arrogance of impatience when the clock was invented.

In the old days, my ancestors would say something like, *Wicokan isamya kin iwahunni ktelo,* or "I will arrive after the sun is in the middle" (meaning noon). Therefore there was no reason for those waiting to get impatient or worry until the sun went down. Though our language identified sunrise, dawn, morning, noon, afternoon, sunset, evening, dusk, and night, those words were not measurements of time, but simply identifiers of the various stages of the day and night. In and of themselves, those words and those realities did not foster impatience.

I agree with my grandfather's theory. I can see the approaching dawn and then the sunrise, and I can discern when the sun is "in the middle" of the sky, as well as when it goes down and when darkness comes. I can experience those realities. Never in my life, however, have I actually seen an hour in the same way. An hour is not real; it is an artificial measurement of something we do not fully understand. Something that *does* foster impatience. Without the artificial concept of time or clocks and watches to measure it, we would not be able to say, "I'll see you in fifteen minutes." The best we could say would be "I'll see you in a little while."

As it is, though, our modern lifestyles are totally dependent on the artificial measurement of time. Our work days and nights start and end at a certain hour. For some of us, the start of our shift arrives much too quickly and the end of it cannot come quickly enough. Reluctance on one end, impatience on the other. Whatever our emotions and reactions, though, the shift begins, we do our work, and it ends. That happens no matter how reluctant or impatient we are. It might, therefore, be preferable to accept the reality of the situation and patiently let it run its course.

Hours, minutes, seconds, and even nanoseconds are part of our lives—so long as the technology is able to measure "time." Measuring time sometimes serves a useful purpose. Airlines, railroads, and bus lines, for example, schedule departures and arrivals down to the minute. On a recent trip, my departing flight was 12 minutes late leaving the gate, and the next flight was behind schedule because that plane was delayed nearly 30 minutes by weather. Already impatient to get home, I was agitated by the delays. But my impatience did not change things one bit. The only way to deal with them was to wait patiently. "Whatever else may be, the day will come and the day will end," my grandparents would say. They also assured me that it would not pass any faster simply because of my impatience.

In the old days, long before the arrival of horses on the northern Great Plains, the people still moved their villages often. It was said they could walk 30 miles in one day. One group on the move descended into a little valley cut by a wide creek and stopped to rest. From the west came a line of buffalo led by an old cow. One by one and two by two they came, paused to drink from the creek, and then moved up the low hills onto the plateau beyond. Since it was early summer, there were many reddish-brown calves in the herd. The people had no choice but to wait for the last of the herd to pass before they continued their journey. One little girl seemed particularly bothered by the delay, so her grandmother came up with a game to help her wait. For every five calves—which happened to coincide with the number of fingers on each hand—the old woman told her granddaughter to place a stone on the ground.

The little girl quickly ran to the creek and gathered a handful of stones. Then for every five calves she put down a stone. Soon she had a long line of stones and had to hurry to the creek several times to gather more. She was so absorbed in counting the calves as the herd passed that she forgot about having to wait. Other children joined the game of counting the calves.

The herd of buffalo was so large that it took until sundown for all of them to pass, so the people camped for the night along the creek. The next morning they departed. The little girl and her friends, of course, left behind a long line of small stones in the meadow along the creek. Thereafter that little valley was known as the Valley of the Calves. It was said that those small stones remained there for many, many years, testimony to a grandmother's inventiveness that served as a lesson in patience.

Winter was the greatest test of my patience as a boy, especially in those carefree years before I went away to school. That season on the northern plains was harsh no matter what. On one end of the scale was tolerable, on the other was just plain brutal. Whatever it was, I dreaded it. But something changed the winter I was approaching my sixth year. Perhaps I simply gained a keener awareness, because the stories my grandparents told me meant more than they had before.

When they sensed my impatience and apprehension, especially after the sun went down—because winter nights were longer—one of them would ask me, "Did I ever tell you about the time Iktomi tried to fly?" Whether I answered yes or no did not matter. The question was asked to let me know it was time for a story.

The story itself was important, of course. But there was more to it than Iktomi's misadventures and how he learned the value of truth or faith, or whatever moral the story espoused. Sometimes the stories were about ancestors, or an event in the past, or a place. But whatever they were, they were always delivered in the same quietly loving and patient manner. That winter was the first time I heard the story of how grasshoppers taught many things to young boys.

One story frequently led to another, and before I knew it the evening had passed and it was time for sleep. All but forgotten were the dark, cold, snow, and howling wind outside. And it was not only stories, but things to do that seemed to shorten the long winter evenings. My grandmother would ask me to string beads for her. Yellow beads on one thread, red on another, and so on. My grandfather taught me how to whittle thin strips of wood from a long, dry branch, in effect making kindling to start fires. Or he had me arrange the wood bin so the wood was in neat stacks.

Interestingly, my grandparents never actually said, "You must be patient." They simply showed me with their own actions and demeanor. They spoke quietly, they faced situations calmly, and went unhurriedly about to do what had to be done. As a child I some-how (and fortunately) knew that it was good to imitate them, and as I grew older I understood more and more that the winter evenings did pass. How they passed—quickly, enjoyably, or with difficulty—depended on the manner in which I chose to deal with the moment. Therefore, at some point I chose consciously to emu-late my grandparents and exercise patience, even in the most difficult of circumstances.

Light-speed technology will be around for a while, seducing us into believing that everything has to happen fast. For example, there will always be those drivers whose cars creep forward at the intersection, indignantly waiting for the light to turn green so they can hurry to the next intersection and stress them-selves out waiting again. There is one essential bit of knowledge every driver has: at some point the light will turn green. No amount of impatience or indigna-tion will make it turn faster. Simple common sense should tell us that there is far less stress in just waiting patiently. As all of my grandparents would say about any situation, "It is what it is." And while it is better to download a photograph in seconds with broadband than to wait five minutes with dial-up Internet, there are instances when slower is good.

There is a line from a popular movie, a Western, that says something like this: You find a thousand ways of running down your time. The reference is to our lives, the time we each have on this earth. Halfway into my seventh decade I have certainly reached that point in my life when things seem to happen fast. As a matter of fact, much too fast. Grandchildren are born and suddenly, it seems, they are already five or seven years old. A few years ago it dawned on me that I have lived most of my life—most of my time has run down, as it were. If there were some way to slow it down now, I would do that. But, of course, the days, the seasons, and the years will pass as they always have. Therefore it is up to me to savor each good moment and endure the difficult ones in the same way—with patience.

I am reminded of that each time I look at those moccasins sitting on a table.

chapter six

The Journey

Long, long ago the people came to live on the never-ending prairie lands. There they found great variety, even in the grass itself. On the eastern half of the prairies it was thicker and taller, while on the western side it was sparse and short. There was variety as well in the beings that lived on the land. Of the many kinds of four-leggeds, some were grass eaters like the enormous buffalo, the majestic elk, and the speedy deer. Others had fangs or claws like the bears, the great cats, short-tailed cats, badgers, wolves, coyotes, and foxes. Still others were small like the squirrels, gophers, moles, and mice. Some beings were crawlers, like snakes and lizards. Then there were the beings who had two legs and two wings and flew, of which there were many, from the tiny hummingbirds to the great hawks and eagles. Finally, there were the unseen ones such as the mosquitoes, gnats, ants, and worms.

The prairies were a place of extremes as well. Winters were very cold and the snows fell deep. Spring was very wet and summer and autumn were hot. In order to survive and thrive on the prairies, any kind of being had to be strong or know how to adapt or both. Each and every being had a way to survive.

Easily the two most powerful creatures on the land were the buffalo and the bear, and these relied mainly on their enormous strength for self-protection. They adapted, too; the buffalo grew thick hair in the winter to protect itself against bone-chilling cold, while the bear simply found a snug den to sleep the season through. Other four-leggeds, such as the deer and white-bellied goat, relied on speed to outrun enemies. As a matter of fact, the white-belly was the fastest on the prairie. The turtle, on the other hand, was one of the slowest beings. To protect itself against attack, it withdrew its head and legs into its extremely hard shell, a shell that even the powerful jaws of the bear could not break.

Of course not all beings relied on strength or speed for survival. The skunk, one of the smaller and weaker four-leggeds, had a noxious spray that it could send great distances: one extremely painful to the eyes and noses of anyone struck by it. No one bothered the skunk. Likewise the porcupine, because he had long, sharp, needle-like quills. Once the quills penetrated anyone's hide or skin, they caused excruciating pain and were impossible to remove.

Other means of defense and protection were extremely sharp hearing and a sense of smell, quickness, hiding motionless, and blending by color into the landscape. Such abilities and characteristics were a natural part of each being, instinctively used when necessary. There was only one being of the prairie lands with no physical abilities that set it apart from others: the Two-Legged People.

Two-leggeds were not the weakest of creatures, but neither were they among the most powerful. Far from it. While they were good runners, just about any other being—except perhaps the mouse—could outrun them. As to size, speed, strength, and quickness, two-leggeds were woefully lacking. Yet they did have one ability that set them apart: the ability to reason. With that ability they developed tools and weapons that enabled them to make use of their limited physical attributes. It was not that other beings did not reason, but for two-leggeds that ability was their fang and their claw. In other words, if they could not reason they could not survive.

A young man named Turtle was beginning to learn and understand these realities that were part of his world. He had been given the name by his mother because, even at the age of five, he was a thoughtful boy and not given to impetuousness as boys usually are. He was deliberate and very observant. Because of those habits he did not play so much with other boys; he had only one friend, another loner named Little Goose. But as they got older even Little Goose found Turtle's ways a little too strange.

As he grew, Turtle did everything required of him in the ways of his people. He was more than an adequate hunter and never shirked his duties as a warrior. He had grown up under the skilled tutelage and counsel of his father, uncle, and grandfather, so his skills and abilities as a provider and protector were no less than other young men in the village, and better than some. But if anything, his habit of putting thought into everything he did became even more pronounced. As a result, when other young men were courting girls, he was often off by himself or sitting near a group of old men. Though the old men teased him, they were pleased that a young man could be interested in other aspects of life.

Turtle was close to his grandfather, No Feather. It was he who taught the boy to make bows and arrows and shoot them, and he who taught the boy to ignore the jibes from other boys. He saw something in Turtle that was different. Most boys grew into young men who were anxious to prove themselves and win glory on the field of battle. Those things were not unimportant to Turtle, but he was much more of a thinker than other young men. That pleased No Feather. It was the thinkers who understood how and why things happened.

One day, just before his grandson's 20th winter, No Feather decided it was time to invoke an old custom, one that had not been done since he had done it as a young man. He had talked to other elders and they all agreed that Turtle was the kind of young man who should do it.

So the old man took his grandson away from the village to the river's edge and told him his thoughts.

"I have talked to the other old men," he began, "and we feel that we should ask you to undertake an old custom. We are asking you to make The Journey."

Turtle knew about The Journey and knew that his grandfather had made it as a young man. It was not to be taken lightly, because it was dangerous. Nevertheless, he was excited at the prospect. It was something that a young man could not decide to do on his own; the elders asked a young man because they thought him worthy of the test. According to the old stories, a few young men in the past had not returned from The Journey. No one ever knew why. One thing was certain: more than physical strength or prowess was necessary to complete The Journey. Those who did succeed invariably became men whose commitment to the welfare of the people was second to none.

"In four days' time the elders of the village will prepare a feast," No Feather said. "Then you will be asked to undertake The Journey. You have the right to refuse, just as well as the right to accept."

That evening the village crier announced to the people that the elders would offer a feast in four days. A feast always meant that something serious or auspicious was going to happen, and usually word got out somehow. But as much as everyone asked, this time no one knew the reason for the upcoming feast.

On the appointed day nearly everyone in the village gathered in an arbor built for the occasion. Women who had been cooking all day long brought the food and the oldest man in the village stood to speak.

"My friends and relatives," he began, as a hush fell. Even the dogs were quiet. "It has been more than a generation since one of our traditions was last done. One man among us, now an elder, was the last to do it. Now we are asking his grandson to do this difficult thing, to make The Journey."

A murmur slid through the gathering, especially among the elders. The Oldest Man went on to remind the people what The Journey was.

"The Journey is a quest," he said. "A quest to find the best in ourselves. For that reason we select a young man we think is worthy to undertake this quest for us. We know we are a strong people, but we also know there must be more to strength than weapons and the ability to fight. Strength is also a will to win, to do what is right, to understand all that is around us. We want the young man we have selected to make The Journey, to finish it, and then bring to us his story of why and how he was able to do so.

"There are things he must bring back to us as well. From the banks of the Bad River to the north, some sweetgrass. Soft gray river shale from the Big River to the east. From the south the blue sage grass, and the flat cedar leaves from where the White Earth River begins its journey. These are to prove that he has walked the land.

"But that is not the difficult thing. The young man we will ask to make this journey must do so without weapons or food. The only things he can carry will be a knife and a deer-hide robe, and the only clothes he takes will be what he wears at this moment."

Another murmur went through the crowd. Now it was the middle of autumn and in another moon the cool winds would precede the coming winter. To be alone without weapons and a shelter was not easy. Yet the elders knew it must be so because life itself was not easy. Anyone who accepted this challenge was accepting that reality.

By now everyone gathered was curious to know which young man would be asked. The young men listening knew that making The Journey successfully would go a long way toward raising their status. But most of them were silently hoping that they would not be asked. And when the name of the young man was spoken, a gasp went through the crowd.

"The young man we ask to make The Journey is the one known as Turtle," the Oldest Man announced. "It is, of course, his right to refuse."

Turtle knew this moment was coming. Among the murmurs in the crowd he thought he heard a few snickers, and there was more than one expression of disbelief. Surely there were those who thought the strongest young man or the most accomplished warrior would be chosen. He was neither. Nevertheless, he walked forward when the Oldest Man motioned for him to approach.

"I know your grandfather has told you," the Oldest Man said to him. "What is your answer?"

"I will go," Turtle said, barely above a whisper.

The Oldest Man was pleased. "Good," he said, then turned to the crowd. "We will feast with this young man and send him on his way with a full stomach and our good wishes."

When it was time to begin The Journey, Turtle stood before the Oldest Man once again and handed over his bow and arrows, his lance and shield. It was an open gesture in view of the whole village to show he was armed only with his knife. The Oldest Man then held out a rolled-up deer-hide robe and an extra pair of moccasins. Turtle was to choose, and as his grandfather had advised, he chose the extra pair of moccasins. It was easier to make good night shelters than it was to make moccasins.

Turtle embraced his mother and grandmother, acknowledged his father and grandfather, then in view of the entire gathering walked north, carrying his spare pair of moccasins. He started north because it was autumn; the sweetgrass he was to gather from the Bad River was already in bloom and would soon begin to wither. Of the two grasses he was to gather as proof of his journey, the blue sage was more durable.

Without a backward glance he walked until he reached a line of hills. From that distance he could just make out the circles of lodges in the village. With a deep sigh, Turtle went down off the hills wondering if anyone other than his family was looking in his direction. Two thoughts coursed through him like whirlwinds: he had never felt so alone in his life, and he might never see his family again.

He dared not stop again, even for a moment, for fear that his doubts would force him to turn back. So he kept walking, briskly at first, and then as the sun sank in the western half of the sky he finally slowed his pace. Over and over as his grandfather had suggested, he thought of what he had to do to get through each day.

Obtaining water was not an insurmountable problem. Luckily it had been a winter with much snow, and rain had fallen throughout the spring and summer, so creeks and rivers were not low. Food was another matter. Only dried and bitter fruit were left on berry trees this time of the year. Wild turnips, however, were in full bloom. If he could fashion a fish trap he might catch a fish or two in one of the larger streams. He decided to keep an eye out for the right kind of fallen branch with which to make a rabbit stick, one heavy and curved. If he threw it with enough force, he could take a rabbit with it, or perhaps a grouse.

Not for a moment did he forget that he would need to keep watch against enemies, especially since he had no weapons. A lance was what he needed, even one without a stone point. But even before a lance and a rabbit stick, he needed something to start a fire. Dropping down into a narrow valley, he concentrated on finding the materials for a bow drill fire starter. Since all but one of the components was wood, it was difficult. Finding some kind of cord for the small bow was the first obstacle he had to overcome, and quickly, with sundown not far off.

Turtle solved the problem by using the thin leather thongs around the tops of his spare moccasins. After he had finished his fire starter he gathered kindling and then firewood for the night. Following an old creek bed, he chose a high bank on the north side, against a bend in the old watercourse, and dug into the bank to make a shallow overhang, just enough to keep the wind off during the night. Then he made his fire. Though it was only a small fire it chased away some of the loneliness he felt. Turtle had been away from home before, several times for many days and nights. But now it was different, because he did not know when he would get home again. He kept his fire burning low until dusk gave way to darkness.

Turtle watched the dawn break and a gray light grow beneath a layer of low clouds. A cool breeze crept along the dry creek. He was hungry and decided it would be wise to find some kind of food before he began growing weak. Following the watercourse north, he found a small thicket of oak and there searched for anything that he could make weapons of. He found a curved branch and carved it into a rabbit stick. Having even such a simple weapon in hand made him feel better. At least he was armed.

Nothing came within range of his rabbit stick, however. Though he had found water, Turtle went to sleep that night feeling the first sharp pangs of hunger. Because he had to keep moving during the day, he decided to fashion snares to be set out during the night from then on. He could hunt as he traveled in daylight.

His plan worked. Though he came close to a rabbit or two with his rabbit stick, it was a snare fashioned with leather thongs from his moccasins that brought success. He delayed traveling the next morning just long enough to cook a rabbit. While it hung over the low flames of his fire he scraped the rabbit hide. He had seen his grandmother sew rabbit hides together to make a coat. There was certainly time for him to do the same; all he needed was enough rabbits.

Turtle was surprised that even a small bit of meat could renew his energy. He did not eat it all, intending to make it last until his next kill. Carrying what was left of the cooked carcass and the rolled-up hide, he broke into a trot to make up the time he had lost. He had never been to the Bad River, but he had heard enough stories told around the fires. Once he reached the Bad River, his plan was to turn south and follow the Big River. By then he hoped to have more substantial weapons, and he resolved to search the next thicket of ash trees he came to. A young ash tree was easier to carve into a bow than one that had dried for many years. His father had taught him that.

The sixth night away from the village was decidedly cool, but it brought another rabbit to one of Turtle's snares. More meat, another hide, and sinew for a bowstring. Feeling rejuvenated, he cut two young trees, one for a bow and the slenderer for a lance, and immediately began crafting his weapons while the wood was still fresh and soft. He paused frequently to look around for two-legged intruders. By late afternoon he had fashioned the bow, and he added finishing touches until the sun went down. In the morning he would find enough wood to build a good fire to make a deep bed of embers. With the intense heat from the embers he would cure his new bow. What he needed now was more sinew for a bowstring, and his immediate source was rabbits. So he set out more snares.

Turtle improved his shelter, making it more difficult to see in the event a two-legged happened along, but mostly to make it as snug as possible since he had no robe to cover himself. He took a long drink from the creek just before dusk gave way to night, then crawled in. Wolves and coyotes were baying and singing in the hills around him, and he heard a nearby cricket chirping and the grunt of a nighthawk diving after insects. These night sounds lulled him to sleep.

A cool dawn breeze woke him to gray light. The first thing he saw was a fox sitting in the grass, no more than three or four paces away. Turtle was startled, though not afraid. Foxes had never been a danger to people. But he was surprised to see that it did not flee when he emerged from his shelter.

And when the animal spoke, it froze him in total disbelief.

"I see you have a warm place to sleep," the fox observed.

Turtle could only stare.

After a moment, the fox glanced about and then returned his gaze to the young man. "Are you traveling far?"

After a moment, Turtle cleared his throat and heard himself speaking to the fox. "Yes," he said hoarsely. "I am traveling."

"I have noticed that your kind move your dwellings often," the fox replied. "It seems you are a traveling people. But why are you alone?"

A fox is talking to me. I am hearing it, Turtle said to himself. There were stories of a time when people and animals could speak to each other. Different animals had the ability to understand and speak to one another as well. But that was very long ago, it was said. Perhaps not.

"Are you afraid?" the fox asked politely.

Turtle shook his head. "No," he said. "I . . . I . . . have never heard a fox speak."

"Then this is a good day," the fox replied. "For I have never understood the language used by two-leggeds. Yet I can understand what you are speaking."

"Why, do you suppose?" Turtle ventured.

The fox smiled. Turtle could discern that it was a smile.

"There are things in life that are hard to believe, hard to understand," the fox said. "That does not mean such things are not real."

Turtle nodded. That was the kind of thing his grandmother or grandfather would say. Perhaps he was speaking with a fox elder. "Yes, I suppose you are right," he replied.

"Which way are you traveling?" the fox asked.

"First to the north," Turtle said. "To the edge of our lands. I will travel to all the far edges of our lands."

"Is there a purpose for such a journey?"

"Yes," Turtle told the fox. "I am to learn."

"That is good. To learn and to know is power. Just as the sun lights the day, knowledge is what lights our journey through all the days we live. As children we depend on the knowledge of others. After that we must begin to learn for ourselves. Then we use it to help others."

Turtle stared at the fox, though he knew it was impolite to look directly into anyone's face. The fox took no notice, however. He pointed with his nose. "It is time for me to see to my duty as the protector of my family. Come with me," he offered. "For you and I have things to talk about."

Turtle glanced at his unfinished bow and the pile of wood at his cold fire pit. In an instant he decided that curing the bow could wait. He stood and followed the fox.

"My name is Old Shadow," the fox said. "My children now have children. More mouths to feed, more beings to protect."

"What are you protecting them against?" wondered Turtle.

"Some enemies can be seen, such as the wolverine and the bear," Old Shadow replied. "When our children are small, they can be carried away by hawks and eagles. Sometimes the owls come at night. The enemies that cannot be seen are hunger, cold, and loneliness. We must face them all."

Turtle followed the fox across a meadow, feeling a bit foolish because he was following a fox. A talking fox at that. But it seemed like the proper thing to do, because whatever else he might be, the fox was wise.

"Where are we going?" Turtle asked.

"I need to know who else has been here, besides you," Old Shadow said, even as he stopped suddenly to sniff at a bare patch on the ground. In a moment he continued with Turtle not more than a step behind. The fox glanced back over his shoulder.

"You are loud," he told Turtle.

Turtle was surprised. He had been taught to move silently since he was a boy. "I cannot hear anything," he protested.

"True," returned the fox, "but yours are not the only ears around, and all of them are better than yours." He stopped and indicated a patch of blue-green grass. "That kind is very loud when it brushes against your feet. Do not let anything touch you as you pass. That is the best way to avoid making noises."

So it went as they probed the edges of the fox's territory: observations and advice. Turtle knew that foxes were good hunters but he had not realized how cautious they were. While Old Shadow's nose constantly sought and found scents and odors, his ears were always alert for sounds. Near a bend of the creek, he suddenly paused.

"Come!" he whispered. "Hurry!"

Turtle followed him as they ducked into a thicket of low sagebrush.

"Down," Old Shadow said. "Do not move, make no sound."

Turtle did as he was told, lying on his stomach and peering through stalks of the bushes around him. A hornet buzzed around the bushes for a moment and a tiny grass snake wiggled past them, but Old Shadow was as still as a stone, and Turtle did his best to imitate him. After several more silent moments, he heard soft footsteps.

A young long-tailed cat walked by their hiding place, cautious and nervous. Lions were hunters and extremely alert. His ears flipped front to back for any sound and his large eyes peered about. Then he jumped across the creek, lowered his head for a quick sip of cool water, and was gone.

"Silence is your best ally," Old Shadow whispered. "And if you can learn to be still, all the better."

Later in the day they paused to rest beneath the edge of a cut bank, the low end of a gully. Old Shadow, as ever, tested the breezes for any errant scent. "We foxes are not as powerful as our cousins, the wolves," he said. "We do not hunt the big animals they do, such as the deer and the elk. Nor are we like our other cousins, the coyotes. Sometimes they throw caution aside, and they are scavengers as well as hunters. It is better for us to hunt smaller animals, those that are not as fast or as clever as we are. It is wisest to stay within what you are able to do."

Old Shadow took Turtle back to his sleeping shelter as the sun was going down. "I hope your travels go well," he said.

"Thank you," Turtle said. "I have learned something this day."

The fox smiled. "That is what life is all about," he said, then trotted away.

Turtle awoke at dawn and immediately looked about, half expecting the old fox to be somewhere nearby. After a small meal, he built a fire to make a bed of coals to dry his new bow. As he worked through the day, he thought of his small adventure with Old Shadow. An adventure that was difficult for him to believe, though he could still see the fox's face and hear his voice.

By sundown he determined that his bow was dry enough to use, and he was restless to move on. Part of him wanted to go home, but he knew that it would be the wrong thing to do. There was no honor in quitting.

At dawn he awoke and gathered his things and turned his footsteps north. Though many beings were moving about on the land, like the white-bellied goats and buffalo in the distance, he did not see a fox anywhere. Of course, that did not mean that one was not around, somewhere. Perhaps more than one. Silence and stillness—those were the ways of the fox.

Several days later he came within sight of a wide river that ran west to east. The landscape around fit the descriptions his father and grandfather had given him of the Bad River country. When he finally came close to the low valley through which the river flowed, he caught the faint odor of sweetgrass on the breeze. If nothing else, he had accomplished the first objective the elders had given him.

Turtle followed his nose to a wide swath of sweetgrass and picked a thick handful. After he set out snares, he braided one strand of sweetgrass and wrapped it in one of his rabbit hides. That braid he would take home, and the other braids he made would be used for smudging as he traveled.

Along the banks of the river he also found willow stalks just right for arrows. He had been picking up fallen feathers all along. Making a well-hidden camp, he decided to stay two days to finish his bow and make arrows. He wanted to finish the lance as well. A good lance was his first defense. Actually, after a pause to think, he decided that any weapon was his second line of defense; constant alertness was the first line.

His camp was on the north slope of a line of hills, inside a thicket of oak trees and plum bushes. Anything or anyone looking down from the hill could not see it, nor was it easy to spot from the north. According to his grandfather, the Bad River—since it flowed into the Great River—was known for large blackfish, so in addition to stalks for arrows he cut thinner ones to make a fish trap.

By the middle of the following day, he had accomplished most of the tasks he wanted to do. His bow was finished and he had six bone-tipped arrows. The lance was nearly done, too. The bones were temporary points, made from the ribs of an elk that Turtle had found. He had a notion to look for the right kind of stone for his lance point and arrowheads along the hilltops behind him. Instead he gave in to a sudden wave of fatigue and leaned back against a tree, just to close his eyes for a moment.

When he woke, the shadows cast by the trees had not changed much, but there was a figure in front of him that had not been there before. A black-tail deer with large antlers stared at him as it lay in the grass, not more than a stone's toss away.

"I have never been this close to a two-legged hunter," the buck said. There was no fear in his voice.

"I have never been this close to one of you," Turtle heard himself reply.

"I trust you are not hunting," the deer said.

"Not . . . not now," Turtle assured him.

"Good. I see you are not burdened with things, the way two-leggeds usually are," the buck observed.

"No. I am traveling light because I have far to go."

Turtle was certain he saw an amused expression in the deer's large brown eyes. All the while his ears were turning, alert for any sound. "We do not have your hands," the deer went on, "to carry anything. But I think even the things that burden the heart and the mind are easier to carry than the things in your hands, or on your back. I have seen two-leggeds carry much on their backs. That must be difficult."

"Yes," admitted Turtle. "But necessary. It is our way."

"We all have our ways," the deer agreed. "My name is Leaper. Come, I have something to show you."

If he had not met Old Shadow, Turtle would have thought he was losing his mind. But if a fox talked to him, why not a deer? He stood.

Leaper, true to his name, was on his feet in an instant. The size and breadth of his antlers showed he was an old buck, but he was still powerful. He pointed with his antlers toward the hills and trotted away. Turtle, close behind, was halfway up the hill before he realized he had no weapon with him. But he did not want to go back.

The old buck paused just below the crest of the hill and gazed for long moments across the wide valley of the Bad River. His large ears were turned back. "Eyes forward, ears back," he said. "That is the best way to stay alert for hunters. Always look and look long, and search through the sounds you hear."

"Eyes forward and ears back—that is difficult for us two-leggeds to do," Turtle said.

"You can find a way," replied Leaper. "And never, ever, stand on the crest of a hill. Find a spot below the ridge, like here. You can still see far, and if you do not move, you will not show your presence to anyone else." So saying, Leaper cast his gaze across the wide valley. Turtle sat next to a bristly soap weed and did the same.

"Tell me what you see," the deer said.

"On the far slopes," Turtle said, after a moment, "are two buffalo, perhaps more in the trees. There are birds everywhere, in the trees along the water and above us in the sky."

"Yes. Your eyes seem to be good, for a two-legged," allowed the old deer. "Do you see in the grass in front of you?"

Leaper looked down and saw the dark squares on the back of the thick-bodied snake wending its way through the grass. He had not thought to look around where he sat.

"Enemies can be where you least expect them. That is a rattling-tail," observed Leaper. "His bite can cause great pain, even death." He stomped the ground hard with a front hoof, twice. The rattling-tail paused, its black forked tongue flicking out from its mouth, and then turned in another direction. "Rattling-tails, and I think all their kind, do not hear with their ears. They hear with their bellies. They feel our footsteps."

Turtle kept watch to make sure the snake was going away, and then looked around to see what else was near. There were many insects but no other dangerous creatures.

Leaper walked to some clumps of soap weed and lay down among them. From a distance he looked like one of the clumps, especially if he did not move. "We will watch," he said. "It is not enough to know you have enemies. It is better to know where they are. Remember, eyes front, ears back."

The day passed as they lay among the soap weeds. Everything else, including the sun and occasional clouds, was moving around or past them. Across the valley the small herd of buffalo had moved over the hills. A coyote trotted along the water and briefly encountered an angry badger before he swam across the gray stream. A herd of white-bellied goats moved into the valley from the east. They drank at the river and lingered, but eventually moved on to graze on the slopes below them. Insects buzzed around them. Turtle made certain no snakes were trying to sneak in close. By turning his head slightly to one side or the other, he found he could hear sounds behind him while he kept watch forward. He heard ducks, the fluttering of a grouse taking wing, and the warning bark of a prairie digger. For some reason he did not feel impatient at sitting so long in one place.

Shadows lengthened, stretching long to the east, before Leaper uttered a sound. "I must go now," he said. "I see no hunters, and when the sun goes down it is time for me to eat."

"Thank you," Turtle said.

"Not at all," Leaper replied. "I hope your journey is good. Remember what I told you about enemies."

Rising to his feet, he shook his great antlers and bounded effortlessly down the slope and disappeared into a grove of trees. Turtle searched the trees with a probing gaze but could not see the big old buck. With a sigh he stood and walked toward his camp.

When he reached it, he saw that it had not been disturbed. In the daylight that remained, he decided to finish his fish trap and put it in the river overnight.

His efforts were rewarded. In the cool light of a gray dawn he walked to the river and found a large blackfish in the conical trap. After he cooked and ate, he gathered his things. His plan was to turn southeast and stay just west of the Great River. He alternated his pace as he went, first walking, then trotting. Thus he covered much ground before the sun went down.

Turtle thought of the fox and the black-tail deer. The words they had spoken to him floated in his mind, like lazy clouds in the sky. He hoped he could remember all they had said, but he wondered who would believe him when he told about Old Shadow and Leaper. He knew his grandfather would.

Four days of hard travel later he came to a high bluff on the west side of the Great River. It was the landmark his grandfather had told him to find. The bluff faced east over the river and its face was gray shale. He would need to gather a few slabs of it to go along with the sweet grass as proof of his journey.

Turtle was gaining confidence with each passing day. In addition to his rabbit stick, he was now armed with a lance and a bow with six arrows. His moccasins were somewhat worn, but not enough for him to discard. And he also had the lessons given him by a fox and a black-tail deer. Taking them to heart, he worked his way silently to the edge of the bluff. There, with a thick growth of sumac guarding his back, he sat for the better part of an afternoon, watching the comings and goings along the shores of the Great River below.

He saw a few raccoons, a short-tailed cat, several coyotes and foxes, and birds of every kind and color. A gray heron walking on long stick-like legs was prowling for fish along the shore. A brown eagle swooped down and took a fish from just below the surface of the water. Above him a falcon circled, as did hawks. Turtle took a deep breath and rubbed his eyes to keep from dozing.

Rustling noises caught his attention, coming from the plateau behind him. His breath stopped in his throat when he saw a large bear. Luckily, the bear was still over 30 paces away, far enough for Turtle to take his chances by sliding down the near vertical face of the bluff.

"Two-legged," the great bear called out. "I know you are there. I cannot see you but I can smell you. Come out, I will not harm you, for today I am your friend."

If not for his encounters with the fox and the black-tail deer, Turtle would have jumped down the bluff for sure. Nonetheless, a fox and a deer were nothing like the most powerful hunter on the land. Turtle knew two things about this kind of large bear: it was immeasurably stronger than a grown man and could outrun even the fastest human.

Turtle rose to his feet, his legs shaking, and moved cautiously out of his cover. Jumping over the edge might still be necessary if the bear charged.

"I am here, friend Bear," he called out, his voice quivering a bit.

The brown bear rose on her back legs, raising her black nose for scent. Locating Turtle, she dropped to all fours and approached.

"Do not be afraid, young two-legged," she said. Her voice sounded tired.

Turtle felt somewhat reassured, though he stayed near the edge of the bluff. The bear was very large, yet not as large as a male would have been. Her coat was a deep, dark brown, though she seemed gaunt. Bears were usually fat this time of the year. Turtle noticed that her teats were small and dry. She was an old bear.

"Thank you, Grandmother," he said. "It is good to see you."

The bear walked to the edge of the bluff and gazed down the slope at the river for several moments, then settled herself in the grass.

"I know that you two-leggeds are afraid of us," she said, "and with good reason. We are much stronger than you and we are faster runners. But you must know that we do not hunt you."

"Yes, we know," Turtle said, taking a seat an arm's length from the bear. He still felt a bit nervous being so close to an animal that could kill him with one swipe of her claws.

"There are ways in which bears and two-leggeds are alike—perhaps you know that, too."

"How so?" the young man asked.

"We are hunters, and so are you," the old bear pointed out. "We eat meat and plants. So do you. That is true of only a few others. Most eat only meat or only plants. There are many ways that my kind are different from your kind, of course. But there is one way that puzzles me."

Turtle cleared his throat. "What is that, Grandmother?"

"Our strength is easy to see. We are powerful and fast. We do not fear any being that walks on this earth. We will face anyone in battle, even elk or buffalo." She paused to lift her nose, searching for smells. "But I am puzzled because I cannot see the source of your strength. I wonder if it is what you carry in your hands—your weapons. Perhaps that is so, because you are weak and slow, you have no claws like we do, or fangs like the great cats or wolves, or horns like the buffalo, or antlers like the elk and deer. Yet you hunt and you take down beings that are stronger and faster than you. It does trouble me."

"Why does it puzzle you?" Turtle asked.

"Because it is the unseen enemy that can cause the greatest harm," the bear replied. "A long time ago one of your kind hurt me with a weapon. A stone piece of it is still lodged in my back. I smelled him but I did not see him."

"You are still alive," Turtle pointed out.

"True," the bear agreed. "But there was a time when two-leggeds had no weapons. Now you have many. Look what you carry."

Turtle had never thought of what the bear said. He thought that weapons were something people always had. Yet how did they come to be? Someone long ago had to make the first lance, the first club. He remembered throwing stones at snakes. Stones became weapons when used in that manner, he reasoned. He had been taught to make weapons. That was what the bear did not know.

"My friend," he said, "when I was a boy, my father and grandfather taught me to make weapons. I have made many in my life. That is our strength—we can make things. We can make our clothing, our dwellings, and our weapons."

The bear nodded her head slightly. "Yes, what you say may be true. I can roll heavy stones aside to look for insects hiding beneath them, or push down a very large tree. But I cannot make anything the way you say you can." She paused for several moments. "You also have fire.

"That is why the source of your strength cannot be seen," she went on. "It is not so much your arms, your legs, or your speed and your size. It is a kind of strength that dwells somewhere within you. I do not know if that is good."

Turtle did not know what to say. The bear's reasoning bothered him, because it was not easy to argue against it. He could not. "I am glad you are my friend today, Grandmother," he finally said.

"My people and yours are not enemies," she said. "Sometimes our trails do cross when we do not expect. If you will walk away when that happens, so will we. You must tell your people this."

"I will, Grandmother," he promised.

The old bear labored to her feet. "Have a good journey, Grandson. My name is Strong Heart. I have lived many, many summers."

Turtle stood and watched the old bear until she was out of sight over the hill. She was thin and he wondered if she would make it through another harsh winter. What she had to say echoed in his mind. She had stayed but briefly, yet suddenly he was sad she was gone.

He did not remember falling asleep, but he awoke curled up in the grass. By sundown he had made a shelter by covering a narrow gully with brush. A large black-fish was in the trap he had left in a shallow eddy of the river. Turtle fell asleep that night with a full stomach, wondering if any more animals would speak to him. In the morning he finished his fish, collected shale from the bluff, and reluctantly continued his trek. The spot by the river was peaceful and he hated to leave.

Of the four items he was to find, he had two. But he knew there was a wide expanse of land before he reached the river far to the south where blue sage grass grew. He had been fortunate so far. He had weapons and his snares had given him food. If he could bring down a deer he could probably take the time to make enough jerky to last a month. However, after meeting Leaper, he decided he would never again shoot a black-tail. If a white-tail came close, he would take a chance. He thought of all these things as he trotted across the prairies. Most of all he wondered who would believe that a fox, a deer, and a bear had spoken to him. Or had they? Maybe it was just his imagination.

Autumn rains, not unusual, began falling softly each afternoon. Walking became more difficult while it rained, especially up hills and slopes, because the ground was soft and slippery. For several days in a row Turtle started in the early morning, then sought shelter as the rain fell steadily in the afternoon. Shelter was not always available. After the third afternoon of rain, everything he owned was thoroughly soaked.

One morning he stumbled upon layers of shale protruding from the summit of a small hill, which was also not unusual. His grandfather called this prairie shale, to differentiate it from the shale found along riverbanks. Intending only to sit and rest, he noticed a bit of an overhang beneath the top layer, behind thick brush. With his lance he poked inside to make certain no rattling-tails were lurking. Pulling out pieces from the crumbling lower layers, Turtle managed to fashion a low shelter. He could sit inside out of the rain.

He hurried to gather kindling and dry wood from nearby gullies and thickets. When the rains came he built a small fire and hung his moccasins and breechclout on sticks to dry, as well as the rabbit hides. He roasted some of his dried meat over the low flames and fell asleep watching the fire.

"This is a good place," said a small, soft voice.

Turtle opened his eyes and sat up, reaching instinctively for his lance. Then he saw the small bird with yellow eyes and long, thin legs. "Did you say something?" he asked.

"I said this is a good place," the bird repeated.

"It is," Turtle replied. "I cleared away the brush and some of the shale. I may need to stay here for a day, maybe longer. Rain makes it hard to walk."

The bird was a small owl, a kind that lived in burrows with the prairie diggers. The bird-with-the-trembling-chin, they were called. In late autumn and early winter they had a high-pitched wavering cry, like someone shivering. It was their way to warn of a cold night coming. Turtle was no longer surprised to be addressed by other beings, yet after the bear, the last thing he expected was a burrowing owl.

"The rain drives my friends crazy," the owl agreed. "Water runs down into their dens. I was going home when I saw your shelter," she said, bobbing down the way they did now and then. "I thought it might be a good place to wait for the rain to stop."

"Yes, it is," Turtle agreed. "Stay as long as you like."

The little owl stayed away from the fire, eyes narrowing when a waft of smoke came near. "My name is Singer," she said. "I have lived here all of my life. In that time the village of the diggers has become larger and larger. Now it is spread over several hills. If you are traveling you might go east to avoid it. There are many rattling-tails who live with us as well. They cannot be trusted."

"Thank you." Turtle was sincerely glad for that bit of news. He did not like snakes, and he knew that rattling-tails lived in the digger burrows because they could not build their own dwellings. He could never understand how the diggers could tolerate a rattling-tail living in their very homes.

"You have come a long way, it appears," the owl said. "I think you also have a long way yet to go."

"Yes. I am not yet halfway through my journey."

"There are many travelers on this land," observed the owl. "The buffalo, most of all. They go from beyond the sunset to the other side of the sunrise. I think they were born with restless spirits."

Turtle's grandfather had said the same about the buffalo. "I think you are right," he told the owl.

"But then, your people are travelers as well," Singer said. "You came to this land from somewhere, because you were not always here. Now you move your dwellings. You do not stay in one place like the diggers or the badgers do. It seems you have restless spirits as well."

Turtle smiled. "Perhaps we have become restless like the buffalo because we follow them. We hunt them and eat their flesh. My grandfather says we take their spirits into us by doing so."

"Your grandfather is right," affirmed the owl. "Does he know what the buffalo have to endure in order to live their life of traveling?"

"Perhaps he does. He has never spoken of it."

"I think he will one day. But consider this," Singer said. "The buffalo are the most powerful four-leggeds on the land, yet that is not enough to keep their enemies away. Wolves hunt them, so do your people. They suffer losses as we all do."

"What does that mean?" Turtle wanted to know.

The owl bobbed her head and shoulders again, and gazed out into the soft rain with her wide eyes. It was stopping, the sun's rays piercing the thinning clouds.

"It means that life favors no one being," she said, a bit sadly. "It does not favor the strong over the weak. We all have our burdens and our victories. We all make our way the best way we can, using the abilities we are given. I must go back to my burrow now, the one that the diggers let me use. I raised my families in that burrow. The rattling-tail took some, now and then. But that is the way it is. I fly low just out of the reach of foxes but not so high that the falcons can dive on me from above. That is the way it is."

"You are wise," Turtle told the owl.

"I have lived a long life," Singer said. "Beyond that hill, there, with the lone tree, is the body of an elk.

He died yesterday, perhaps of old age. His flesh is still fresh, his hide will be very useful to you. The rains have kept his scent from floating far. Go, before others find him."

"Thank you, Grandmother," Turtle said.

"May all your journeys be good," the owl said. She flew out of the shelter. Turtle jumped up and watched her go, flying low over the land. Then, grabbing his lance and his knife, he hurried toward the hill with the lone tree.

Two days of hard work, from dawn to dusk, yielded all the meat he could carry, along with a large hide. He scraped the inside clean, pounded it with stones, then smoked it over a fire. All the while he kept watch. He could not take all the meat from the elk carcass, only one hind leg and part of the rump. But he also took the hamstring sinew, the cord that ran from the base of the skull down to each ankle. Now he had a stout bowstring.

From the hide he made a small shirt without sleeves and a robe he could sleep under. It would also serve as a coat and shed rain and snow. Strengthened by good meat, he traveled south for eight days until he came to a wide river with clear water. Water that came from mountains far to the west, which he had never seen. Along the banks of the river was the blue sage grass.

He tried his fish trap and caught two fish, of a kind he did not know. He rested a day to work on his hide and dry out his bowstring. At dawn the second day he turned west, now wearing his second pair of moccasins.

Turtle was thankful for the elk hide because the nights were growing colder. He thought about the little burrowing owl. She was the size of one of the bear's paws, but no less wise. Never in his life did he think animals could be wise, but why not? They were born and lived their lives, the same as humans, and on the same earth. Each of them that had come to him had been an elder. All the elders back home in his village knew things, more than anyone who was younger. It made sense, then, that an old black-tail deer would know things a young one did not.

The fourth night away from the river with the clear water, Turtle stared into his small fire. A cold breeze slid over the land outside his snug shelter, a small, low dome of interwoven branches and leaves. He was tired. His feet were sore because he had never traveled for so many days in a row. At least 48, if he had not lost count. For certain he knew that he was also much leaner. Though he had food, he ate sparingly. *A man needs so little, just to live and breathe,* he thought. Just before he extinguished his fire he saw the fox, the deer, the bear, and the owl. They knew things that he did not, perhaps never would. Somehow, that awareness bothered him. After the fire was out, he lay in the dark under the elk robe wondering where this journey would really take him.

Nearly ten days later he passed north of a land that seemed bare of grass and trees. At least the hills and slopes he could see had nothing growing on them. Turtle held back his curiosity about the place, resisting the urge to explore this patch of desolation in the middle of the prairie lands. His grandfather had warned him to stay out of it. That was another journey for another day, he had said.

A day's travel north of the bare hills were rocky ridges, many of them covered with cedar trees. Turtle stared at them with a deep sense of relief. A kind of fatigue he had never known made his legs weak. He had been away from home for 60 days. Perhaps his family thought he was injured or dead. Wasting not another moment, he climbed the closest ridge and cut several flat branches with the flat cedar needles. He had the proof he needed. Now it was time to go home.

Below the ridge of cedar trees, he found an old blown-down tree, its roots exposed. By weaving brush through them, he made a solid shelter, a place where he would rest for a few days. Then taking his bow and lance, he climbed to the crest of a ridge and crawled in under the lower branches of a cedar. For most of the afternoon he watched the land all around.

There was plenty of activity. An elk whistled some-where and a buffalo bull bellowed, its voice thinned by the distance. Coyotes could be seen everywhere, as well as rabbits and white-bellied goats. Turtle was reassured because he did not see any two-leggeds. Any people here would probably be enemies—that was an assumption the warrior side of him had to make. But, of course, not seeing an enemy did not mean one was not there. Anyone encroaching into enemy lands did everything possible to stay out of sight. One thing was certain, however. A cold breeze was prowling the land and he knew that autumn was nearly gone.

Turtle decided to close off his shelter and make a fire inside. Nights were colder now. As dusk settled across the land, he prepared a bed of small cedar branches and needles, then gathered fallen branches to cover the shelter, not only to keep the wind out but to keep the fire's glow from being seen. Returning to the shelter with an armload of sticks, he saw a low, shadowy form blocking his path.

"You hide well," a gruff voice said. "For a two-legged."

Turtle saw the small eyes of the badger glistening in the dusky light. He kept his hand around the handle of his knife. He knew about badgers. They were extremely ferocious. One had chased him up a tree when he was a boy.

"Thank you," he said, watching the badger look around. "I am glad to know that." Turtle could see the dark stripes from the sides of his face and down his back.

"You have traveled far," the badger said.

"Yes," Turtle said, nodding slowly. "My feet hurt."

"Now you can go home."

Turtle paused. How did the badger know that he could go home? He decided to let it pass. "It will be good to go home. Come to my shelter. I have a few tubers. I am sure you are hungry."

He decided not to build a fire after all, since he knew animals were afraid of it. The badger sat on his haunches off to one side and nibbled on the handful of tubers Turtle put before him.

"You have built a good shelter," observed the badger. "My name is Digs. My dwelling is not far from here, high on a hillside."

"High on a hillside?"

"Yes. There is a hard winter coming," Digs said, taking more bites. "Our kind move to a hilltop or below the rim of a high bluff when there will be deep snow. That way it will not bury us and we will be above the water when the snow melts."

"What if there is a drought, or a winter with not much snow?" Turtle asked.

"Then we move down the hills, closer to the creeks and rivers," the badger said.

"That is good to know, and a wise thing to do," Turtle pointed out.

"Everyone must have a home," the badger said, finishing the last tuber. "Everyone must defend it. We badgers do not like anyone coming near our homes. We will fight fiercely to drive enemies away."

"Is that what you came to tell me?" Turtle asked.

"Perhaps," Digs replied mysteriously. "But also that two-leggeds passed by my dwelling days ago. I think they were carrying weapons, of the sort your kind use to hunt, or make war."

"Where did they go?"

"That I cannot tell you," the badger said. "They were traveling from the land of the Owl People."

The land of the Owl People meant south. People from the south, likely going north. Turtle was worried. "I am glad to know that. Now I must hurry home. Those two-leggeds may be enemies of my people."

"Thank you for feeding me," the badger said cordially. "I must return to my dwelling. It is dusk now; darkness is not far and the nighttime hunters will be out. Travel well, two-legged."

After the badger departed, Turtle built his fire. He wanted to sleep comfortably and rest well. In the fire's light he wrapped his bundles and checked his weapons. At dawn he would begin the last part of his journey, as fast as he could manage. If the badger was right, enemies from the south could be somewhere out there.

Dawn came cold and clear. Turtle's breath misted lightly in the air. After his legs had loosened, he broke into a trot. He traveled in a straight line, picking out a spot on the skyline ahead. When he reached it, he picked out another. Going over hills and ridges could not be avoided. Thus at the crest of each rise and hill, he hid and paused to rest and scout the land ahead. Many animals were moving, as he had expected. Except for bears and big cats, there was no outright danger from animals. The danger he was looking for was enemies from the south. Not until the fifth day, however, did he find them.

He smelled the smoke from their fire at dawn and saw them when they moved from their night camp. Seven men, all armed with lances and bows and quivers full of arrows. Stopping them was out of the question; he was badly outnumbered. There was only one way and that was to reach his village before they did.

For two days he followed them, conserving his energy and hoping they were not going in the direction of his village. His hopes were dashed. The intruders entered a river valley he knew well, southwest of his village. Home was four days away.

That night he did not sleep, but kept going, bending his line of travel to the east and then back to the north. It was cold and he was glad for the elk robe. Walking all night, he slept briefly at dawn.

At midday he stopped and slept again. He kept moving in this way, sleeping only in brief snatches. Though thoroughly exhausted, he was confident that he had left the intruders far behind. Pushing through a second night he reached a line of hills south of his village.

The dogs were the first to greet him as he stumbled past the outer circle of dwellings. His mother and grandmother were overjoyed to see him. Before he fell asleep he told his father about the intruders coming from the south.

Not until the next morning did Turtle awake. His mother told him that his father had led warriors to meet the intruders. After he bathed in the stream he took a meal of hot soup and mint tea from his grandmother. Several elders came to see him, to welcome him home, anxious to hear of his journey. There would be a rebirth ceremony in the sweat lodge, they told him, after the warriors returned. Then he could tell them all he had seen.

But Turtle was not certain if the elders would believe what he had to recount—or even his grandfather, whom he told first. No Feather listened quietly, inscrutably, it seemed, to his grandson. After Turtle told him of his last visitor, the badger, the old man nodded thoughtfully. Finally he spoke.

"There was a time, it is told, when two-leggeds and animals spoke to one another," No Feather said. "It was not a different language that they spoke. It was that they could understand one another, just as you understood the fox, the deer, the bear, the owl, and the badger and they understood what you were saying to them."

The next day his father and all the warriors returned with good news. There had been no fight, because the enemy had been surprised and surrounded in an ambush. The warriors had taken all their weapons away and sent them back to the south.

Everyone in the village came to visit Turtle as he rested, even some who had thought him strange. Most brought gifts and all were anxious to hear of his journey. After the rebirth ceremony he was taken into a special lodge where the elders met, and there he told them the story. No one scoffed when he told them of the fox, the black-tail deer, the bear, the owl, and the badger. But Turtle had expected that the elders would listen courteously and not scoff at him. The old ones had lived long lives and nothing seemed to surprise them. A feast was prepared the next evening to welcome home the traveler, and all the people came.

The Oldest Man spoke again. He did not tell the people that Turtle had spoken with animals and they with him. But he did say this:

"We are what we are. The wisdom of the Creator made us so, and made us to share this place, this earth, with all the other beings who are here. With some we are friends, with others we are enemies. We welcome our friends and face our enemies. There are other enemies as well, which cannot be seen—hunger, cold, and loneliness. They must be faced as well.

"Throughout our lives, our journeys, we are burdened. Some burdens we carry in our hearts, others we carry on our backs or in our hands. We must strive to travel light, without burdens, and when we can we must take on the burdens of others.

"Every being on this earth has a way, a power, be it strength or speed, sharp eyes and ears, or the ability of silence or stealth. Ours, as two-leggeds, is to reason, because we are weak and slow. We can reason to rise to the level that all others have, and it is my prayer that we do not lift ourselves above others. But whatever our power is, life deems that we will not be favored because of it. We must always remember that.

"We must use that power always to fiercely protect everything that is precious to us, our families and our homes.

"These words I have spoken rise out of The Journey of the young man we call Turtle. He has learned that knowledge is the best weapon, the greatest tool. Knowledge will light our path throughout our lives.

"Along the way he has been taught that each of us—no matter who or what we are—looks at life from what we are and how we live it. We look at the world from our path, whether it is high or low, hidden or in the open. If all that every being knew could be collected, there would be more knowledge than anyone could imagine. Each of our journeys is necessary because if knowledge is the key to wisdom, then all beings must learn as much as possible during their journeys—their lives.

"Finally, we give a new name to our traveler. Though his journey has not been easy, neither has it been without gain. From this day on he will be known as His Good Trail."

Wawoslolye

(wah-woh-slol-yeh)

Knowledge

Be Quiet, Watch, Listen, and Learn

In the land of the blind the one-eyed man is king, so says an old axiom. The reason that the one-eyed man is king is obvious: he can see and no one else can.

There are over four thousand public and private colleges and universities in the United States where students are ostensibly beginning their pursuit of knowledge. Every year thousands upon thousands of them graduate from these institutions with basic skill sets and knowledge specific to their chosen professions. Yet, after they spend 40 years or so acquiring valuable experience and building on their knowledge base, society will deem them of no further use. After a career and several jobs, where they have certainly acquired more knowledge than they ever did in college, these people will be unceremoniously ignored, if not forcibly retired.

The United States, like just about every Western country, is a youth-oriented society. The energy and good looks of youth are preferable to the seasoned experience and knowledge of anyone over 40. Old equates to useless. If that seems difficult to believe, then consider the fact that most organizations, companies, and governments have a mandatory retirement age. Granted, the U.S. government has recently raised the retirement age, but the reason has nothing to do with keeping an experienced, knowledgeable work force in place; fewer people retiring means less drain on Social Security funds.

Even in qualifications for public office, knowledge and experience seem to take second place. Among the requirements to run for office at any level of government is a minimum age, usually 30 or younger and often as young as 21. Other basic requirements are citizenship and residency. Meaningful, relevant experience and a broad base of knowledge are not mentioned.

It is interesting to note that youth rights groups regard minimum age requirements for candidacy for elective offices as age discrimination. In comparison, I think of how my ancestors developed leaders. There, experience and a record of achievement were the first requirements. Young men used the arena of combat as well as civilian life to build this record, distinguish themselves, and demonstrate their courage and common sense. For all aspiring leaders, whether as warriors or civilians, it was necessary to be selfless, compassionate, honest, courageous, intelligent, and humble. As young men worked to demonstrate those qualities, they gained experience and knowledge. Elders knew that a man with several years of experience was the best one to handle the inexperienced exuberance of young men, especially in a combat situation. Several years of experience and useful knowledge gained gave assurance that this first line of leaders, who were about 30 years old, knew what they were doing more than the 18- to 20-year-olds did. Any thought of age discrimination was met with the patience of experience and the assurance that those young ones would one day realize why 18- to 20-year-olds were not leaders. They would learn that after several years of "doing"—serving the needs of the people—they would gain the experience and knowledge to be considered for leadership. There is no substitute for knowing what you are doing. As a matter of fact, it was basic knowledge, and the willingness to gain more, that enabled my ancestors to successfully face a major change in their lives about three hundred years ago.

The Lakota people (along with the Nakota and Dakota) once lived in the region southwest of Lake Superior. How long our ancestors were there as forest dwellers and canoe people and fishermen is not known. We do know approximately when they migrated farther west. In the late 1600s French trappers and voyageurs arrived and formed alliances with other indigenous people. The French tipped the balance of military power by providing the Hahatunwan (a.k.a. Anishanabe, Ojibwa, and Chippewa) and other tribes with firearms, and drove the Lakota, Dakota, and Nakota out of the region.

In this instance discretion was the better part of valor. Common sense told the Lakota and their allies that any military confrontation with their better-armed enemy would decimate their populations, especially males between ages 20 and 40, since those were the fighting men. The regions farther to the west were not totally unknown to them, since adventurous young men had occasionally wandered beyond known areas and brought back information. But when they left the thick forests and plentiful lakes of what is now northern Minnesota, they realized that a change in lifestyle was necessary because the northern plains were a drastically different physical environment. And adapt they did to that new environment because of one simple and strong value: knowledge.

As hunters and gatherers, all indigenous people knew the basics of survival, such as finding food (which included hunting and fishing) and procuring raw materials for shelter and clothing. But procurement was only the first step. Harvesting or gathering was followed by processing. For a game animal—be it rabbit or elk—this meant skinning and butchering and taking all usable material from the carcass. The hamstring cord of elk and deer, which was attached on either side of the spine from the base of the skull to the ankle bones on each hind leg, was extremely strong; it was dried and separated and used for thread and bow strings. Hooves, when boiled and cooled, produced a glue stronger than most chemical glues today. Sewing needles were made from leg bones and awls (for piercing holes in hide) from antler tips.

The Lakota, Dakota, and Nakota lived by their knowledge of the world around them in all its aspects—such as plants. They categorized these for use as food, medicine, construction or crafting materials, or dyes. Plants that did not fit into those categories were used in ceremonies or as additives or ingredients in cooking, processed into soap, made into toys, or burned as smudge or incense. Medicine plants were used to treat a variety of ailments and illnesses, such as colds and coughs, headaches, gastrointestinal disorders, toothaches, diuretic needs, dizziness, snake bites, and aching joints, to name a few. Just as important as knowing how to use them was knowing where to find them, when to harvest them, and how to process or prepare them for use. It was also necessary to know which part of the plant could be used: the leaf, root, bark, or fruit.

Similar banks of knowledge, if you will, existed for social customs, spiritual beliefs, hunting techniques, warfare, friends and foes, seasonal weather patterns, animal habitats and habits, and weapons, utensils, and tools, all of them obviously handcrafted. The products of technology, then as now, did not and could not exist without human skill and ingenuity, not to mention knowledge of materials and construction methods. Then, it was human energy that literally drove the functioning of tools, utensils, and weapons. But the driving force behind it all was knowledge.

Thus it was knowledge that enabled the Lakota, Dakota, and Nakota to live in their forest home, and knowledge that allowed them to adapt to life on the northern plains. Some of the information and knowledge specific to the forest environment was of no use in the new reality; it was not totally discarded, though, but replaced with new information that led to building a new body of knowledge.

The only bodies of water on the plains were creeks and streams and the many small rivers. The largest was the Great Muddy River, now known as the Missouri River. It was along these watercourses that trees grew in groves and forests, but nowhere near as thick as the woodlands around the lakes of Minnesota. Fishing would no longer be a primary method of procuring food. Canoes would no longer be necessary and neither would canoe-building skills. The lack of trees meant that the old ways of ensuring comfort and safety no longer held; in the forest, lodges or dwellings had been mostly permanent dome-shaped structures, a framework of wood poles covered with layers of woven branches. There was an immediate impact on hunting, too. Since forests provided food as well as shelter for game animals, such as deer and elk, it was not necessary to go far to find them. The wide-open grassy and virtually treeless plains meant not only that hunting tactics had to be altered, but that hunters had to travel great distances to find game. The Lakota, Dakota, and Nakota realized almost immediately that the plains environment was much more unforgiving than the forest. Survival would require adapting, and adapting meant developing a new knowledge base.

They also learned immediately that the northern plains was a place of extremes. Though sparsely populated by humans—a testament to the physical and mental toughness that two-legged beings needed to survive there—it teemed with animal life. Seemingly numberless herds of bison and pronghorn antelope wandered over the vast and endless landscape. The extremes played out with the weather as well. Summers could be scorching hot with powerful thunderstorms, and winters brought bone-chilling cold, with wind-driven whiteout blizzards. There were only two choices, equally extreme: stay or leave. The Dakota and Nakota chose to stay east of the Great Muddy River, where they found the rolling hills of the tall-grass prairie more to their liking. The Lakota, on the other hand, crossed to the western short-grass prairies.

Because herds of bison, the most readily available resource, were almost constantly on the move, anyone who hunted them had to be mobile as well. So the once forest-dwelling, sedentary Lakota shifted to a nomadic lifestyle. Permanent dwellings made of wood were no longer practical. What to replace them with was the obvious problem.

Any dwelling had to meet three requirements: portability, suitability for cold weather, and sturdiness to withstand strong winds. The answer was a conical lodge made of hides and wooden poles.

Bison were plentiful, in the hundreds of thousands if not millions, so there was a ready source of hides. The Lakota knew the characteristics of the trees in the environment around them—essential knowledge that was second nature to them after countless generations of living in direct daily contact with it—and since the poles had to be straight as well as strong, they knew that young pine trees were the logical choice. The resulting shelter was easy to put up, take down, and transport, snug in the cold winter, and able to stand up to merciless winds: the perfect product of old and newfound knowledge.

To make what would become the iconic dwelling of the plains—known as *tipi*—about 10 to 12 bison hides, with hair scraped off, were cut and trimmed and sewn together to form two triangular halves. The base of each triangle was curved. The two halves were laced together with hardwood skewers (usually choke-cherry shrub) to form a half-circle-shaped covering. That covering was draped over a conical framework of 10 to 12 poles. These poles of softwood, such as young pine, were straight and when dried were rigid and strong enough to bear the weight of the hides. They were about three inches at their base and 12 feet long, yet they were light and easy to transport. Bison hides had the tensile strength necessary to be stretched tightly, as they were over the framework of poles.

Loops of braided cord were attached to the curved bottom edge of the covering, and long hardwood pins were twisted into these loops and then pounded into the ground. This accomplished two things: it stretched the covering tightly and it enabled the structure to withstand wind. Though the basic floor design of the dwelling was circular, with the door facing east, the Lakota learned that an elliptical or egg-shaped design was more effective against the wind. Thus the back end, to the west, was narrower.

The dwelling was approximately eight to nine feet high inside, or just beyond the reach of a tall man with an arm stretched upward, and about 10 to 12 feet wide at the floor level. It was a dwelling that could hold four to six adults comfortably. To make the lodge snug and warm for the winter, an inner lining was added—two narrow lengths of bison hide, about four feet wide, tied to the lodge poles. Grass was stuffed between the inner lining and the outer covering, creating effective insulation.

Interior fire pits were necessary for cooking and heat, especially in the winter, so one other crucial design element was a smoke hole. The new conical lodge had a narrow opening at the top, with two square flaps on either side of that opening on the outside, propped up by two long poles that faced them away from the general direction of prevailing winds. The conical shape of the dwelling allowed smoke from the fire to rise and slide out of the smoke hole. The outside flaps created an eddy that sucked out smoke in even the slightest breeze.

Since dogs were used to haul possessions and household goods, the design and size of the conical lodge made it easy to transport (from the point of view of the people, if not the dogs). Each dog pulled two drag poles to which a light frame of wood was attached. Onto and into this frame, household goods and possessions were placed and tied down. Larger and stronger dogs could pull one half of the lodge covering, essentially the weight of five to six buffalo hides. One dog could also pull at least six of the long support poles. So four dogs were required to transport one lodge: two halves of the covering and 10 to 12 poles. With the coming of the horse, it became possible to transport bigger and heavier loads, so the tipi grew larger; eventually up to 20 buffalo hides went into its construction, with longer and sturdier poles to support the covering—another transformation made successful by knowledge and the willingness to learn.

But knowledge encompasses much more than just the artifacts and physical realities of a culture. There are aspects of culture that have no physical dimension but profoundly shape a society: values, beliefs, traditions, customs, laws, and norms of human behavior. For the Lakota as a culture, this kind of knowledge was as essential to survival as knowing how to build a shelter.

On the plains, surviving with and within the natural environment was often a struggle, and to ensure survival it was necessary for people to live and work together. To make this possible, societies established and applied rules, roles, and behavioral expectations—which meant that awareness, hence knowledge, of individual and collective human behavior was a critical necessity. Observation over time was the best teacher, and among other things it revealed one reality at the core of group dynamics: most humans preferred to be part of a group rather than live in isolation. That essential bit of knowledge formed the basis for the community's punishment of the most serious offenses, such as assault, bodily harm, and murder: ostracism and even exile.

Ostracism meant that the offender was no longer part of the community, either for a prescribed period of time or forever. The offender, for all intents and purposes, ceased to exist as far as the community was concerned. He was escorted out of the village with nothing but the clothes he was wearing, and the people were told that under no circumstances were they to have any contact with him. After that, word was sent to other villages, and sometimes even to enemy villages. The offender, therefore, was utterly alone in the world. If his family chose to follow him, then the sentence applied to them as well. This punishment defused the inclination for revenge in the community, and the threat of it was such an effective deterrent that murder and aggravated assault were rare (until the arrival of alcohol).

On the other side of the coin, recognition within the group was a powerful motivator and a way to guard against the vice of arrogance, especially when it came to exploits on the field of battle. An arrogant man more often than not put his own needs and welfare and reputation first. Warfare was a proving ground for young men, especially those who aspired to be leaders. The dilemma was to encourage them to do their best as warriors when it was necessary—to the point of laying their lives on the line—while keeping their egos in check and learning the value of humility. To solve that dilemma, a special recognition ceremony for Lakota warriors was devised.

The ceremony was called *waktoglakapi* (wahk-toh-glah-ka-bee), or "to tell of one's victories." A few days after warriors returned from a patrol or mission, the village gave a feast and invited the warriors to stand before the people and recount their exploits in battle. This was done for two reasons. First, the telling of significant and courageous action taken on behalf of the people was a gift to the people. Once the story was told by a man, the action he described was no longer his; it belonged to the people. Secondly, any and all accounts had to be verified by others who were involved or present when it occurred. This ensured that stories could not be fabricated. Thus the ceremony was both an affirmation and recognition of the warrior and an effective safeguard against arrogance. Someone with keen insight and firsthand knowledge of the fragile egos of young men was certainly behind the creation of the *waktoglakapi*. Chances are it was an elder.

Elders, of course, were the best source of information and knowledge in the Lakota world. Not only because of the knowledge they had gained from a long life, but also because they were the connection to the previous generation's thoughts and ideas. Interestingly enough, an elder would be the first to tell you that he or she really did not know much. Which was, of course, spoken out of true humility. In reality elders were the repository of knowledge: walking libraries, if you will, and a most precious resource. In spite of American and Western societies' tendency to be youth-oriented, this is still very much true. Elders today are an untapped resource. This was not the case for my ancestors, the pre-reservation Lakota. They developed a social hierarchy based on experience and knowledge that enabled them to stay a strong and well-organized culture for hundreds of years. And the elders were the first to tell children and remind everyone that the pursuit of knowledge must be a lifelong endeavor.

No one, of course, can know it all, but each of us can know as much as is in our power. There are choices, of course. We can know a little about many things, which is better than knowing nothing at all—though the axiom "A little knowledge is a dangerous thing" is a word to the wise. Or we can accumulate voluminous and specific knowledge regarding just a few things.

In this day and age the pursuit of knowledge begins with a formal education, and then what we learned in those 12 to 20 years is either affirmed, disputed, altered, or obliterated. Whatever we do with a formal education, or after it, the most significant truth that each of us can embrace is that life is the greatest teacher. And it is not selective about what it teaches us. It will teach us how to be as well as how not to be. It will teach us how to do something and how not to do it. My grandparents all had the same advice when it came to living life. They said "Be quiet, watch, listen, and learn."

The more we see, the more we know, and the more we know, the more empowered we are. In the land of the blind, the one-eyed man is king.

chapter seven

The Shield Maker

No one knew exactly how old they were, the man and the woman who lived near the village but never in it. Their modest little lodge was within sight of the village, and when the people moved to another site, the old couple always took down their lodge and packed their belongings on seven dogs and joined in.

The man's name was Good Hand, and he was a shield maker. His wife was White Shell and she was a weather woman. She knew about the signs in the sky and on the earth, and those revealed by the plants and animals, that told her what the weather would be in the days and months ahead. Good Hand and White Shell did not have children of their own, and no one could remember why they chose to live outside the village. It seemed to most that this had always been so. Even in the childhood of those people who were 60 years and older, Good Shield and White Shell had been there, just outside the village. They were old then, it was said.

Both had snow-white hair and faces deeply lined and coppery brown, signs of a life spent in the sun. And because they were so elderly, the men in the village gave them fresh meat from their hunts. Though Good Hand had two bows hanging in his lodge, and sometimes displayed outside on a willow tripod, he was not known to hunt. The elderly couple never turned down a gift of fresh meat. In the winter, they always had plenty of firewood piled near their lodge, though no one had ever seen either of them gathering wood.

But Good Hand and White Shell were not needy or dependent on people in the village. They were always glad to have visitors, feeding anyone who came, and were always especially happy to welcome children to their lodge. If a change in the weather was approaching, especially a storm, White Shell always sent word by one child or another. And she was never wrong.

One thing about the old couple was evident to anyone who was invited into their buffalo-hide lodge. There was a calmness and serenity inside their home. It seemed to hang about them like an unseen mist, wherever they went and whatever they did.

Except in the winter, Good Hand was always busy making or preparing to make shields. The strongest and most durable shields were far and away those made of buffalo, and of the kinds of hide available he preferred that from the front shoulders. Good Hand's shields, it was told, easily repelled arrows and lances. It was not unusual, now and then, for a warrior to bring him a gift because his shield, made by Good Hand, had saved his life. Over the years many warriors came with gifts.

Warriors came also to thank Good Hand for what they had learned from him. Those men often asked him to make a shield for a son. There was always a specific reason for such requests, and Good Hand always complied, asking only that the young man bring the buffalo rawhide and stay to help.

One such young man came from another village early one summer, sent by his father. He was a strong, skilled, and reckless warrior with aspirations to glory. His name was Two Lance. Though he was polite, he was not impressed with the shield maker. Good Hand, however, was not unused to youthful arrogance.

Two Lance brought the required piece of buffalo rawhide and courteously told his hosts he would make his own camp nearby. His first task the following day was to dig a large pit and haul water to fill it. Then he was to soak his rawhide until it was soft. For several days he had to keep the pit full until Good Hand determined the rawhide was ready.

While the rawhide was soaking, Good Hand instructed Two Lance to dig two other pits in the bank of the nearby stream, one at the top of a bank and the other at the base. After the pits were dug the young man's next task was to gather firewood enough to burn two fires for three days and two nights. Two Lance did as Good Hand requested, mainly because he had promised his father he would be on his best behavior as a guest of the shield maker and his wife.

As it always happened when a young man came or was sent to help make his own shield, he had one question for Good Hand: "Why do you make shields?"

"When we dig up your shield I will tell you," Good Hand said, and Two Lance saw the sadness in the old man's eyes.

Several things had to happen before the shield was dug up. First, Good Hand asked the young man to join him by the creek. There the old man filled his black stone pipe with red willow tobacco and offered it to the Sky, the Earth, and the four directions—West, North, East, and South—and then to the Creator. He prayed for good things in order that he could make a strong shield for Two Lance.

Next, Good Hand declared that the rawhide had soaked enough to be soft and pliable. It was as thick as a small child's finger. Placing it on the flat, bare shoreline of the creek, he marked a perfect circle on it using a sharpened stick, a cord as long as one of Two Lance's arrows, and a piece of charcoal. Then with his knife he cut along the scribed line. The result was a round piece of rawhide. After that he placed the wet rawhide in the round pit at the top of the creek bank and covered it with a thick layer of dirt, which he compressed by pounding it with a large stone.

Next, Two Lance was instructed to build two fires, one in the pit in the side of the bank and the other atop the compressed dirt above the buried rawhide. He was to post himself beside the bank and keep a bed of red-hot coals in each pit, until the firewood was gone.

The young man discerned that the fires would warm the dirt from above and below the shield, and he guessed the rawhide would shrink.

White Shell brought the young man food and a willow chair so that he would be comfortable as he kept watch over the fires. The first night he nearly let the lower fire go out, but he did not let that happen again. At dawn on the third day Two Lance estimated that there was firewood enough to last until noon. He was right. At midday Good Hand came.

"When the top embers cool, it is time to dig up your shield," he announced.

"Grandfather," Two Lance said politely. "You said you would tell me why you make shields."

"Yes, I did. While we wait for the top embers to cool down, I will tell you why I am a shield maker. However, there is one thing I must ask. This story is for you and you alone. You must not tell anyone else, ever."

The young man was puzzled, but agreed.

"Good. When the old woman comes with tea and stew, I will tell you my story."

White Shell came moments later with bowls of stew and large horn cups of mint tea. She said not a word, only gave a motherly smile to the young man and walked away to the lodge.

After a sip of tea, Good Hand cleared his throat. "You remind me of how I was when I was young," he began. "My name was Stone Arrow then. Our village was along a river that flowed into the big river far to the east of here. I joined other warriors going north to raid against a new people. They were not like us. They did not move their lodges as we do. They kept them in one place along the river, and the lodges were made of logs and earth."

◀◀◀ ▶▶▶

Late autumn it was after a long, hot, and dry summer. Snowfall had been thin the previous winter, so the great river was low. Eleven men walked most of the way across on the many sandbars showing. They had been following the footprints of intruders that had crossed into their territory, then turned back. A young hunter had seen the footprints coming from and returning to the north, where it was known that strangers lived. Warriors had been north the year before and had seen people living along the rivers, in earthen dwellings. Where those people had come from was not known. Whether they had come south was not known. The 11 men were now farther north than most of them had ever traveled.

Stone Arrow was among them, an experienced warrior. He had turned 21 and his wife of less than a year was expecting a child. In four years he had not ignored a chance to prove himself against any enemy. His ambition was to become a leader of warriors before he was 30, a status never before achieved by any man. Though he had courted and won his bride by following all the rules and rituals of courtship, his burning desire was elsewhere. His young wife was dismayed when he joined the war party going north, but he knew she would understand when—in the years ahead—she would be known as the wife of the most glorious warrior there had ever been.

After two days of watching from across the river, the 11 warriors crossed at night. By dawn they were hidden in the tall grass south of the few earthen lodges on a plateau above the river. The leader chose Stone Arrow and one other to crawl closer to the village.

From the distance of a short arrow cast, the two young warriors watched until dusk. Their main concern was the number of grown men in the village and the weapons they carried. It seemed to be a small village, because there were only six of the earthen lodges. They surmised, however, that more than one family likely occupied one dwelling.

Stone Arrow and his companion were crawling away through the tall grass, intending to rejoin the other warriors and slip away under cover of night, when they heard someone shout. Assuming they had been spotted, they jumped up and ran, expecting pursuit. The shouting continued behind them. Looking back they saw a figure chasing them, wielding a short lance in one hand and a sling in the other.

Stone Arrow tripped and fell, then realized a cord was wrapped around his ankles. Tied to each end were heavy round weights: stones wrapped in rawhide. He recognized the weapon, used to bring down game birds. By the time he untangled himself, the pursuer was only a few paces away.

Stone Arrow stood to face him. Even in the fading light he saw that it was a slender youth. A boy on the verge of manhood, but only a boy nonetheless, a combination of fear and determination on his face. Still, the lance in the boy's hands was no less dangerous than it would be in the hands of a man. Stone Arrow sidestepped the charge, tore the lance from the boy's grip, and pushed him down into the grass.

The boy cowered in the grass. Stone Arrow tossed the lance aside and trotted away. A warning shout from his fellow scout made him turn, in time to see the boy running at him again with lance in hand. For a second time, Stone Arrow easily disarmed the inexperienced youth. Once again the boy fell, but this time he scrambled to his feet, stone-bladed knife in hand.

What happened next occurred in less than a heartbeat, but it would haunt Stone Arrow for a lifetime. The boy's inexperience collided with the warrior's annoyance bursting into anger. Stone Arrow saw his own hands thrust the lance, and saw the boy fall and twist in pain, the end of the lance broken off in his side.

Stone Arrow's companion appeared and looked down at the dying youth. "A boy. He is only a boy," he said.

No one spoke of the boy on the trek home. Stone Arrow feared he might have damaged his chances to become a war leader, but he kept his regrets to himself. He knew his fellow warriors would talk after they were home. Yet he knew he would have the opportunity to tell his side of the story, too. Though he thought about the boy from the earth lodge village, he decided that the unfortunate incident was unavoidable. That was the truth of it, as far as he was concerned.

Stone Arrow described the incident to his father before whispers and rumors ran amok in the village. He assured his wife that he had acted in defense of his own life. Though she was shocked, she accepted his assurances. Four days after the war party was home the elders called Stone Arrow to the council lodge. There once again he told his version of events. The elders listened but expressed no opinions.

Warriors did not cease patrols that winter. Watchfulness was necessary as always. Stone Arrow did his duty and more. On several occasions he went out alone to keep watch along the outer borders. He did not, however, reveal to anyone that the real reason for those lonely forays was to face down the guilt that whirled within him. Stone Arrow did not want his family to see his turmoil. During one such outing his wife gave birth to a daughter, which only affirmed his belief that strong and unyielding warriors were the best defense any people could have. He was determined that his child would grow up safe.

It was once again a winter of little snow. The elders fretted that they might see another spring of sparse rain as well, and the summer and autumn would be dry. If that happened the animals they depended on for food were certain to move nearer to the bigger streams, since those did not dry up as fast.

It was as the old ones had feared. By late summer most of the smaller creeks had dried up, forcing the people to move their village north to a river that flowed into the big one. They found that the deer, elk, and buffalo were staying close to the big river. So, late in the autumn the elders sent a large hunting party on the first of two big hunts to lay in meat for the winter.

The previous autumn's incident in the earthen lodge village to the north had become less and less of a topic for rumor and gossip. Most of the men who had been in that war party could not say with certainty they would not have reacted in the same manner. Many times a warrior had less than a heartbeat to make decisions that carry the weight of life and death, they reasoned. Furthermore, though some men shunned Stone Arrow, it seemed not to affect his dedication as a warrior. As time went on a drought was more of a concern than one warrior's aberrant behavior.

That incident, however, did not go away for the father of the boy who was killed. It stayed with him day and night, as if it had happened only the day before. He could not forget that his only son had been taken from him. His wife was inconsolable, which turned the father's anguish into a darkness that would not go away. Soon the grief turned to anger and then a desire to take revenge. As winter slid into the next spring, summer, and then autumn, the man observed all the necessary rituals of grieving to help his son's journey into the spirit world. Then one morning, just as dawn was graying the sky, he gathered his weapons and left the village on the plateau above the river.

It was known who the men were who had been caught scouting the village. They were the people of the buffalo-hide lodges from the south. Two young men had followed them to make certain they returned to their own country. After a month they returned, having trailed the intruders to their own village. They recognized the one who had killed the boy, and they were able to describe the man's lodge to his father. He would know it by the yellow lines on either side of the door.

Armed with this knowledge and pushed by a rage that boiled within him, the grieving father traveled south with a determination to exact revenge.

The elders decided that, while the men were hunting, the village would move north to a wide valley through which a river meandered. After two days on the trail a runner from the village caught up to the hunters with a message for Stone Arrow. He was to return to the village immediately. His wife and child were missing.

The village's move north had been delayed, he was told, after unsuccessful searches in every direction. Stone Arrow could only wonder what might have happened as he stood in front of his empty lodge. Two more days of searching revealed no sign of his wife and daughter. It was not until the third sleepless night in the lodge that he saw the lance. Tied to a lodge pole near the smoke hole was a broken lance with a stone head. It was the lance carried by the boy from the earthen lodge village, and its message could not be mistaken.

Stone Arrow could think of nothing but avenging his family. He gathered his weapons and asked his mother to prepare food. His father did not encourage him.

"I do not know what has happened to my daughter-in-law and granddaughter, your wife and daughter," he said. "Yet I am certain of one thing. The man who took them has learned that revenge does not change things back to the way they were. It never does and it never will. You may learn that as well.

"Punish this enemy if you think you must, perhaps take his life. But remember it was you who drew first blood, and you may not strike the last blow, and you will never feel at peace."

Anger prevented Stone Arrow from hearing his father's words. Bristling with weapons and hate, he departed on his quest—a quest that took him in a direction he never imagined.

At first the power of anger pushed him, giving him the strength to walk and run at an unrelenting pace. He traveled until he was too weary to take another step, found a hiding place to sleep, and then started walking and running again as soon as he awoke. Then, one morning, try as he might, he could not crawl out of the hole he had found to sleep in. Strength had left his legs and arms, and he began to weep.

Faces and images swirled in his eyes—his wife and daughter and the boy he had killed. It did not matter if his eyes were open or closed, he saw them. Summoning every last vestige of will, he crawled out of the hole. It did not seem to matter which way he was going, he was simply driven to move. Down hills, across watercourses, up hills, through brush and meadows he stumbled. At sundown he found himself on a hill and realized he had nothing in his hands. He was lost and unarmed, his clothing torn, his arms and legs scratched. He was hungry and thirsty, and barefoot. Stone Arrow thought to retrieve his food and weapons, but he could not remember how he had gotten to the hill. *What happened to me?* he wondered.

His only weapon was a knife, still in its sheath on his belt, which was still tied around his waist. The landscape around him did not look familiar and he could not decide what to do. So he found a narrow gully and curled up in it. The next morning, shivering in the cold air, he ignored his hunger and wondered again what he should do.

Around midmorning he stumbled onto a small creek, took a long drink, and tried hard to find a landmark he could recognize. Nothing at all was familiar, only the images that flowed through his mind: a dead boy and his own wife and daughter, over and over again. His father's words came to him:

. . . it was you who drew first blood . . .

He wept, and this time he could not stop. A reality pierced him like a battle lance. Whatever had happened to his wife and daughter, he had caused it. In the back of his mind was the thought that he would never see them again in this world.

Day passed into night, and day came once again. Stone Arrow saw these things, but it was only as a watcher, as though he were not part of it. He wandered aimlessly, sometimes stumbling, sometimes crawling. He fell asleep only when exhaustion overtook him, and he awoke alone and cold. Hunger and thirst had no effect.

One day he awoke in daylight next to a small creek, not knowing how many days had passed or where he was. When he sat up he did not recognize the dirty, gaunt, shadowy face looking back at him in the water, though he knew he was seeing himself. Never in his life had Stone Arrow known such a moment. He felt empty and powerless, a leaf at the mercy of the wind, his only purpose to feel anguish and guilt. Out of that utter helplessness he cried out.

"Help me! I am pitiful! Help me!"

He crawled to a small tree and sat against the trunk. Day passed until long shadows told him sunset was near, and another long, cold night lay ahead. It took a moment for him to realize that something was moving in the grass near him.

"Grief is no place to be lost," an old voice said.

Stone Arrow was shocked and afraid. When he tried to speak his own voice was nothing more than a croak. "I know this to be true."

The young man wiped his eyes and looked up to see the thin frame of an old man with long, white hair. He was leaning on a short lance.

"That is good to know," replied the old man.

Stone Arrow was still wiping his eyes, trying to make out the old man's face. It was someone he did not know.

"I do not understand, Grandfather," he said.

"When you are lost, the only way to find your way is to know you are lost."

Before the young man could reply, the old man sat down. In a moment he opened a bag and held out a piece of dried meat. "First we eat and drink," he said, "then we talk."

The old man built a small fire while Stone Arrow ate the dried meat and drank from a water skin. Even small bites of food revived him, and he was starting to think clearly. Yet he had never felt so much despair in his life.

"Grandfather," he said, "how did you find me?"

"Grandson," the old man replied, "I am a finder of lost souls. I followed the whirling anguish you left behind. It leaves deep tracks."

Stone Arrow was thoroughly puzzled. The old man was sitting with his back to the low sun sliding behind the horizon, and therefore his face was in shadow. There was a stillness around him, it seemed.

"I do not understand, Grandfather."

"You have wandered far across the land, a long way from where you lost your weapons. But you have wandered in a darkness as well. A darkness where the soul of a man can wither. A kind of darkness that can pull you in deeper and deeper, so deep that you can stay lost."

"My wife and daughter," Stone Arrow whispered. "They are gone."

"Yes, and what was the cause of that?"

"Something I did," the young man admitted.

"Something to start the fire of revenge?" the old man asked.

Stone Arrow could only nod.

"Fires of revenge are usually ignited by injustice or unfairness, or what the aggrieved person perceives as such," the old man said.

"You are right, Grandfather. I killed a boy not yet a skilled warrior."

The old man nodded, a grim expression on his weathered face. "Yes. Such a thing would drive a man to retaliate. I think that man knows that your own death means little to you. So he chose to cause the same pain he suffered. The kind of pain that will deny you peace."

"I wish I could change it, go back to that day, so I could make another choice," Stone Arrow admitted.

"Yet you know that cannot happen."

The young man took a deep breath to stifle a sob. "Is this to be my life, Grandfather?"

"If you so choose."

"Choose? What must I choose?"

The old man added sticks to the fire and glanced at the disheveled young man. "That is for you to decide. Life is making choices. Choices lead to consequences."

"What is the use of making a choice now? What I have done cannot be undone."

"True enough," the old man agreed. "The choice you made to fight that boy has brought you to this day. The choices you make now will take you through the days of your life ahead. It will be so, whether you choose wisely or foolishly."

Stone Arrow had no memory of falling asleep. He awoke with the sun just over the eastern hills and an elk robe covering him. The old man was near the fire, cooking fresh meat, a whole rabbit carcass.

"Today I will leave you," the old man announced, "so that you can search your heart and mind."

"Search my heart and mind? What will I find there, Grandfather?"

"One road, or another. Both will take you on the journey that is your life. One is easy, one is hard."

The young man was perplexed. Not only did he not know who the old man was or where he had come from, he seemed to talk only in riddles.

"What lies on the easy road or the hard one?" he asked.

"Ah, there is the rub," chuckled the old man, turning the rabbit on the spit. "The easy road is wide, easy to travel, but on it there is weakness, emptiness, and darkness. The hard road is narrow, much more difficult to travel, but it leads to strength, light, and enlightenment. Therefore, you must search your heart and your mind and choose which road you will travel. If you choose the easy road, be on your way."

He pointed to a nearby hill. "If you choose the hard road, make a fire on that hill and burn these pine boughs." So saying, he tossed a bundle of green pine boughs to the young man. "If I see gray smoke, I will return."

The old man stood to his feet. "The rabbit is nearly done cooking," he said. "Eat, and think with a clear mind."

Before Stone Arrow could respond, the old man was gone from his sight and only a strange silence stayed behind. He waited for the rabbit to finish cooking, wondering again who the old man was. A thought seeped into his tired mind. In the old man's parting words was the answer. *If you choose the easy road, be on your way.* Without telling him what to do, the old man had revealed the correct choice.

After he ate some of the rabbit, Stone Arrow huddled beneath the elk robe and fell asleep again. He awoke to a late afternoon. Looking around, he saw the mostly uneaten rabbit still on the spit above cold ashes. At the creek he washed, and then on unsteady legs he gathered kindling and wood for the fire. When it was burning he grabbed more kindling and a burning twig and climbed the hill, carrying the green pine boughs.

Thick, gray smoke rose and floated like a banner after he dropped the boughs on the second fire. Stone Arrow worried that enemies might see it as well as any old man could. Back at the meager camp along the creek he ate more of the rabbit meat and waited. Just before the sun went down he heard a rustling in the grass. It was the old man, and over his shoulder was a large bag.

"You have made a good choice," he said.

In the morning Stone Arrow awoke to find a small, half-round lodge nearby, covered with buffalo hides and its door to the west. It was the kind of lodge used for the renewal ceremony. Stone Arrow could only assume that the old man had built it during the night. The old man sent him to the creek. "Gather stones, as many as you can carry in your arms."

Next they dug a pit several paces to the west of the lodge. After that they gathered firewood and arranged the stones and the firewood in the bottom of the pit. The old man ignited the kindling and soon the fire was burning high. They sat and waited for the stones to heat until they glowed red.

When the fire had burned down to glowing embers, the old man deftly retrieved the hot stones among them with the forked tips of elk antlers. Then he carried them into the lodge, placing them in a small round pit in the middle of the floor. Next to the door was a large skin of water.

They entered the lodge naked and covered the door. Stone Arrow knew the ritual well, since he had participated in many. Water poured over the hot stones heated the interior of the lodge, causing the men to sweat profusely. It was a ceremony of purification, of cleansing, and of rebirth. The old man sang sacred songs and prayed on behalf of Stone Arrow. This he did four times. After the fourth time they emerged from the lodge, drenched with sweat, and immersed themselves in the creek.

After they smoked the old man's black stone pipe, he invited Stone Arrow to sit near the pit with the still-glowing embers. There, he gave him water to drink.

"The spirits have offered you a new purpose," the old man said. "It lies on the hard road, the road you have chosen. You are to be a maker of shields. It will be your way to find peace."

"Shields?" Stone Arrow asked. "I do not know how to make shields."

"I will teach you," replied the old man.

"Why am I to make shields?"

The old man cleared his throat. "In wars between people, animals go to the place between the territories of the warring tribes. In that place there is no conflict. There they find peace. We all search for that place, for that moment, where there is no conflict. You are beginning that search.

"You ask, 'Why am I to make shields?' Let me ask you this: what is the purpose of the lance you carry in your hand as a warrior?"

"To fight an enemy."

"True. Therefore the lance is not an instrument of peace, it is an instrument of war, of conflict. Whether you use it to defend or attack, its purpose is to injure or kill. This is not true of a shield."

"Warriors carry shields," Stone Arrow asserted.

"Yes, you do. But what is the purpose of a shield?"

"To protect against the enemy's weapons," the young man replied.

"True. A shield is not a weapon; it is used by the warrior to defend. It absorbs the blows of lances, arrows, and war clubs because it is made to do so. It defuses conflict without retaliation. A shield is a haven between life and death, much like that moment between dusk and darkness."

Stone Arrow had never heard anyone speak of shields in this manner. "Then, Grandfather, is the shield an instrument of war or of peace?"

"That is determined by him who carries it."

"I do not understand."

"It is necessary to be a warrior," the old man said patiently. "But we are not at war every moment we are awake. We are also hunters, husbands, and fathers. There are enemies, war does come, but so does peace. Which should you live for? Should you be a man who lives for war, or a man of peace who is willing to face war?"

"I think it is wiser to be a man of peace who is willing to face war."

"Then tell me this, Grandson. Which kind of man killed that boy?"

Stone Arrow took a deep breath and exhaled. "It was the man of war, Grandfather."

From a small bag the old man removed a small, round, reddish stone and handed it to Stone Arrow. "Carry this always, to remind you that on this day you have placed your feet on the road of peace."

In the days that followed the old man taught Stone Arrow the art of making shields, and the young man learned well. In return the old man asked one thing.

"War may be the path to glory and status," he said, "but peace is the way to strength. When you find a young man who is troubled about which path to take, you must make him a shield and tell him your story."

◀◀◗▶▶

"I never saw my wife and daughter again," Good Hand told Two Lance. "In the days and months after I left the old man, I did search for them now and then. As each day passed I reminded myself that anger or regret was not the way to peace. Still, peace did not come all at once. It came a little each day. In time I met White Shell and we have been together since."

"Do you still think of your first wife and daughter?" asked Two Lance.

"Yes, I do, as well as the boy I killed."

"Is it not better to forget?"

"Perhaps someone with a heart of stone can forget," reasoned Good Hand. "I have not yet met such a person. I could not bring back my wife and daughter, nor that boy. So I honor them by remembering them." He opened a small bag hanging around his neck on a cord, opened it and showed the young man a small reddish stone. "This reminds me that I chose the path of peace, and to think of them. Now, it is time to dig up your shield."

Under the old man's guidance, Two Lance scraped away the cold embers and the layer of dirt beneath. It was as he had surmised. The round piece of rawhide had shrunk to about the width of the young man's chest from side to side. It was also thicker, the size of a man's finger. It was the most amazing transformation the young man had ever seen.

Good Hand leaned the rawhide against the creek bank and asked Two Lance to pierce the shield with his lance. The young man was not surprised when the stone point of his lance broke. So did the stone head of the arrow he shot at it.

The shield maker next covered the shield with tanned deer hide, laced on the back side, and there he added loops to fit over the young man's forearm and wrist. On one side of the front of the hide, Good Hand painted a spiral that symbolized the whirlwind. On the other side he painted four circles, each inside the other. The whirlwind was red and the four circles blue.

"Whirlwinds are the storm of war," he explained. "Circles mean life, balance, and peace. Red is the color of honor, and blue the color of victory," he said to the young man. "As a warrior, you must strive for honor because it gives meaning to victory. But you must also know that even in war, honor must come first. And that the greatest victory is peace."

The next morning, as Two Lance was about to leave, he had one last question for the shield maker.

"Grandfather," he said, "who was the old man who taught you to make shields?"

"He never told me his name," Good Hand said. "I never saw him again. He was a spirit, a being who came from the other side."

Several mornings later it was another cool, quiet dawn in the middle of autumn. The early risers from the village were starting outside fires. Birds were already calling and singing and bull elk were whistling when someone noticed that the lodge of Good Hand and White Shell had been taken down. The elderly couple, it could only be assumed, had moved their lodge nearby.

An old man walked to the edge of the meadow where the lodge had stood and others joined him. The site looked as if no lodge had ever stood there. The outside fire pit was gone, as was the circle of stones that had ringed it. For that matter, there was no hole in the ground to mark where the inside fire pit should have been. The meadow grass was tall; nothing had disturbed it.

Word went back to the village swiftly, as it does in such moments. Soon nearly everyone approached the small meadow where a lodge had stood only the day before. There was nothing to indicate that the old couple had been there. No dogs, no piles of firewood, and no moccasin tracks in the dirt. The war leader sent four young men to search a wide circle around the village, on the chance that Good Hand and White Shell had simply moved elsewhere. In a while, however, the young men returned to report they had seen nothing.

Wing, the old man leader of the village, was not surprised by the news that Good Hand and White

Shell were gone. He was sad as well. When someone asked him why the old couple had gone away so suddenly, he invited anyone who was curious to sit by his fire. There he told the story of the shield maker.

"Where did they go?" someone asked, after the old man had finished.

"To a place of peace," said Wing, "because they fulfilled the purpose they were given."

Wowahwa

(woh-wah-hwah)

Peace, a quieting

THE POWER THAT IS PEACE

On the north wall of the Visitors Center at Little Bighorn Battlefield National Monument at Crow Agency, Montana, are words displayed in Lakota and English:

> *Wohwahwa tawowashake kin slolyayo*, or "Know the power that is peace."

There is nothing like conflict—or, as in the case of that famous battle of 1876, unfettered violence—to teach us the value of peace. Indeed, in one sense peace is simply the opposite of war; many definitions of the word refer to the "absence of war or hostilities between nations" or "a state of harmony between peoples." Only further down the list of definitions do we see words like *silence, stillness, tranquil,* or *untroubled.* Yet the absence of war or hostilities between nations does not necessarily mean that there is true peace within a nation or society, much less that individual human beings are at peace in their own lives.

For each and every one of us in our daily lives (as it often is between nations), peace is elusive. There is always uncertainty, stress, or some form of trouble lurking somewhere. Some of us reach the end of the day and look forward to rest and sleep that will, at least for a few hours, give us some respite. Some of us, on the other hand, spend sleepless nights because our troubles are overwhelming enough to hold peace at bay.

There are, of course, many reasons for us to be troubled or bothered at any given time in our lives. Depending on political or social circumstances and where we live in the world, the absence of peace in our lives can range from merely bothersome to absolutely terrifying. We may face illness, separation, no job, no money, guilt, lack of answers, or the reality of loved ones serving in a combat zone half a world away.

Peace and war between nations occur for reasons that individual citizens will never know. The real reasons are rarely revealed, even in circumstances that seem transparent or obvious. Deals are made, convenient situations are exploited, and in some cases obvious lies are told. Our collective welfare as nations and societies is determined by people who hold power and influence that we ordinary individuals can never imagine, people who do not care about our daily lives. People who are as out of touch with our below-the-headlines social and economic situations as we are ignorant of their hold on power. Consequently, peace between nations is illusionary, war is always a probability, and the lives of ordinary people are pawns in the game.

One of the sad consequences is that governments send young people to engage in combat, after investing thousands of dollars in each one to train them to defeat the enemy by attrition and giving them state-of-the-art equipment and weapons to do just that. And when they do their duty, the first wound they suffer, the one that never really heals, is to the spirit. Because of those wounds, former combatants find themselves in an often lonely struggle to find peace, and in a tragic irony, the same government that sent them into the situation does not invest anywhere near the same amount of money or effort to help them out of it. In this case the peace they seek is the cessation of horrific memories and dreams, the dissolution of survivor guilt and self-recrimination, and a stop to the parade of sad, perplexing, and grisly images. They seek the kind of peace that they hope will restore their souls.

Among the pre-reservation Lakota there was a ceremony, now long forgotten, that was a first step in helping warriors—combatants—find that peace and forgive themselves for things they had seen and done. Warriors who had seen combat lined up beyond the outermost circle of lodges in the village. They wore the habiliments of war and carried their weapons, even painted their faces for war. Then at a signal from the elders, the men turned to face away from the village and walked backwards until they reached the very edge of the line of lodges. There they divested themselves of all the things of war, leaving their weapons on the ground, and washed the war paint from their faces and bodies. These acts meant they were symbolically leaving outside the village the "shadow man," that part of the individual that had to emerge from the psyche in order for the man to fight as a warrior. Another way to describe it was "putting the war back in the bag," some said, because they were putting their face paints into their "war bag."

After those symbolic acts the warriors continued walking into the village, backwards, until they reached its center. There, children sprinkled their faces and bodies, and sometimes actually washed them, with water—a symbolic cleansing of the spirit. Then the men were taken into the *Inipi;* that term, for what is now known as the "sweat lodge" ceremony, actually meant "rebirth" or "renewal." After the sweat ceremonies, the warriors were asked to sit in a circle in the center of the village, and they were fed to strengthen their bodies as well as their spirits.

Every man, woman, and child participated in this ceremony for their warriors because they—the warriors—had put themselves in harm's way for everyone. Thus everyone assisted in the healing process. The ceremony was not meant to glorify the warrior or war itself. It was an acknowledgment that peace had just as much of a place in life as war did. It was intended to heal the spirit by forgiving the "shadow man," which Lakota society considered a necessary first step for the warrior to forgive himself and be at peace.

A movie from the 1980s addressed this issue from a different angle. The film was *Uncommon Valor* and the lead character, played by Gene Hackman, was a Korean War veteran searching for his son who was missing in Vietnam.

In the film, Hackman explains to a Vietnam veteran how he dealt with an incident during his tour in Korea, when the frozen bodies of dead soldiers were piled on tanks and trunks like so much cordwood. He could not ever shake the image of those soldiers from his memory, but he did finally find a way to come to terms with it. "I made friends with them," he says.

In the real Korean War there was a retreat by American troops during an extremely harsh winter. Many of those killed in action were recovered and transported on tanks and in trucks. Frozen dead bodies were a jarring sight, even for hardened combat veterans. But they were part of the reality of the circumstances, and for Hackman's character in *Uncommon Valor*, it was more sensible to accept the situation than to deny it. Acceptance enabled him to be at peace.

When I was growing up, I heard one axiom many, many times: *Hecetuwelo* (heh-cheh-doo-weh-loh) from a male speaker, *Hecetuye* (heh-cheh-doo-yeh) from a female speaker. It meant "That is the way it is." It meant that, good or bad, it was smarter to accept the reality of any given circumstance or moment. I recall my grandparents having to turn back at a flooded creek one early spring, and retrace our path to go around it, even though it meant going at least two miles out of our way. My grandfather simply said, "Hecetuwelo," it is the way it is. In no way did he like the situation, but neither he nor my grandmother allowed their emotional reaction to interfere with the necessity of dealing with the problem at hand. In that way they met a difficult moment with peace.

Over the decades there have been countless conversations inside and outside the Lakota culture about the difficult (to say the least) transition our ancestors had to make when Euro-Americans came on the scene. To put it in a nutshell, a nomadic society had to give in to a life lived within definite boundaries, and a society of hunters had to learn how to farm. Our social norms and spiritual beliefs had made us a strong people for countless generations; now forcible measures were taken to wrest those cultural strengths from us.

The obvious changes were environmental and tangible. No more buffalo-hide lodges, no more wandering over the prairies in tune and time with the land and the buffalo. Now lodges were made of canvas and people donned Euro-American clothing. Their new style of square houses were heated with iron stoves and lit with candles and kerosene lamps. Food came from the "annuities" provided by the U.S. government: beef, beans, rice, flour, and sugar. Some Lakota espoused the necessity of giving up the old ways and adopting, more or less wholesale, the ways of the society that had overwhelmed them. Many chose to adopt Christianity, and some disdained and even ridiculed their friends and relatives who did not. Others wanted to hang on to their values, traditions, customs, and language, all the factors that made them who they were.

In 2012 there is still a Lakota culture and a Lakota nation. We are scattered across the northern plains on various reservations, though many of us live off reservation in just about every state in the country. We are part of American society and now the global community in this age of instant communication. But how we evolved from our great-great-grandparents' time is a story of the way a people confronted change.

As I have written elsewhere, my grandparents' parents were born in the 1860s and 1870s. That generation of Lakota was on the cusp of change. The wise men and women among them realized that survival among the whites was the sensible path. They accepted the reality of the circumstance, no matter how galling it was. They made peace with how things were, and relied on the strength of their cultural values—still embedded in each man and woman and child—to enable them to confront change in the hope that they would emerge on the other side of it mostly intact. Mostly intact was preferable to losing all semblance of being Lakota.

One of the stories I heard as a child was how my mother's and grandparents' band of the Lakota, one of seven, came to be known as *Sicangu* (see-chan-ghoo), which means "burnt thigh." It originated in the time before horses, when our nomadic ancestors traveled on foot and their belongings were transported by dogs.

A group of them were moving camp one late summer day. As frequently happened in that season, clouds formed in the west, thunder rumbled, and lightning struck the prairies and ignited a grass fire. Pushed by a wind from the west, the flames soon grew and rolled east toward the travelers. The people hurried to outrun the fire, at least to find a sizeable creek or river, which would be a barrier between them and the oncoming flames. But they were too far from any kind of water and the flames raced toward them.

The people realized that they could not outrun the flames, and panic made many of them flee blindly. Soon the elderly could not keep up the pace and had to stop to rest. Many of the younger people stayed with them. Then an old woman made a suggestion that seemed to be born of desperation or senility. She said it would be best to run back through the flames to the other side, because the fire would certainly catch them in any case. Many of the people disagreed, and some fled. But others saw the wisdom in the old woman's idea. So they doused themselves with what water they carried, turned loose their dogs, prayed, and waited. When the flames came close, they ran into them.

Understandably, some perished, mostly the old and the very young whose lungs were not strong enough to withstand the intense heat. But some did survive the flames, though their clothes were burned off and they suffered horrible wounds. Because of the height of the flames, most of the burns were to their legs and thighs. So the name Burnt Thigh is, to me, a name that speaks of courage. It reminds me of how an old woman's wisdom and courage compelled her people to make peace with a devastating decision, then act on it.

My grandparents, in my childhood during the 1950s, did not like the fact that their generation of Lakota were not in control of their own lives. But they accepted how things were, instead of bemoaning at every turn and resisting everything that came down the road. They were happy and grounded people because of this. They were at peace, and that sense of peace enabled them to thrive. It was not because they liked the circumstances, but because they had the ability to find peace within themselves, no matter what was happening around them. Though both of my maternal grandparents spoke often of "how things were" and tried to explain the realities to me, never did I hear them rant and rave in anger, though I know they were angry and sad over certain realities, such as the tragedy of Wounded Knee.

We modern Lakota are different from our ancestors, because of the changes and circumstances each generation has had to confront and adapt to. Our history has been passed down by each generation to the next, and much of it has not been easy to hear and learn. Some of us are angry over that past, and rightfully so. But no matter how righteous our anger is, we cannot allow it to prevent us from accepting the realities that were, and are. This does not mean accepting harsh realities as good or justified in any sense, or forgetting them or brushing them aside. Making peace with harsh realities means, to me, accepting that they did occur and no amount of grief or anger will change them. Once we do this, we may even derive strength from them, because no matter how horrific those events were, we are still here. We are still here because generations before us accepted how things were and made peace with the circumstances they found themselves in. If our ancestors did it, so can we.

Peace is elusive, but it is also empowering. To be at peace with circumstances, especially those over which we have no control, does not mean we should not strive to deal with them. It means that we deal with them with the strength of clarity, reason, and deliberation, because that is what peace enables. That kind of peace means that we individually are sure of who we are, what we are, what we want, and where we are going. If that is not strength through peace, than I am at a loss as to what is.

Our world is noisy and loud, it moves fast, and if we let it, the noise can constantly invade our awareness. There are still places in the world, of course, where we can go to separate ourselves from it all and find quiet and solitude, that outward peace that can calm troubled spirits. Not all of us have the ability to go to those places, but the truth is that peace is not just a place, it is a state of being. And all of us can go there.

We can keep the world at bay, as it were, to recover, rejuvenate, to recharge. There are several roads to that state of being; meditation and simple quiet time are two that work best for most of us. It takes a bit of practice to focus and concentrate on something, someone, a place, or an event that is calming and empowering. I often think about the plateau above the Little White River where I lived for a few years with my grandparents. Our log house stood on a rise above a gully, and we had a panoramic view of the prairies and hills around. My childhood there was happy and carefree, and the image of it in my memory always chases away the cares and worries of the moment. It always strengthens me, drives away stress, and lets me pause to reflect, renew, and find peace.

In such moments, when I go back to that place, I feel the presence of my grandparents, and I am reminded that peace is not so much the absence of conflict and chaos as the ability to be centered, calm, quiet—for one moment or many—in the midst of chaos.

I wish you peace.

chapter eight

The Hunter

Long ago on the northern plains, it was necessary for large villages to break up into several smaller ones for the winter. Large villages and many people scared away the game animals. Because winter was an unpredictable season on the plains—one year there was little snow, while the next the snow lay deep and it was difficult to travel or hunt—laying in enough meat in the autumn was the best approach.

In the time before horses, one small group located their winter village in a deep gully that led down to the Great Muddy River. It was a small village, only six families and a few elders. They were led by a head man named Uses Cane. Up and down the river were other villages, each no less than a day's travel from the next. All were sheltered against the south- or east-facing slopes of deep gullies. In the first days of the winter moon, the men of the village were busy hunting before the snows came. They were working hard to bring in enough meat to last through the long prairie winter, so that no one would be hungry.

Of the 36 people in the village of Uses Cane, 10 were full-fledged hunters and warriors. Each lodge had at least one hunter, except for one. In that lodge was an old woman, a widow, and her grandson. Her name was Gray Grass, his was Slow. (Author's note: we met Gray Grass and Slow in Chapter One.) Theirs was a sad story. In two years they had lost three members of their family. Slow's mother and father had died in a flash flood two summers past, and a winter ago his grandfather had broken his leg while hunting and had frozen to death. Though they had been close before, now the boy and his grandmother were absolutely devoted to each other. Slow was 12, leaving his boy-hood behind but not yet ready to be a man. But by the time the last snows of spring would finally melt, he would be well on his way to being a good man.

Winter was intent on punishing the land and all its inhabitants, it seemed. Blizzards howled out of the northwest, leaving a thick blanket of snow. The people were not alarmed, because they had prepared as much as possible. Food containers were full. Firewood was piled high outside of each lodge. Behind the inner lining in each lodge, plenty of grass had been stuffed to create a thick layer of insulation. But not only did the snows come early, they did not let up.

Hard winters were nothing new. Spring always came no matter how long or how hard the winter, so the people went on with life. But those in the village who had seen hard winters before knew that overcon-fidence could be dangerous. Though the elders advised everyone to be judicious with the food stores, very few took heed.

Gray Grass was very careful, however, mainly because she and Slow did not have much to begin with. Though hunters shared with them, the old woman nonetheless stretched their supply as much as possible. When the weather permitted, she encouraged her grandson to hunt for small game to supplement what they had. The boy was a good hunter, well taught by his father and grandfather, and he had heeded his lessons well. Not only that, he was more than an average marksman with his bow and arrows.

Toward the end of the Mid-Winter Moon (December) there was no longer any doubt that the people were in the middle of the severest winter in memory. Not only would snow fall for days without stopping, the wind blew and created drifts nearly as high as the tops of the lodges. All of the village's hunters, like Slow, pursued small game, such as rabbits, until there were practically none to be found. When the elders asked the people to take stock of their food supplies, they were not surprised to learn that supplies might not last until the first snow melt. That was normally early in the Moon When Geese Return (April). The prospect of hunger seemed certain, and the elders advised everyone to cut their daily consumption of food in half. In the meantime they would hope and pray for a break in the weather so the men could hunt.

Gray Grass, like the other elders, watched and listened. There were good men in the village, many good hunters, but few of them had seen such a winter. One or two of the elders made quiet suggestions that were largely ignored. But Gray Grass had a plan, though she knew the men in the village would not listen to anything she might suggest about hunting. She had grown up there and knew every hill, meadow, and gully. She also knew the habits of animals like the deer, elk, and buffalo during hard winters with deep snow. She decided her grandson was good enough to carry out her plan.

She sent Slow out on short hunting forays, giving him careful instructions about landmarks to look for. Though sometimes he returned empty-handed, nonetheless he was gaining firsthand knowledge of the land, and gaining confidence as well. One evening Gray Grass opened a bundle and revealed her husband's hunting bow. Though she had given away all of his personal possessions after he had died, she had kept the bow with a specific purpose in mind. She had planned to give it to her grandson one day, and though that day had come sooner than she anticipated, she knew it was time.

Slow was astonished to see his grandfather's hunting bow, and speechless when his grandmother told him it was his now, along with the arrows. She helped him adjust the tautness of the string to suit his size and strength and showed him several replacement strings. Those strings were made of thistle, instead of sinew, and were used in wet weather because they withstood moisture better than sinew strings.

While Slow practiced with his new bow, his grandmother sketched a map for him on a tanned deer hide and prepared a special wolf-hide cape. At night she told stories of his father's and grandfather's hunting escapades. Finally one evening she told him her plan.

"Buffalo look for grass even in deep snow," she said. "They will go to the meadows and dig, scraping away the snow. When they find it, they will stay and graze. They will run, even in the deep snow, when they see human hunters. Yet they will not be alarmed when a single wolf comes among them."

Slow had heard such stories before, but he sensed there was a reason his grandmother was telling them again. So he kept silent and listened.

Gray Grass showed her grandson the map she had sketched and the wolf-hide cape. "Since I was a little girl, the buffalo have always gone to a certain meadow when the snow was deep, as it is now. Your grandfather would find them there and crawl in among them wearing his wolf hide. Now it is up to you to go out there or not."

Slow listened to his grandmother's plan, his eyes full of excitement and his heart pounding. She was asking him to do a man's task. That night he was too excited to fall asleep, not certain that he could do what his grandmother was asking, but certain that he must try.

Two mornings later Slow departed the village. Across his back were his encased bow and quiver of arrows, and he carried a short lance. Anyone who saw him leave assumed the boy was after rabbits again. The snowshoes he was carrying were not unusual and no one seemed to notice that he was also carrying half a buffalo hide rolled up into a bundle. They couldn't see that he had a bag full of pounded dried meat mixed with chokecherries, a staple for hunters—enough for several days. Nor could they see the map he had carefully hidden in his shirt or the wolf hide wrapped inside the buffalo robe. On his hands were elk-hide mittens and on his feet were thick elk-hide moccasins. In his heart burned fierce determination.

Back in her modest lodge, Gray Grass burned sweetgrass and prayed, asking the spirits to watch over her grandson. She had sent him on his mission with all the meat they had left.

Slow followed his grandmother's instructions down to the smallest detail. Before sunset he found the first landmark she had described—a sandstone outcropping with the outline of an elk carved on it. There he made a snow cave and built a small fire to keep himself warm for the night. The danger he faced was mainly from the cold and another hunter, the great cat, which some called a mountain lion. That was the reason for his lance and the second reason for the fire. Bears were in their winter dens and wolves did not bother people.

As dawn broke, Slow doused the fire with snow and resumed his trek, buoyed with confidence because the weather was good and because he had found the first landmark. But early in the afternoon, gray clouds gathered low and snow began to fall. Wisely, Slow made camp out of the wind against a high bank in an old creek bed. He was able to keep a very small fire burning through most of the night with the wood he had gathered along the way. But when the fire sputtered out, he was still safe wrapped in his buffalo robe.

Slow waited for the weather to clear the next day, then strapped on snowshoes to travel. Before sundown he found another landmark, an ancient cottonwood tree that had been split by lightning. There he camped and found enough wood to build a good fire so he could dry his wet moccasins. He was now in territory new to him, but he was encouraged that his grandmother's memory of the landscape was so dependable. By another sunset, he estimated, he would find the last landmark, a grove of giant cottonwoods on a river bottom with four of the trees standing in a straight north-south line.

Wolves howled and coyotes barked during the night, strangely comforting and familiar voices. Though he strained to hear the bellow of buffalo bulls, he heard nothing. The fire of determination still burned in him, however. At times he imagined, or felt, the presence of his father and grandfather. That chased away the loneliness and the reality that he was farther away from home by himself than he had ever been. During those moments of loneliness, he took out his grandmother's map. That simple act reassured him and he could hear her voice describing the land-marks he was to look for.

When he did find the grove of leafless cottonwood trees along the river bottom the next day, he was reas-sured to see tufts of grass poking up from the snow. But no buffalo. In spite of a pang of doubt, Slow built a hunting blind as his grandmother had instructed, making it appear like a mound of snow. Inside it he prepared his weapons and wrapped himself in the buffalo robe—and waited.

Sometime in the night, he heard a strange noise and imagined it might be a large, fierce animal of some kind. Though he looked out of his snow blind, he saw nothing. The rest of the night he tried to stay awake. When a cold dawn came, he heard the noise again, and for the first time on his quest he felt a real fear. Slow realized, again, that he was alone and far from home.

He was right about the noise. It was made by the largest animal on the plains—the buffalo. Several of them, as a matter of fact, in the meadow not far from his shelter. Their enormous forms were like large shadows in the dawn light. His grandmother was right. Now a different kind of apprehension took hold: a fear of failure.

Even at this distance, at the outside range of his bow, the animals still loomed very large. Suddenly Slow felt weak and puny—and cold. He had slept without a fire, curled inside the folds of his buffalo robe. Outside his shelter snow was falling quietly in large, lazy flakes—the kind that brought a sense of connection. But the only things on Slow's mind were his cold fingers and the thick hides of the buffalo digging for grass in the meadow. Was he strong enough to pull his grandfather's bow? Was he good enough to hit the mark?

For a time he pulled his head back into the robe, considering the idea of going home and saying he had not found the buffalo. At the same time, he knew his grandmother had asked him to do something important. She did not say she expected him to succeed. She only wanted him to do his best. If he tried and missed, he knew he could go home with the knowledge that he had done his best, and his grandmother would welcome him home. Slow threw off the robe and reached for the bow and arrows.

A while later a wolf crawled out of the snow shelter. In its right hand was the sinew-backed ash wood bow with its thistle string. In its mouth were two arrows; on each tip was an extremely sharp flint point and on the ends a notch and three goose feathers. Two more arrows were in his left hand.

The wolf-hide cape fit Slow perfectly. For all intents and purposes, he was a wolf stalking the buffalo. Of course, the snowshoes tied on his back were not something a wolf would carry, but they would mean nothing to the buffalo. He estimated the distance at about a hundred long paces. He needed to get 20 paces from the enormous animals to take a good shot.

"Remember," his grandmother had instructed, "act like a wolf. Stop and sit on your haunches now and then. Lift your head, sniff the air. Do not crawl straight toward them. Go off to the side, as if circling them. It is what a wolf does. Go to the right. Shoot at the right side, behind the ribs."

Her words played over and over in his head as he crawled. He became the wolf, stalking his prey. He had heard the stories of how powerful buffalo were. How with one shake of their great heads they could toss a man high into the air. But he wasn't a man on two legs. He was the wolf, stalking and circling. Though the buffalo did see him when he was within 40 paces, they stared for a moment and then returned to digging and grazing on the grass they found. Now and then one would stop and gaze at him. Slow wondered if they could hear his heart pounding like a drum in his chest.

Like the wolf, he selected his prey. A cow with an injured leg, limping as she moved through the deep snow. Slow, mimicking the wolf, circled to the right until he was at 20 or so paces. He sat back, his mouth going dry as the cow turned her head and stared at the wolf sitting on its haunches. Only then did he realize that his hands were trembling.

When the cow turned away and began digging again, he raised his bow and placed an arrow on the string. Heart pounding, he pulled, aimed, and released. He missed!

The arrow had flown just below the cow's belly, but it had flown silently and the great animal was not in the least alarmed. Taking deep breaths to calm himself, Slow took the second arrow from his mouth and prepared to shoot again.

Quietly, snow was still falling. Slow's leggings from his knees to his ankles were soaked, but he barely felt the cold. The morning air was frigid, and he could feel it in his lungs with each excited, nervous breath he drew. He paused a moment to blow on the fingers of his right hand so he could hold the arrow and pull the bowstring. With a deep breath, he took aim again.

He heard the soft *twang* as he released the arrow. In the next instant he saw the cow jump forward and stop broadside to him, her tail curled upward. Slow nearly forgot to notch the third arrow. But he did, and drew back on the string again, heart thudding in his chest. Holding his breath yet again, he released. This time he followed the brief flight of his arrow, watched it slice into her chest. As did the fourth and final arrow, which he barely remembered shooting at all.

With a grunt of surprise and confusion, the wounded cow bolted through the deep snow. Slow watched partly in disbelief, mostly with awe, as the other animals joined her brief flight. Though the others heaved their way up a small slope and over, the wounded one was obviously struggling. She paused at the top and fell on her side. Though she tried to rise, she could not.

Slow's hands shook and he found himself panting as though he had run a race. He rose and walked back to his snow shelter. He needed a fire to warm himself and dry his wet leggings.

At midmorning a cold-looking sun broke through the clouds briefly. On the slope the cow was down and not moving. Sooner or later, however, he knew the coyotes, wolves, and ravens would arrive. According to his grandmother's instructions, he still had several chores to finish.

Sometime in the afternoon, a bundle of sage in his hand, he trudged through the deep snow to the cow. She had expired. There was no feeling of elation, however, only sadness. The words of his grandfather ran through his mind.

We do not kill because we can, we do it because we must. For that, the hunter gives thanks and humbles himself for the animal's gift of life.

Slow laid the bundle of sage next to the cow's head. Then, drawing his knife, he set about finishing his chore.

He stayed the night in his snow shelter, cheered by a warm fire on which he roasted a piece of the flank meat he had cut away. In a special bag he had placed the proof of his hunt, as his grandmother had instructed. Through the night he heard the barks and growls of wolves as they came to feast on the carcass. But that was just as his grandmother had said it would be. He had hunted for those hungry relatives as well, so the meat would not go to waste.

When he left his shelter after sunrise, the wolves were still at the carcass. On a nearby hill a family of coyotes were patiently waiting their turn. Such was life.

Four days after he set out, Slow made it home. That evening Gray Grass made soup and invited the head man Uses Cane and the leader of the hunters to her lodge. They were surprised to see she had fresh buffalo tongue to feed them. They ate while they listened to the boy's story of his journey to a far valley and his hunt. Neither man had any reason to dismiss offhand what they had heard. When they asked the boy to lead the hunters back to the valley, he did not hesitate for a moment.

And so it was that Slow became a man, though he was only 12, that hard winter. He led the hunters to the valley of Turtle Butte Creek, once again following his grandmother's map and his own memory of the trek. There the hunters found the skeleton of the cow, all that was left of the carcass. From there they tracked the small herd and found them.

There was just enough meat from that hunt to feed the people of the small village until the spring snows melted. When they rejoined the other villages, they boasted of the new hunter among them. Along with him, however, there was another gift. They had been reminded that the older the man or the woman, the greater the knowledge and the deeper the wisdom.

Woksape

(woh-ksah-peh)

wisdom, to be wise or discerning

THE INTELLIGENCE OF THE PAST

Most of us who live in industrialized countries and use technology daily to make life easier forget that humans also have roots in the past—farther back than we care to or even can imagine.

As a case in point, someone goes home to a modern apartment on a cold day and pushes a button to ignite a gas fireplace, but has no inkling that a distant ancestor laid the foundation for that modern convenience. That ancient ancestor rotated a softwood rod between his calloused palms to create friction between it and a hardwood base, grinding off tiny hot embers. He blew softly to turn the tiny embers into live coals, which he then transferred to dry, light kindling, such as grass, or seaweed, or lichen. When the kindling erupted into tiny flames, he placed small twigs or dry wood shavings on it to make a larger fire. In elapsed time, this process probably took 20 to 30 minutes, only because he was highly skilled at the art of making fire.

The modern apartment dweller pushes a button and has a cheery fire burning in all of three seconds, perhaps less. Furthermore, he probably thinks ancient fire making had something to do with wooden matches, if he thinks about it at all. If he knew truly the atavistic connection he had to the convenience of fire, it is possible he would appreciate the eons of process that brought him to his moment of comfort, and gain understanding and respect for it.

Perhaps that is the solution to many, if not all, of the problems we confront daily in this technology whirl we call modern life—chief among them greed, arrogance, apathy, and the loss of respect. We need to go back to the beginning and remember the foundations for the values that are antitheses to greed, arrogance, and apathy, such as compassion, respect, and humility.

To solve our current problems, perhaps even to save ourselves from ourselves, we must make a necessary journey into the past. The stories in this book come from the past. And if we go back of our own accord, we may not have to repeat many of the mistakes we made along the way the first time.

It is probably safe to state that most of us who live in industrialized countries think of advances in civilization in terms of technology. There is significant pride in how high and fast an airplane can fly, how instantaneous communication is, how telescopes enable us to see across our universe, how our cars can tell us where to go with the help of a satellite, and so on and so on. As a matter of fact our modern societies, especially in the West, are defined by technology.

Technology has definitely made human existence more comfortable. We live, work, and travel in controlled environments. Medical technology has contributed to the increase in our longevity, and the list goes on. Many, if not most, of us tend to think that our grandparents who lived in a time without movies on DVD or cellular telephones had a primitive existence. We tend to feel sorry for them because they did not have the comforts we do. But we also may think less of them because their technology was not as good as ours is today.

Russia and the United States engaged in the "race for space" after Russia orbited the Sputnik satellite in 1957, vying to develop the technology that would gain them any advantage in that "new frontier." After an expenditure of billions of rubles and dollars, the United States was the first to land a man on the moon, a grand contest that schoolchildren can read about in the history books. But our contemporary fascination and love affair with modern technology often obscures the intangibles that are also part of culture and lifestyle, such as values and character, as well as genuine human need. (What nation is openly, with the same publicity and resources as the space race had, working to solve the homeless problem?) Furthermore, what we tend to overlook, or forget, is that every nation that has risen to power and asserted and identified itself by the physicality of power has fallen—great societies such as the Romans, Greeks, Minoans, Phoenicians, Persians, and Chinese. The markers of power, such as large armies and navies and complex infrastructure enabled by the technology of the day, could not save them.

Most of the trials and tribulations inflicted on humankind by humankind, from the beginnings of civilization to now, can be attributed to imperialism and greed. It can be safely said that greed instigates imperialism because there is the need and desire to have more, if not all. But once having most or all of it, there is then the need for control in order to keep it all—whether it be land or gold or the resources that enable comfort and power.

In order to acquire territory and resources and maintain control over them, the greedy imperialist control freak must have the inclination and means to wield the power required. Thus the concept of military power was born to implement the means to maintain and control. Not everyone had the means to put armies in the field. And so the few preyed on the many, and one need only study the feudal age in Europe to understand this tragic dynamic of human interaction.

The many, the masses who had not the means to resist, had two choices: capitulate or try to resist anyway. Resisting with force was out of the question. There was only one other way: to develop fortitude so that, no matter the savagery of the outward assault, enough of the essence of the person and the identity of a group would survive. It was the only viable "counterattack," one that could be carried out without weapons. Therefore, military might could not entirely wipe out courage and fortitude, compassion and generosity, and all the other values that were the basis for survival and eventually became the core of many cultures and societies.

We know that Thomas Edison invented the lightbulb; that the Chinese invented the compass, the clock, gunpowder, and a printing press before Johann Gutenberg; that Galileo invented the telescope, and so on; but do we know with the same certainty who invented compassion, tolerance, generosity, honor, respect, or humility? I suggest that these human values were not invented by one person or by one group of people, but that they emerged because they were the only defenses against cruelty, imperialism, and hopelessness that did not have to be funded or constructed; they were intrinsic in most people. And these values are the weapons that those perceived to be powerless use to confront and overcome the trials and tribulations of life.

Another reality is that some, or perhaps many, of those trials and tribulations are self-inflicted. That is, we humans can be our own worst enemy, especially when we forget the path we have traveled over time to reach the point where we are today. A wise man once likened human memory to a beam of light passing through the darkness. It is easy enough to see what the light illuminates, but once the light passes on, what was once visible returns to the darkness and is forgotten.

The metaphoric beam of light for our time is our fascination and daily identification with technology, whether or not we can fully understand it. It does obscure the hard-won lessons of the past, like the wisdom of an old woman in the story of The Hunter. Therein we are reminded that wisdom, one of the core values of many cultures past and present, is just as powerful and critical as any tangible tool or weapon. It was the knowledge and wisdom of the old woman, Gray Grass, that placed her grandson in the position to wield his skills with the weapon. Therefore we must ask the question: Which was more powerful, the weapon or the wisdom? In this case, wisdom is much more powerful.

Which should logically lead to other questions, such as *Can technology solve all of our problems? What place should values have in our modern world?*

In 1990 a columnist for the *Casper Star-Tribune* of Casper, Wyoming, wrote: "The greatest arrogance of the present is to forget the intelligence of the past." I firmly believe that we modern humans are so enamored with our industry and technology that we look with disdain on the primitive lifestyles of our ancestors. We forget that there are aspects of our lives that do not require tools, utensils, or weapons. The people of Egypt demonstrated that in 2011. They showed the world that while technology is critical, human initiative is still a powerful driving force. In this case, technology—the Internet and social media—enabled Egyptians to unite with one another and the world. While that in turn enabled the ousting of a dictator, it might not have occurred if the people did not have the basic value of courage to take to the streets and face the mechanical and technological power wielded by the military rulers.

Most of us in the Western world cannot think that we will ever be without the technology that enables our lifestyles. We flip a switch to have light, we turn a dial to heat and cool our homes, and now we can carry on "face-to-face" conversations using our laptop computers. Many of us have lived in a time when fast communication was a handwritten letter (or one typed on a manual typewriter) that reached its destination in two days via the U.S. mail. Now we grow impatient and indignant when an attached file does not download in a few seconds.

To be sure, modern technology has improved our lives, and that is critically important for those of us who are physically challenged or depend on medicines in order to function every day. But technology should not obscure or diminish our basic humanity, that part of us that can be self-reliant, compassionate, moral, and ethical, as well as having faith, tolerance, patience, and selflessness. Such values are what define us as human beings because they are part of us, or can be. Anything external—a cell phone, automobile, television remote, for example—is only a useful tool, nothing more and nothing less.

Basic values do not need to be changed or improved, the way tools, instruments, and weapons are. We simply need to remember that they have been part of us since before we learned to write. If we look past our modern arrogance to see the intelligence and wisdom of our ancestors, we will connect with the timeless values that can be as powerful as any product of industry or technology. We will shine a beam of light into the darkness and find again what we have lost.

EPILOGUE

The Crooked Cane

On a cool autumn evening, a sedan passed a man walking in the ditch of a rural county road. Its driver saw the thin, slightly stooped man in the beam of the headlight, carrying a small duffel bag in one hand. But it was not the man's bag or his posture that caught the driver's eye. It was a slightly crooked light-colored cane.

The cane was made of the gnarly roots of a tree. This the driver learned after he stopped, reversed, and asked the man if he wanted a ride. Without a moment's hesitation the man accepted the offer. After he was in the front seat and the car was back on the road, the driver glanced at the man and his cane. It was hard to tell how old he was, since the interior of the car was dim and the man's skin was dark. Age was often hard to discern on dark-skinned people, it seemed.

"My name is Wentworth," the driver said, keeping his hands on the wheel and casting only quick glances at his passenger. "You know, I never take this road. You are lucky I did tonight. Where are you going, if I may ask?"

"To the nearest hotel room," replied the man, in an old, melodious voice. "My name is Wolf."

"Well," Wentworth chuckled. "Mr. Wolf, that is a very specific answer that tells me exactly nothing."

"Forgive me," said Wolf. "Beyond the next hotel room, I have no plans. Thank you, nonetheless, for stopping and giving me a ride."

"You are most welcome. Actually, I was curious about your cane. My father—God rest his soul—had one very similar to that."

Wolf patted his cane. "What a coincidence," he said. "This is my father's cane. Made from the roots of a cottonwood tree, nearly a hundred years ago."

"Unique, then, for at least two reasons," decided Wentworth. He pushed his steel-rimmed glasses up on the bridge of his nose and concentrated on the road ahead. That he had actually picked up a hitchhiker on a lonely, little-used road began to bother him. He watched out of the corner of his eye as Wolf took a small bottle from his bag. From the bottle he shook out two pills and swallowed them with a drink from a small canteen.

Wentworth sighed inwardly. Luck seemed to be on his side. The man seemed frail, and likely not given to violence. He was dressed neatly and his hair was thin, worn in a long braid down the back. But who knew what kind of past he carried, along with that duffel bag and gnarly cane?

"Tell me, Mr. Wolf," he ventured. "If you don't know where you are going, can you tell me where you are coming from?"

The man chuckled. "From west of here, a small town called Mormon Crossing. I grew up near there, on the Indian reservation."

That explained the dark skin. "I haven't heard of it, but I'm afraid I have spent much of my life poring over ledger entries rather than maps," Wentworth admitted. "I am from the town at the end of this narrow road, River Bend."

"I see. You are a banker then, I wager."

"Yes. It was my father's business, and his father before him. Pray tell, what is it you do, Mr. Wolf?"

"I fix things," replied Wolf.

"A repairman?"

Wolf nodded. "You can say that."

"One thing puzzles me, sir. How did you—I mean, why this road? This is as backcountry as there is around here. The main highway is miles and miles north."

Wolf chuckled again. "A trucker gave me a ride to a crossroads. I chose this road because it seemed like the thing to do. Life gives us many choices, but I am certain you know that, Mr. Wentworth."

Wentworth sighed. "Indeed I do."

"Do you travel this road often?" Wolf asked.

"No. I arrived at the same intersection you did and made a right turn, and here we are. I guess I was not in a hurry to get home. Perhaps I was wishing for time to think."

Wolf nodded, glancing for an instant at the driver's face. "I apologize, then, for disrupting your plan. Quiet time to think is much overlooked these days. Especially if what one must think about is not pleasant, or—"

"You got that right," Wentworth interrupted. "Difficult situations I have always wrestled with alone. However, I am facing one I have never faced before."

"We all come to those moments, I have learned," Wolf said softly. "More than one, I am afraid. But there is always one that will eclipse the rest."

"Right again," agreed Wentworth.

"And we wonder if there are answers, or where they are," Wolf pointed out. "Perhaps on a lonely road."

"Well," sighed Wentworth, "a lonely road might really be a place to hide. Yet I know better. We can never hide from those moments in life that require us to step forward."

"You do not strike me as one who avoids tough circumstances," observed Wolf.

"I haven't in the past, but the current situation is the toughest for me," Wentworth confessed. "It involves family."

Wolf nodded. "I have been there," he said. "Most of the time we would rather take the suffering on ourselves, instead of holding a loved one to the fire. At least that has been my experience. It has cost me dearly, however. I do not recommend it."

Wentworth found himself squeezing the steering wheel. How did this total stranger know of his situation? This moment went against the grain of his well-ordered, tangible, tactile life. But life was more than numbers on a ledger page. He decided to take a leap of faith, hoping it was not a leap of foolishness.

"Mr. Wolf," he said, hoarsely, "my son-in-law works in my bank. He is next in line to become branch manager after I retire in a few weeks. He started out as a teller, as I did. Some months ago, however, I discovered that he had been diverting funds to an offshore account. He has apparently been doing this for many years, a few dollars and even pennies at a time. But over the years, it added up."

Strangely, Wentworth felt a sense of relief. It was the first time he had given voice to the situation. He was terrified of telling his wife because she thought their son-in-law could walk on water.

Wolf nodded as he gazed out the windshield, his eyes probing the darkness with the headlight beams. "I have often wondered," he said gently, "which is more of a thief, the person who steals one dollar or the person who steals a million dollars. Yet the hard reality is that a thief is a thief because he has stolen. It matters not how much."

"Perhaps I can't accept the reality that my son-in-law is a thief," Wentworth admitted. "But more than that, I can't destroy the lives of my daughter and grandchildren by turning him over to the authorities."

"Begging your pardon, sir," Wolf countered immediately. "You will not destroy your daughter and grandchildren's lives. Your son-in-law has already done that. The question that comes to mind is how long you will enable him to live the lie."

Wentworth sighed deeply. "I have thought of that as well."

"What about the people who put their trust in your bank, as well as their money? Unless I am mistaken, there are mechanisms in place for banks to recoup financial losses. Perhaps you have a way to rebuild trust as well."

"You have a point," Wentworth said, after several moments of silence. "I have made that point to myself over and over again. I carried on after my father developed the business. We were a small community bank providing the usual services in a rural area. My father was known for his compassion and his honesty and our default rate was much smaller than other banks, because of his reputation. Twenty years ago we were bought out by a much larger regional bank because of our customer base. A loyal customer base, I might add."

"Your son-in-law has violated that trust," Wolf pointed out. "He has harmed the human equation."

"The human equation?"

"Yes. I am not a rich man," replied Wolf. "But I have worked hard to make a living for my family. By the sweat of my brow and the ache in my back I put food on the table, clothes on their backs, and shelter over their heads. That was my responsibility. The people who put their money in your bank have done no less. Therefore, when you look at the bottom line, your profit and loss statements, and your quarterly earnings, you are looking at more than dollars and cents. You are, sir, looking at the sweat equity of hundreds if not thousands of people who trust that you will care for their money. They are entrusting more than their money, as you well know. They are entrusting their futures, their families' welfare. By putting their money in your bank, they are trusting that their aching backs have paid off. So your son-in-law is not just taking someone else's money. He's taking their humanity."

Wentworth glanced at his passenger. "I have never heard such an eloquent and forceful argument from a simple repairman, ever," he said, smiling.

Wolf waved a hand. "Be that as it may, I think you see my point."

A soft glow of lights appeared on the skyline. "We're getting close to River Bend," Wentworth said, pointing to the lights. "There are several reputable hotels, and I'm sure they are comfortable. May I recommend one to you?"

"Please do, keeping in mind my modest means," Wolf replied.

They rode in silence until Wentworth turned onto the main street and then into the entryway of a hotel. "I know the couple that own this place," he told Wolf. "They are good and honest people. Please tell them that I brought you here."

"I will. Thank you for the ride."

"It was my pleasure, I assure you." Wentworth held out a hand. "Thank you for a stimulating and enlightening conversation."

Wolf shook the offered hand. "I will think of you in the days to come," he said. "Just remember, life goes on." Then he opened the door and stepped out of the car. Wentworth watched as his passenger stopped at the front door of the hotel, holding up his gnarly cane in a salute, then disappeared inside.

Twenty minutes later, in the confines of his living room, Wentworth telephoned the River Bend Hotel and asked the owners to bill him for Wolf's accommodations. Then he made coffee and invited his wife to share a cup with him.

"I have something to tell you," he said to her.

"If the look on your face is any indication," she said, "we may need something stronger than coffee."

Morning came as it always did. It had been a long night, but Mrs. Wentworth prepared breakfast for her husband as she always did. Her eyes were puffy from weeping, yet there was an inner strength emerging, too. Wentworth saw it in the way she carried herself and in the certainty of her movements. *Wolf was right,* he thought, *life does go on.* When he left the house to face the difficult tasks of this coming day, she embraced him long and lovingly.

On his way to the bank Wentworth stopped at the River Bend Hotel. He was told, however, that the man with the gnarly cane had checked out early and had insisted on paying for his own room.

"Where did he go?" he asked the proprietor.

"He asked for directions," the man told him. "It seems he is walking to his destination. So we sent him to the truck stop because he was hoping for a ride."

At the truck stop on the edge of town, Wentworth found two people who had seen and talked to the man with the cane. It seemed he had caught passage somewhere with a long-distance trucker.

The banker drove a mile out on the main road that led from town. Before he turned back he gazed at the rolling hills stretching away, and watched the several vehicles heading east. Wentworth knew he would never see the man with the gnarly cane again. Yet he seemed to sense his presence, and in no way did that feel strange.

He managed to arrive at the office at his usual time, and answered the usual greetings as he opened the door to his corner office. At precisely nine o'clock, 30 minutes before the lobby was opened for the day's business, he dialed his son-in-law's telephone extension. When the younger man knocked on the door, Wentworth knew exactly what he needed to say.

"Jim," said Tom Clements, tall and fair-haired, dressed in his usual blue suit. "What did you want to talk to me about?"

Wentworth sighed deeply. "Choices," he said. "You need to make some choices."

Two mornings later the man with the gnarly cane sat at the counter in a restaurant. He had finished breakfast and was reading the newspaper while he sipped his coffee. On the inside of the front page, a headline in bold type caught his attention:

> Assistant Branch Manager of Local
> Bank Surrenders to Authorities After
> Admitting to Embezzlement

Wolf read the story, which described how Thomas Clements had voluntarily confessed to banking officials that he had been siphoning funds. The article went on to say that Clements's lawyer would likely arrange a plea bargain; Clements had promised to return the stolen money, since none of it had been spent.

There was much the article did not say, but not because the writer was withholding facts. Wolf guessed that Wentworth had walked a fine line in order to soften the blow for his daughter and grandchildren. The article did say that Clements had been released on bail, though he had lost his job and a promising career with the bank.

"They sure do take care of their own, I think."

Wolf turned toward the speaker, a husky black man with salt-and-pepper hair and a broad, friendly face. He was pointing at the article in the paper.

"Ah, yes, well, it does seem that way, on the face of it," Wolf said.

"Yeah, I mean someone steals thousands of dollars and then promises to give it back, so they slap him on the wrist." The man leaned over, conspiratorially, and lowered his voice. "If that was me, or you, they'd throw away the key even if it was just ten bucks. Know what I mean?"

"I know exactly what you mean. That is the nature of things around here."

The man nodded, sadly and thoughtfully. "The thing is, it used to be worse. My daddy grew up in the South. He was in the army and it was bad there, too. Served in a segregated unit in Korea. After he got out, he went north thinking it would be better there."

Wolf nodded and waited for the rest of the story.

"Wasn't as bad, but the attitudes are everywhere. I'm sure you know all about it. By the way, name's Walker. Thad Walker. I drive a truck."

Wolf shook the man's thick, strong hand. "Name's Wolf," he said. "I fix things. Glad to meet you."

Walker pointed to the duffel bag on the seat between them, and the gnarly cottonwood cane. "You a traveling man, Mr. Wolf?"

"I am."

"Headed anywhere special?"

"Up north, past the big city, to see my youngest daughter," Wolf said.

"Hey." Walker grinned. "I just happen to be taking a load of appliances up that way. Got an empty seat if you need a ride."

Two hours later Thad Walker's 18-wheeler was humming along on the interstate. "Up ahead is a weigh station," he said drily. "I've had to stop there eleven times in the past six months. I own this rig, believe it or not, so I can freelance, pick and choose my loads. Seen every part of this country." He punctuated the air with a thick finger. "But that station there, they always give me grief."

"What do you mean?"

"Well, the last time I was hauling a bulldozer, a small one," he said, exasperated by the memory. "They held me aside for four hours while they measured the load, front to back and side to side. They knew I was within the regs and it wasn't a wide load. I just gritted my teeth and waited. Nothing else for me to do."

"They were doing that just because they could. They were within their authority but on the outside of being a pain in the ass."

Walker laughed, the booming laugh of a big man. "Yeah, you got that right! Sounds like you been there and done that."

Wolf nodded. "Got out of the service in sixty-eight," he said. "I had a U.S. government check, back pay for hazardous duty, eight hundred dollars. None of the banks on or near the reservation would cash it."

Walker shook his head, lips set grimly. "What's your take on stuff like that, Mr. Wolf? I mean beyond the obvious reasons they give about 'authority' and 'policy.'"

"It's power," Wolf said. "I remember going with my grandpa when I was a boy, back on the reservation, to a white rancher's place to collect lease money he owed us. My grandpa was a quiet, dignified man, and physically strong even into his midseventies. But when we arrived at the rancher's house, we waited in the wagon. We did not get down and knock on his front door. We waited until he felt like coming out and giving us 20 dollars.

"Fact of the matter was, my grandpa could have taken that rancher, easily, in a fair fight. He knew it and the rancher knew it, but there was something else they both knew. If my grandfather had even looked at that man crossways, the sheriff would have come knocking on our door.

"My father came home from his war, shortly after I was born, full of spit and vinegar. He took on all comers, didn't back down. He was more than a match for any one man, or even two at a time. So they hauled him off to jail, beat him badly. They almost sent him to the penitentiary. After that he got the message."

Walker nodded knowingly. "They have that kind of power. My game, my rules."

"There's still a law on the books in a town in the western part of the state," Wolf said. "If more than three Indians gather, they can be shot by a peace officer."

"You got to be kidding!"

"I'm afraid not. It hasn't been enforced since nineteen hundred, and that's good," Wolf went on, shaking his head as well. "I'll be impressed when the town fathers repeal it. That would show me they're growing up."

Walker sighed, a deep, sad sigh. "So what do we do until they do grow up?"

"Stay low, pick the fights we can win, decide which issue is worth dying for."

"Doesn't sound like an easy way, but I guess it never has been."

Wolf took out a pocket watch and opened the cover to check the time. "It boils down to this," he said, taking a pill bottle from his duffel. "We need to be strong to beat it, take a few punches now and then, but we get up each time we get knocked down. We'll win in the long run because racism doesn't thrive on strength, it thrives on weakness and mean-spiritedness."

"You mean we have to outlast them."

"Absolutely." Wolf paused to take two pills then put the canteen and pill bottle away. "We can outlast them; we have to. Part of the victory came in our parents' generation, part of it in ours, another piece will happen in our children's time. I read that in fifty years or less most of the world's population will be dark-skinned. That means that our values, our beliefs, our philosophies will have the opportunity to prevail. The answer is to stay strong, teach our children to stay strong, and so on."

Walker nodded and geared down to slow for the turning ramp onto the weigh station. "Well, here we go," he muttered under his breath. He eased his rig onto the scales and waited uneasily, watching the two scale operators inside the building as they checked monitors in front of them.

"There is my friend," Walker whispered to Wolf. "The short one. The good thing is they have a bathroom inside, just in case we're here for a bit."

After a minute a metallic voice came over the loudspeakers. "You are cleared to go, big rig. Thanks for your time, and have a good day."

Thad Walker's jaw dropped. "That's the last thing I expected," he said, shifting the transmission into first gear. "We're leaving before he changes his mind."

Back on the interstate the 18-wheeler flowed back into the line of traffic. Walker grinned at his companion. "Hey, if you got nothing to do sometime, give me a call and you can ride with me anytime. I think there was something magic back there, and it might have been you."

Wolf chuckled. "I'll keep that in mind."

Two hours later Walker turned his big rig skillfully in a cul-de-sac at the end of a suburban street. The big man reached out his hand to Wolf.

"Thanks," he said. "Sure enjoyed your company, and thanks for your wise words."

"Not at all. I owe you for the ride." Wolf shook hands with the smiling Walker. "Maybe I'll see you on down the road somewhere."

As he watched the big rig ease its way out of the neighborhood, a growling, rolling behemoth, a voice called out from a nearby house.

"Dad!"

Over coffee at the kitchen table, Doreen Talman gazed at her father's tired face. "How long can you stay?" she asked.

"Until you get tired of me. Where's my granddaughter?"

"School. Bus will be here shortly. Why didn't you tell me you were coming?"

Wolf smiled. "I did. I wrote you a letter two weeks ago."

The young woman threw up her hands. "Dad, you didn't say when! But I'm glad you're here. Randy is coming home, next week I think. His unit will be flying back into the city airport. Mary and I will go meet him."

Wolf studied her face. "You're worried."

She nodded. "This was his third tour, Dad. We were just getting things together from the last one, he was settling back in at his job and then his unit was activated again. I . . . I don't know what to expect. So I'm glad you're here."

"Are you still laid off?"

"Well, in a way, I guess. I'm back on half time, money's tight. I'm hoping Randy will get his job back."

Eight days later Sergeant Randy Talman dropped his rucksack inside the front door and gazed at the Welcome Home banner hanging on the wall. Above the left breast pocket of his Class A uniform, above his shooting badges, were three rows of service ribbons—one more row than he had after his last combat tour. His mouth was smiling but his eyes were not. In a moment he noticed his father-in-law standing in the corner.

"Hey, son," Wolf greeted him. "Good to see you back. Welcome home."

Randy crossed the room to shake hands. "Thanks, Dad. It's good to see you, too."

After midnight Wolf was in the kitchen waiting for the coffee maker to finish brewing, and listening to the soft footsteps enter behind him. "Almost done if you want a cup," he offered.

"Coffee was on my mind, thanks," Randy said, taking a seat at the table. They sat quietly for several minutes after Wolf poured coffee. The wall clock seemed especially loud. Wolf waited, giving his son-in-law the first opportunity to say whatever he wanted. The older man had never been one to be pushy or intrusive. He wondered how Randy felt about him being here.

"I wish you could have met my dad," the younger man said suddenly. "He was a talker. He'd walk up to anyone, even someone he didn't know, and strike up a conversation. I think the two of you would have hit it off."

"Likely so, because I like to listen to people talk," Wolf replied, smiling.

"He had one withered hand," Randy went on. "Don't know if you knew that. Anyway, it kept him out of the service, and he was kind of ashamed of that. If he were here, I'd tell him he's got nothing to be ashamed of. He didn't miss nothing."

"I think your mom mentioned it to me, about your dad's hand," Wolf recalled. "And I think I would have told him the same thing. He didn't miss nothing."

The younger man stared into his coffee. "Yeah, but I don't know if he would have understood. My cousin told me not to enlist, after his first tour. I know now that he was trying to spare me, but it's too late."

"We're all the same way when we're young," Wolf assured him. "We don't know how to listen. We learn the hard way. Trick is to listen once you know how."

"Are you sorry you enlisted?" Randy asked.

"For the most part, no. I learned things, met good people. I don't know how other guys felt, but combat gave me an appreciation for life. There's a lot a person can do when no one's shooting at you."

"You never had the guilt syndrome?"

Wolf sighed and nodded. "Oh, yeah. Big time. Then one day my mom got exasperated with me and told me I should be glad to be alive. She said the guys who got killed would choose to be alive. That pulled me up short."

Wolf saw the pain and confusion in the younger man's eyes as Randy rubbed his face. "I know our casualty rate wasn't as high as you guys in Vietnam," he said, exhaling sharply. "Seven guys in our platoon were wounded, one lost his left arm and leg from an IED. I can still see the torn stumps as the medic worked on him. The guy lived, as far as I know, he was only twenty. We did lose three KIAs. I see them all the time, hear them talking, laughing. I didn't see them die, but I saw them dead. Seems like they won't go away."

Wolf stood and refilled their cups and sat down again. "You know," he said, sighing, "the thing is, they won't go away, not completely."

"I was afraid of that."

"No." Wolf waved a finger. "No, don't be, and I'll tell you why. Your memories of them are their last hold on this life. In a very real way, they still live in you. Don't make them go away, or try to. Let me ask you this: Don't you think those young men have earned something by dying? Don't you think they've at least earned the right to be remembered?"

After a deep breath, Randy nodded. "Yeah, they have."

"Then remember them. Let them come into your memory. Keep them there."

Randy's blue eyes filled and a tear slid down his pale cheek. "Yeah, yeah, I will." Then, in a moment, he whispered, "Who ever thought war is the answer to anything?"

"No one wise," Wolf replied.

Two days later when no one was looking Randy took down the Welcome Home sign, folded it neatly and put it away. In the afternoon he and Doreen went for a walk before the bus brought Mary home. "I have a plan," he told her. "I talked to the manager of the warehouse and there is an opening there, not my old job so the money's a little less. But it's a job and it'll help us get caught up.

In the meantime I think you should go back to school—you're only two semesters from finishing. Go part-time if you like. When you finish and get a job, I'll go to school since the army will pay my way."

"I like your plan," Doreen said. "When do you go back to work?"

"Next week. How long is your dad planning to stay?"

A worried expression slid across the young woman's pretty face. "I don't know, he didn't say. Is there . . . is there a problem?"

"No, no, not at all. He and I have been sitting up nights talking. He knows a lot." Randy paused, a frown wrinkling his brow. "But I noticed he's lost some weight and I think he's taking pills. Is he sick, do you know? Because the last time he came to visit he drove."

"I think he is sick, but he hasn't said anything."

Doreen broached the issue of her father's health in the only way she could. She asked him about his pickup truck.

"Is your truck still running?" she said over lunch.

"Still running," he replied.

"Then why didn't you drive, like the last time you came to visit?"

Wolf smiled, a nearly imperceptible upward bend to the corners of his mouth. Doreen had seen that smile many times. There was always something mysterious behind it.

"The spirits told me to walk," he told her.

"You mean hitchhike? That's kind of dangerous these days, Dad."

Wolf chuckled. "So what about life isn't dangerous, these days? You live on the edge of the largest city on the plains, one with a high crime rate. How does that compare to hitchhiking?"

"Is this your way of turning the conversation into another one about us moving away from here?" she asked suspiciously.

"No. I thought we were talking about hitchhiking."

Doreen shook her head. "Okay. So the spirits told you to walk. Does that mean you're going home the same way?"

Wolf smiled patiently. "No, I thought I'd take the bus. Is this your way of telling me I've worn out my welcome?"

"Oh, for heaven's sake, Dad! No! I'm just . . . I'm just worried about you, that's all."

"You noticed the pills."

Doreen reached out and grabbed her father's hands. "What are they for?"

"An infection in my gastrointestinal tract," he told her.

"Are they helping?"

He nodded. "Seem to be."

"Okay. Have you gone to another medicine man? Isn't that what you do when one of you gets sick? You treat each other, right?"

Wolf smiled. "I have." He patted her hands reassuringly. "It will be okay. I promise."

Something in his tone bothered Doreen. On their way to a movie that evening she mentioned the conversation with her father to Randy.

"You don't believe him?" he asked.

"Yes, I do, but I don't think he's telling me everything."

In the days after Doreen could see that her father was getting restless. So she did not object when he talked about buying a bus ticket home. Her older sister, Lucinda, who made her home on the reservation, had called a few times. She would meet their father at the bus station, she promised.

Wolf left the city on a bright but cold day. Randy, Doreen, and Mary watched the big silver- and-blue bus blend into the traffic and then disappear. When they returned home they found a small envelope, with all their names on it, sitting on the kitchen table. Inside was a blank card.

Taped in the fold of the card was a postal money order for a thousand dollars.

Wolf leaned back in his seat and watched the rural landscape beyond the city flow past his window. Taking a moment, he found his reading glasses and looked at the face of his paper ticket. Five hundred miles and three bus changes and he would be home, or at least close. Lucinda would drive him the last 20 miles.

He sensed the stares before he glanced sideways and saw a young couple across the aisle, whom he guessed to be Asian, smile and wave at him.

"Forgive the intrusion," the man said, pointing to Wolf's crooked cane. "We noticed your unique cane, but we are curious. Are you a native North American?"

Wolf chuckled under his breath. *Native North American.* Well, that was the most accurate of all the labels favored by one group or another. "Yes," he said. "I am."

"Wonderful!" the man exclaimed. "A pleasure to meet you. We are from China."

Wolf reached across the aisle and shook hands with the couple. A hundred miles later they sat at a table in a roadside convenience store doubling as a bus station. Their next bus was not due for an hour.

"This is my wife, Sarah Wu," the man told him. "I am John Tay. We are from Yulin, which is north of Zhanjiang, which is on the coast on the South China Sea."

"If you say so," Wolf smiled. "I am afraid my geographic knowledge of your part of the world is woefully lacking. Your names, a combination of English and Chinese, I presume?"

"Yes," said Tay. "A necessary thing. How we Chinese give and use names is a source of confusion for most people here. Such a combination of English and Chinese is easier to do. Both of us were doctoral students at the university. We are going home, to fly from the west coast. We take the bus to Denver, then fly to Los Angeles." "I'm glad you will not ride a bus the whole way to the coast," Wolf said.

"We thought to see some of the country, the landscape, especially the plains," explained Sarah. "There was little opportunity for us to travel while we were in school."

"Please," interjected Tay. "May we know your name?"

"Ah, forgive my poor manners. Yes, my name is Wolf. I am going home."

They shook hands all around again.

"May I ask what it is that you do?" said Sarah.

"I fix things," Wolf told her.

"I see. A repairman?" she said.

"You can say that. Are your doctorates in the same field, or different?" Wolf asked.

"I am an archaeologist," replied Tay. "My wife is a hydrologist. I am the romantic, she is the practical one. I am the past, she is the future."

They laughed together. "Well," said Wolf, "it takes both to run the world. We have to understand where we have been to know where we're going."

"You seem also to be a philosopher," observed Sarah.

"I'd rather be a realist," Wolf replied.

After a waitress refilled their coffees, Tay leaned across the table. "There is one thing I am curious about."

"Would that be the Bering Land Bridge theory?" Wolf guessed.

"This is astonishing! Yes, it is."

"And are we native North Americans related to present-day Asians, Mongolians, and indigenous Siberians?" Wolf went on. "I should think that you are in a better place to answer that question than I."

Tay nodded thoughtfully. "Evidence strongly suggests so, of course. DNA testing is incontrovertible. Biological connection is one thing, Mr. Wolf, but what about culturally? How do you, for example, feel about that ancient connection?"

"Who are we and where do we come from? That's the ultimate question, as far as I am concerned, Mr. Tay."

"Why is that, for you?" wondered Sarah.

"Because if we ever factually prove that and we truly come to understand it, we might have a chance to eliminate some basic misconceptions that we've labored under for millennia. For example, if we can accept that all biological human variations are less than one-tenth of one percent, and that we are the same on the order of ninety-nine and nine-tenths percent, maybe we can see beyond the archaic myth that the color of our skin matters."

"Indeed," said Tay, nodding.

"So, to answer your first question, yes, I think your people and my people, and the Koreans and the Japanese for that matter, are related. How do I feel about that culturally? Well, let's throw caution and politics aside and strengthen the ties that bind."

"How and when will that ever happen?" asked Sarah.

Wolf sipped his coffee. "When wisdom rules the world," he said.

"Mr. Wolf," she said, smiling nervously. "I think you are something more than a repairman."

"No. That is what I do, what I have done for most of my life. I fix things."

"Do you meditate?" asked Tay.

"Yes, I do."

"What do you meditate about?" Tay pressed.

"Connections," Wolf replied. "I am a traditionalist; that is, I live according to the spiritual beliefs my people have had for God knows how long. There is a prayer that we use in every one of our religious ceremonies, a very simple prayer. *All my relations*. That phrase includes everything that is; not just humans, but everything in the world.

"When we pray or meditate and say *All my relations,* we invoke the essence of all that is in the world. Think of the power that is there. It's not magic, it is unbridled and awesome power. We must bring it together unselfishly, for the good of all that is.

"Now, the next time I say it I will think of you, my new friends."

After a moment of silence, Sarah reached across the table and touched Wolf's hand. "We will be indebted to you for that."

"Not at all," he replied, "because you can do the same for me."

At the next stop Wolf had to part company with his new friends. John Tay and Sarah Wu waved as they boarded the southbound bus to Denver. Tay was holding a small, sealed envelope Wolf had given him. On the front was scrawled a short note:

To my friends Sarah Wu and John Tay.
Do not open until you arrive home.

Inside the station Wolf took his pills and sat down to wait for the westbound bus. When it came, it was a smaller bus and nearly full. As always with connecting routes, it stopped at just about every small town along the way. Wolf tried to sleep but managed only to doze off and on. They came to his stop at one o'clock in the morning.

Lucinda Wolf Day watched her father get off the bus and walk toward the pickup truck where she waited with her husband, George. The old man seemed a bit unsteady to her as he picked his way, leaning on his cane. He seemed thinner as well. She hurried forward to meet him as Doreen's concerned voice played in her memory. "What's wrong with Dad? I know he's sick, but he wouldn't tell me exactly what's going on."

"Dad," Lucinda called out. "It's good to see you. I just called Doreen to tell her your bus was pulling in."

"Ah, thank you," he said, his voice somewhat hoarse. He hugged his oldest daughter and shook hands with his son-in-law.

Though it was only a 20-minute drive to Lucinda's house, Wolf was asleep 5 minutes after they left the small town. He awoke at ten the next morning in Lucinda and George's spare bedroom, barely remembering how he had gotten there.

Though he soaked for over 20 minutes in the guest bathtub, in water as hot as he could stand it, the pain in his back did not subside. Dressed in gray cotton sweat clothes, he walked stiffly into the kitchen to join Lucinda. It was just past ten thirty.

She noticed how pale he looked, but did not mention it. It was hard to mask her concern, however, when he could not finish his breakfast. "Dad," she said softly. "What's going on? I know you don't feel well."

Wolf nodded slowly. In a tired voice he said, "I think you should take me to the hospital."

Lucinda was shocked when the doctor at the Indian hospital admitted her father after reading the results of a blood test. At just past two in the afternoon she sat, stunned into silence, as she listened to the doctor break the news to her. Her first tearful call was to George, who took time off from work to be with Lucinda while she called Doreen.

"Yeah, hon, that's what it is," Lucinda said to Doreen, trying to sound brave. "Pancreatic cancer, advanced. Even if it had been detected sooner, it wouldn't have made much difference, according to the doctor. Dad's known about it for months."

After two weeks in the hospital Wolf insisted on going home, back to his own house. His attending physician agreed and signed the discharge order. He sent Wolf home with pain pills. Lucinda moved in with her father.

Every day a nurse from a rural hospice program came to administer morphine. In spite of the pain, Wolf was lucid, telling stories and visiting with anyone who came.

After a week two medicine men came and stayed, sitting with Wolf day and night. The day Doreen arrived Wolf gave his daughters a scrap of paper with words scrawled on it. "Just simple requests," he told them. Requests they promised to carry out.

On a cold, late autumn night the spirits came for Wolf. Lucinda would swear that she saw something misty and shimmering rise from her father's chest. The two medicine men sang and prayed, then announced to the nearly 30 people packed into the small house, as well as an equal number waiting in the cold night outside, that their brother Wolf had finished his earthly journey.

Over 200 people came to Wolf's funeral. They buried him on a hill overlooking a river valley, next to his wife. That had been one of his requests.

A month later a stone carver came and erected Wolf's marker, a slim red granite slab that matched his wife's. The man labored for most of a morning and left behind the new marker connected to the first with a three-foot length of steel chain. Sometime later Lucinda and George came to finish fulfilling Wolf's final request. George attached the crooked cane to his father-in-law's stone.

Before the first heavy snows of winter, two men came to Lucinda's house, one several days ahead of the other. The first was a big black man and the other was a white man in steel-rimmed glasses and a gray suit. Both said the same thing to Lucinda; they had seen an obituary in a newspaper, and they wanted to see Wolf's grave.

She took each of them to the graves on the hill, and they smiled at the words on the new headstone. "I wish I could have visited with him a lot longer," they both told Lucinda. "I never learned so much in such a short span of time."

Lucinda never saw either of them again. But before they drove away, each of them asked her a question: "He said he fixed things. I know he was much more than a repairman. What did he do, really?"

Lucinda told each of them with a smile, "He was telling you the truth. When you translate our native word for 'medicine man' into English, it literally means 'the man who fixes.' He healed people, took away their cares, their pain. Took them onto himself. He fixed things."

On the other side of the world a young couple finished building their new house. A small house, to be sure, but it would be a fine place to raise children. One of the first things they pinned to the wall in their small living room was a card. On it, in Wolf's writing, were a few words. Words that Sarah Wu and John Tay looked at each day and vowed to live by. They were the same words on his headstone:

Wisdom travels many roads and knows no boundaries. It is a fleeting gift. Grasp it while you can, for it is not yours to keep, but to use and pass on.

ACKNOWLEDGMENTS

This is the third project I have had the pleasure of doing with Patty Gift, the first two when she was executive editor at Sterling Publishers. *Returning to the Lakota Way* is the first with her at Hay House, and hopefully not the last. I appreciate, to say the very least, her faith in me, and her willingness to do this particular project after only one inquiry from my agent.

Thank you to the editors at Hay House who worked with Patty to provide order and cohesiveness to a manuscript that had substance but not much else in first draft.

To my friend, Donald Montileaux, a fellow Lakota and an extraordinary artist who created a dazzling cover. This is the third he has done for me.

As ever, and always, I am grateful for all the Lakota elders who graced my life as a child and young man. Many of them were family, but all of them were certainly part of the "village" that nurtured Lakota children and young people in the communities of Swift Bear and Horse Creek on the Rosebud Reservation and Kyle on the Pine Ridge Reservation. Their influence was considerable and it was gifted through advice, stories, and the examples they set simply by living their lives.

Those elders (as I have said more than once) were a direct connection to the past, where we all come from. They brought that past alive through their knowledge, a priceless gift that I've tried to share—because they wanted the world to know who we Lakota were and are. But of that group of unforgettable people I must mention my maternal and paternal grandparents: Albert and Annie (Good Voice Eagle) Two Hawk, and Reverend Charles and M. Blanche (Roubideaux) Marshall. Without a doubt they were the four people most influential on my life. Not a day goes by that I do not think of them.

Finally, to my late wife, Connie West Marshall—a farm girl, a child of the western North Dakota prairies, a beauty queen, an adventurer, an entrepreneur, and a devoted and fierce mother. She was my agent, best friend, the love of my life, and my soul mate. She took my breath away the moment I first met her, and again at the moment she left our daughters and me for the Spirit World. In between she blessed our lives with grace, style, and unconditional love. As the saying goes, "Death leaves a wound no one can heal. Love leaves a memory no one can steal."

Connie, I will always love you.

ABOUT THE AUTHOR

Joseph Marshall III was born and raised on the Rosebud Sioux Indian Reservation and is an enrolled member of the Sicangu Lakota (Rosebud Sioux) tribe. Because he was raised in a traditional Lakota household by his maternal grandparents, his first language is Lakota. In that environment he also learned the ancient tradition of oral storytelling. Marshall is an author with nine non-fiction works, three novels, a collection of short stories and essays, and several screenplays to his credit. He is also a speaker and lecturer, having appeared throughout the United States and internationally.

Marshall has also appeared in television documentaries, served as technical advisor for movies, and served as the narrator for the six-part mini-series *Into the West,* as well as playing the on-screen role of Loved by the Buffalo, a Lakota medicine man.

www.josephmarshall.com

NOTES

NOTES

NOTES

NOTES

NOTES

NOTES

NOTES

NOTES

We hope you enjoyed this Hay House book. If you'd like to receive
our online catalog featuring additional information on Hay House
books and products, or if you'd like to find out more about
the Hay Foundation, please contact:

Hay House UK, Ltd.,
Astley House, 33 Notting Hill Gate, London W11 3JQ
Phone: 0-20-3675-2450 • *Fax:* 0-20-3675-2451
www.hayhouse.co.uk • www.hayfoundation.org

◀◀ ▶▶

Published and distributed in the United States by:
Hay House, Inc., P.O. Box 5100, Carlsbad, CA 92018-5100
Phone: (760) 431-7695 or (800) 654-5126
Fax: (760) 431-6948 or (800) 650-5115
www.hayhouse.com®

Published and distributed in Australia by: Hay House Australia Pty.
Ltd., 18/36 Ralph St., Alexandria NSW 2015 • *Phone:* 612-9669-4299
Fax: 612-9669-4144 • www.hayhouse.com.au

Published and distributed in the Republic of South Africa by: Hay House
SA (Pty), Ltd., P.O. Box 990, Witkoppen 2068 • *Phone/Fax:* 27-11-467-8904
www.hayhouse.co.za

Published in India by: Hay House Publishers India, Muskaan Complex,
Plot No. 3, B-2, Vasant Kunj, New Delhi 110 070 • *Phone:* 91-11-4176-1620
Fax: 91-11-4176-1630 • www.hayhouse.co.in

Distributed in Canada by: Raincoast, 9050 Shaughnessy St., Vancouver,
B.C. V6P 6E5 • *Phone:* (604) 323-7100 • *Fax:* (604) 323-2600
www.raincoast.com

◀◀ ▶▶

Take Your Soul on a Vacation

Visit **www.HealYourLife.com®** to regroup, recharge, and reconnect
with your own magnificence. Featuring blogs, mind-body-spirit news,
and life-changing wisdom from Louise Hay and friends.

Visit **www.HealYourLife.com** today!

Free e-newsletters
from Hay House, the Ultimate
Resource for Inspiration

Be the first to know about Hay House's dollar deals, free downloads, special offers, affirmation cards, giveaways, contests, and more!

 Get exclusive excerpts from our latest releases and videos from **Hay House Present Moments**.

 Enjoy uplifting personal stories, how-to articles, and healing advice, along with videos and empowering quotes, within **Heal Your Life**.

 Have an inspirational story to tell and a passion for writing? Sharpen your writing skills with insider tips from **Your Writing Life**.

Sign Up Now!

Get inspired, educate yourself, get a complimentary gift, and share the wisdom!

http://www.hayhouse.com/newsletters.php

Visit www.hayhouse.com to sign up today!

  HealYourLife.com ♥